A Man Without a Story

A Man Without a Story

a portrait of a man who was
four-fifths of a champion and a virtual parricide,
in search of a story and a woman to love

Bill Wheatley

"A Man Without a Story," by Bill Wheatley

ISBN 978-1-62137-635-4 (Softcover)   978-1-62137-636-1 (Ebook)

Library of Congress Control Number: 2014921855

Published 2014 by Virtualbookworm.com Publishing Inc., P.O. Box 9949, College Station, TX 77842, US. 2014, Bill Wheatley. All rights reserved. No part of this publication may be reproduced, stored in a retrieval system, or transmitted in any form or by any means, electronic, mechanical, recording or otherwise, without the prior written permission of Bill Wheatley.

in memory of

R.M.H.

"How you doing, babes?" Hugh always greeted me.

"How *you* doing, Hugh?" I always answered.

"Not too bad, not too bad," he would reply, even when things had turned very bad.

PART ONE

Whodunit?

When I began writing about Hugh, the first thought, the first sentence that came to mind sounded like a joke or a parody:

My assignment was to find out how Hugh had died and if anyone was at fault to bring them to justice...

I don't know where that line came from, that old detective story style, because it was absurd. I had no way to bring anyone to justice, and besides, I knew exactly how Hugh had died and it wasn't anyone's fault. Except maybe his own, since he'd tried several times to erase his existence or withdraw from it, to evade it somehow. If there was any mystery it wasn't how he died, it was how he lived. Why had his life stumped him so completely, like a puzzle he couldn't solve? It was a tangled, twisted, labyrinthine quandary intensified by some force that drove him on almost furiously, yet simultaneously it was opposed or nullified by some other force or condition that held him in place, as if he was paralyzed. There was another conflict running along parallel to this one: How do you live by a code, or a philosophy, that's at odds with the entire surrounding culture? This could be seen as an attempt to solve the first riddle—how to live—but ended up creating its own insoluble difficulties.

In one of Hugh's notebooks I found a thought he had written that sounded like his own way—one of them, anyway—of describing what I'm now trying to do, and the inevitable mystifications involved when trying to understand anything as complex as another human being.

1

"The living resist our 'stories' about them," Hugh wrote, "the dead cannot. The living must betray all the themes we devise for them, all our knowing. They must insist on being unknowable, unfinished, unapprisable."

Unapprisable. That was Hugh. As much as he wanted to love and be loved, he did not want to be known. Now that he's stopped moving, maybe I can finally grasp him.

2.

On that gray March morning with his cardiovascular system pumped up close to its limit, Hugh had climbed off his exercise machine—a contraption with rollers you could mount your bicycle on to ride indoors—then picked up his stopwatch and sat down in a chair to monitor his heart rate. Every day he did some form of physical exercise in a regimen that was extreme by any normal standard, and he often recorded the stats of his workouts in a small notebook in his scanty left handed scrawl. The words could be hard to decipher but the numbers were always clearly inscribed, as if he trusted their certainty more than words and had to respect them by making sure they had no ambiguity (even if no one but him would ever read them).

But at this moment Hugh is not writing numbers in his book, he is counting off the beats per minute of his heart. His resting rate is unusually low, 43 or 44 b.p.m., and since he has never had his maximum heart rate tested on a treadmill while hooked up to an ECG, he doesn't know the exact number for his "heart rate reserve"—the difference between the rate at rest and his maximum heart rate—but he does know that he has pushed his system above the standard HRmax for his age. This isn't surprising since the formula is based on an average: 220 minus your age is the usual estimate, which for Hugh, at 62, would be 158. A more refined, non-linear equation puts Hugh's slightly higher, at 164, and his goal is to push his "training heart rate" to between 65% and 85% of the max. That rate has been calculated to give the heart and lungs the most benefit from a workout. For Hugh it would work out to be between 107-139 b.p.m., and he would definitely aim for the higher number, roughly 3x his resting rate. Because of his passion for measurement, for knowing maximums and limits for all kinds of human endeavor, Hugh's brain contains many numbers, and he is aware that when applied to him all the numbers that measure strength and cardiovascular fitness project him as a much younger man. The entries in his little notebook of heart rate, miles ridden or run or swum, stadium steps climbed, ropes jumped, weights used for various exercises and the number of repetitions for each all tracked a slight decline over the years, but these were Hugh's numbers, not those of a normal man. To say he was 62 years old seems wrong. It's on the wrong scale, it conjures up the wrong person. No one looking at him for the first time would guess his age. It should be written as something like 42+ to be accurate. A value all his own. If I use that number, 42+, as his age, then I could say I knew him for 5+ years because when we met he was 37. In fact, we knew each other for twenty-five years. A quarter century, a generation, a long time, and this is a typically convoluted Huvian way to express that simple fact.

It wasn't just his cardiovascular system. Everything about Hugh both physically and mentally was off the charts. Compared to the rest of us he seemed a little less mortal, as if because of his strength and vigor Hugh would still be out there, keeping pace with only himself, after everyone else had run their race. His end would eventually come, the way it had to, but none of us would see it or know what it was. He would ride off into the sunset on his bike, unseen, out of sight, no longer mortal, into infinity.

Yet today, on this cool wet early spring morning—which is why he was riding inside—as Hugh sat there counting the beats, the rapid thumps suddenly stopped. His heart wasn't beating. One can wonder whether the message that the beating had stopped was received in his cortex in time to be understood before he lost consciousness. This lethal fraction of a moment grabs my attention because Hugh's brain was so acutely attuned to his body. I try to recreate in my own mind what it feels like to receive a message that something is about to happen. If you smash your finger with a hammer there's an instant after the blow before the pain signal screams in your head. Short as it is, the moment is palpable; it's long enough to be recognized. In fact, it seems unnaturally long. You know that you know something. Before you know what it is. Yet you do know, exactly. The pain is coming. Did he know the end was coming? Why am I so hung up thinking about this? Do I really want to know what he knew in a dying instant too brief for any words, or is it just a way to try to feel close to him, to recapture my friend, to hold on to a last moment? My attention has already shifted to the scene of Naomi finding him. Home from work, walking in, calling his name, whatever their routine was at the end of the day. Wherever she expected to find him. In the kitchen, making supper, like he usually did. No. He's in the chair in the room beyond, unmoving, in the wrong position for life.

At this point, hardly begun writing his story, his non-story, I stopped. I went to find Sherwin Nuland's book *How We Die*. I'd bought it a couple years ago, curious to know what happens when the body stops living, then realized I hadn't the stomach to read it. I'd gotten some of it second hand reading Joan Didion's account of her husband's sudden death in *A Year of Magical Thinking*. Didion was a writer Hugh liked and I'd thought of him reading about John Gregory Dunne's final moments with an EMT crew laboring over him on his dining room floor. It was the kind of book certain people (like Hugh) could read thinking if they could just learn enough about an event the knowledge might enable them to control it, even change it. When I started looking for *How We Die* on the shelf I got distracted by a row of Hugh's books which

Naomi had given me. There was Richard Rhodes' fat book on building the atomic bomb, one on Einstein the philosopher-physicist, Eugene Genovese's *Roll, Jordan, Roll*, Gleick's *Chaos*, Frederick Crews' *The Freud Files*. Noticing the Crews book was a reminder of Hugh's fascination with Freud as a writer, and his even greater disgust for Freud's methods and secrecy, all framed by Hugh's antipathy toward the art and quasi-science of psychology. It was a huge fraught subject which he returned to again and again as if it were a thumping heart under the floorboards, something he had to tear out and destroy. Destroy by understanding its falsehoods, its reinforcing delusions, its deflating truths.

Nuland's description of what happens in "sudden cardiac arrest" when blood is no longer moving through the heart was just what I'd remembered from Didion's book. The victim Nuland described was middle aged, a stockbroker who played "a lot of tennis" and on the court he appeared to "drop dead." His heart stopped and went into ventricular fibrillation, the muscle fibers all twitching uselessly instead of flexing together. His partner, a doctor, started doing CPR on him and saved him. Hugh was alone when his heart stopped pumping, he wasn't playing tennis with, say, me, and even if he had been I'm not a doctor and don't know CPR, so I couldn't have saved him. I'd have run around shouting for help or stood there stupidly trying to remember how to do artificial respiration from Boy Scouts' exercises fifty years ago.

What did Hugh go through when his heart stopped, what was the last moment of his life like? The answer was reassuring if you cared about Hugh and didn't want him to suffer, disappointing if you wanted to hear something profound about a mind, an unusually perceptive and self-aware one, and what it experienced as it shut down. According to Nuland, the sensations the stockbroker felt (would Hugh feel the same thing even though he was a socialist?) were the initial physical collapse, then the lights going out as if slowly turned down by a rheostat. The stockbroker said later he was aware of both sensations; he could remember the collapse and the dimming, but there was no pain, nothing else to mark The End. It just felt as if he was deflating, a balloon losing air, inside a room gradually going from light to dark. It had happened so fast—in no more time than it takes to say, "sudden cardiac arrest" or "How you doing, babes?"—that Hugh probably didn't have time to become fully and self-consciously aware of what was happening to him. Nuland describes how the cells in the brain need to have oxygen supplied continuously. After they use what they have, they stop functioning, fast. It was disappointing, and disturbing, to have a doctor confirm what I'd guessed, and seemed not just wrong but profoundly unjust for a mind as tuned and ramified as Hugh's to be deprived of some kind of summing up moment. I shuddered for him, as if he were a modern, secular version of the saint who died unshriven, with no time to confront his Maker. That was nonsense of course, especially given Hugh's antipathy toward religion, and the movie technique of replaying his life in a flash of images was too trite for him, unless it was done as a parody. But I couldn't help feeling that he had been denied an experience that should have been his. It also seemed perversely appropriate, standing for everything else he missed in his life.

It wasn't because Hugh's mind was so unusual that I linger on this moment, or that I expect a person's last moment to reveal something unique about them. No. All this probing is because Hugh died from the same cause and just as abruptly as his father, and it was that death, and that person, and his absence, which dominated Hugh's life. A nineteenth century novelist might even have said, in the manner of the time, that when Hugh's father died, he took his son's life away with him.

PART TWO

Four-fifths of a Champion

I first met Hugh just after I met Kate. She introduced us. They were working together on a public television show which debated a current issue in the news using lawyers and witnesses in a courtroom format. I was working on a different program at the same station, and since my office was in another building we hadn't run into each other. I was talking to Kate when Hugh appeared—he's walking out of my memory now—down the corridor between the moveable walls forming office cubicles and she is holding out her hand in a gesture of introduction almost as if she's emceeing a show and a guest is coming out of the wings as she says, "This is Hugh...."

"I knew a guy named Hugh once," I started to say, like a wiseguy, but caught myself. Kate would say there's a certain tension, a competitive male one, underlying our meeting because she's been talking about him for a couple weeks, what an unusual guy he is, a student of philosophy with a quirky mind, and how much Donald, the guy they're both working for, likes him. Hugh has his own girlfriend, but since Kate and I have recently met it would be logical—if we were all in one of the soap operas Kate watches—if her new romance was complicated by her boyfriend's jealousy over the man she works with. I think it's just two guys sizing each other up. Hugh is barely taller than average and looks fit, but he wears his pants high and seems on first glance to be a flaky Cambridge type, the kind of guy who may stay in shape riding a bike or jogging but isn't athletic.

I sure got that wrong.

Yet maybe that was just the right note for meeting Hugh because misunderstanding was such a big theme in his view of life. "Almost everything everyone thinks they know is wrong," he said on that first occasion when we met. He said it with a dry, raspy laugh—his private laugh track that often accompanied his own comments—and I heard him repeat it many times over the years. One of his goals in life was to learn whether what he thought he knew was supported by facts or evidence and if it wasn't to correct it. He wanted to cleanse his mind of misapprehensions so what was left in it was information about the world as it really was. The way everyone saw a world distorted by their own peculiar cache of misinformation could be funny to think about and if you pooled the misinformation you could ask whether the collective mind was even more misinformed than any random individual one with only solo delusions. Or did the skewed views cancel each other out? Mostly it frustrated and depressed him. If he corrected everything he heard that was wrong he'd be a nuisance, a pedant, a pain in the ass, and some of the time that's just what he was. Besides, many of things people believed and lived by were opinions not facts, and the realm of opinion was itself ruled by a fact that made Hugh seethe with anguish: bad ideas don't die, they have to be killed again and again. It was his mantra for why one couldn't believe in progress. At best it was no more than a cycle. Hugh's outrage made you feel that if yours was any less you were part of the common mental sloth which agreed to live with delusion. You too were willing to trade the "truth" for "happiness."

So the first time we met, for a moment, I got him wrong. It was a minor thing, and my false impression of him was almost instantly corrected because just seeing Hugh walk you couldn't miss his physical grace. He was bow-legged, like many athletes, and light on his feet like a springy big cat, as if his legs were meant to carry a heftier body or do something more feral than walk down the street.

A few weeks after we met, Hugh and his girlfriend Debby came over for dinner. It was a sweet summer night; after a hot day the temperature was dropping toward the ideal, and by dark the climate felt like what it would always be if the planet had been made just for us. Kate and I lived in a dingy duplex in Cambridge, but she had made the apartment cozy and stylish, and there was a patio in the small side yard where the four of us had eaten and were now talking, laughing, drinking. The midnight breeze dragged the wicks of the candles out horizontally, making them gutter and smoke, dripping wax through the gaps in the lattices of the metal table we sat around. Kate and Debby were talking in pleasant, musical voices—enjoying each other—and Hugh was sitting back in his chair, torso shadowed by the branches of the mountain ash above us, his face nearly invisible under the dark bouffe of his Einsteinian hair—maybe it was more like Abby Hoffman's—his hand enclosing a wine glass or beer bottle; in the dark I can't see which it is. This was the first time we'd talked more than briefly, and as if he was spilling the secret, telling me the end of the mystery before I even knew there was one to be solved, Hugh was confessing the most crucial event in his life. In an even softer voice than his usual speaking tone, he was telling me about his father. About his father's death.

"He died when I was sixteen. He had a heart attack playing baseball. Running out a double. He was sliding into second."

The dust settles over the man lying by the bag, the fielder bent over him holding the ball in his glove, tagging him. Out, I think, he was really out.

"He'd hit four singles during the game but it was his last at-bat and he was looking for extra bases so he tried to stretch it. He slid into second with the throw and just lay there. They drove the ambulance out on the field and took him to the hospital where he died. I was sure it was my fault. I'd just had a big argument with him so I felt like I'd killed him."

Hugh's voice is coming out of the dark, the dark summer night, the dark crown of his hair, the dark of the past so indelible to him, but what I see is a square-jawed, flat-bellied, lean and muscular man—another Hugh, slightly older, an American ideal, a middle-aged Wheaties man—running with competitive fury and hurling himself at the second base bag. He isn't wearing a uniform, he's wearing industrial grays, like the men I used to watch after supper on summer evenings playing behind the school at the end of the street, hubba-hubba, hubba-hubba, easy out, easy out, way-to-go big guy, way-to-go.

"You felt as if..." I leaned forward across the metal table trying to hear Hugh's muted voice against the counterpoint of the women talking and laughing beside us.

"I killed him," he said. "Because we were always fighting, we argued all the time. But this was different...we'd had a real bad one."

Hugh probably can't see me in the dark either. But maybe he can; the long candle wick bends in the night breeze as I lean even closer.

"How old was he?"

"Forty-four."

"Jesus."

"He'd had a serious heart attack several years before but he'd gone back to bad habits like smoking a couple packs of cigarettes a day."

"Jeez," I repeated, still absorbing this strange confession. "Was he..."

The women's voices filled the pause.

"...he smoked but was he in good shape? Otherwise?"

"He was an athlete. He played a lot of sports."

"And you'd had an argument with him just before the game, so when it happened, when he had the heart attack—"

"I was sure it was my fault," Hugh repeated. "I thought I'd killed him."

"It wasn't the effort of running the bases, and smoking. Things like that."

"We hadn't been getting along. A lot of arguments. If I hadn't had a fight with him, he would have been all right."

"But doesn't that sound like—"

I stopped myself. Hugh was blaming himself so assertively, so proprietarily—it was as if his father's death was something he owned and tempering his guilt would take it away from him.

How had we gotten into this? I hardly knew him.

"That was what it felt like," Hugh said.

"And you were...sixteen?"

Hugh didn't answer. It seemed he had dropped it, and didn't want to go back over details again.

"Jesus," I said softly.

We sat. The women were talking.

"I was a catcher," Hugh said, picking up an earlier subject. "My father played all the other positions. Nobody wants to be a catcher," he laughed.

"The tools of ignorance," I laughed with him. That's how we got into this. Someone had told me Hugh was a hell of a baseball player and he'd had a chance to play professionally. When I asked him about it, he jumped to his father.

"I liked running the game, I liked calling pitches. I could make the throw to second. I didn't like the competition. I don't like the feeling that in order to win you have to beat someone. I had that experience—I wanted to beat my father, and we fought— we argued and he died."

"But don't you think—if you can explain the connection so clearly—it sounds to me like it was a coincidence, really. I mean it's not so unusual to argue with your father at that age—I certainly did— but you had, you both had the bad luck...to have something happen."

Hugh didn't say anything. Something moved in the dark. He was sipping from the glass or bottle in his hand.

"Plus you said he'd been sick before."

"He was a talented athlete," Hugh said. "All-American in lacrosse, a tennis player, a sprinter. He could play any position in baseball. I was eight when he had his first heart attack and by the time I was twelve I could throw a ball farther than him, because of his condition."

"How did he, the fact that his kid could throw a ball farther—"

"He quit playing with me," Hugh said.

"You quit playing and just argued," I said facetiously.

"We argued all the time. Any subject, sports, politics, anything. The weather," he laughed.

Hugh talked in that whispery voice I would get to know so well, rapidly, clusters of words coming out in bursts, the voice so low he might be talking to someone he didn't want to alarm, like a child, or it might be more like someone giving you a final urgent instruction before you rushed off on your mission. In the dark I couldn't see the expression on his face, only that his head was inclined slightly forward, tilted down, and in the pauses or when I said something he'd answer softly, "Yup...uh-huh..." with the two large pods of fuzzy hair on each side of his head bobbing like a clown. His sudden confession had utterly changed my response to him. Earlier in the evening I'd been annoyed at the way he carried his opinions to tiresome length and held them so tenaciously, and I'd been thinking that at least I wouldn't have to see him any more after tonight. I'd tell Kate not to invite him and Debby again. But when he spoke about his father the way he did, I was instantly converted to a potential friend, even a soul brother. I wasn't drunk but I was under the influence and fathers and sons was a subject I knew well. I felt an impulse to grab his hand, hold him, cry for him, make his life well for him.

"You seem to understand the whole, the relationship with your father—I mean how you feel about it—it's something you seem to understand very well," I said, still wanting him to explain more.

Kate and Debby had gone into the house and I hoped they wouldn't come back right away and interrupt.

"It was impossible to compete in any sports my father had played," Hugh's voice went on in the dark, bypassing my comment. "Like catching, I loved it because it was a position he hadn't played. Or basketball. I was thrilled when a coach told me if I were three inches taller I could have played professionally."

"Really. No kidding. Grow a foot," I said, laughing sympathetically. "Work on that part of your game."

"That's what I think I like about running. My father didn't run, he didn't do any distance running. He ran sprints. But I seem to have a desire to fail," Hugh said in the same voice, the low soft voice in the darkness. "I get close and then back off, like when I'm running at the track if I'm out in front I start worrying about the guys behind me—are they all right, are they hurt?—then I don't want to win."

It was too easy to do the psychoanalytical dance with the past Hugh was describing—to explain it all a little too glibly, as glibly as Hugh was describing his unwillingness to play to win because it would hurt his opponent (his father, always his father), so he had to do something to sandbag his performance. But diagnosing the cause of your neurotic unease doesn't make it go away. It was much later in our friendship when Hugh said the same thing himself, that the insights of psychological probing hadn't changed anything. The very idea made him laugh humorlessly as if it was such an old joke it wasn't worth telling again. He had read Freud like a jilted lover, his indignation exploding with every self-confident assertion about how minds and emotions worked. Hugh was outraged by Freud's own glibness, his manipulations, his shamelessness, and at the same time impressed by his brilliance;

not as a scientist but as a writer, a concocter of his own kind of fiction. He was a completely unreliable guide to the territory he'd claimed, and part of that territory was inside Hugh's own head, as much as he'd tried to evict all the witch doctors of psychology. If Hugh was a parricide of some kind he was also aware that as much as he suffered it was also darkly funny—funny because the deepest, the most disabling emotions could be summarized so suavely, so painlessly, so ineffectually. This fact, both superficial and profound, was a fixed part of his life. As were physical culture and competition, along with the life of his mind, and he had to do something with all these powerful urges. His answer was to compete with himself. Who might—or might not—also be doubling the ghost of his father.

"My goal is to run a five-minute mile," Hugh said, shifting in the dark. "I figure that would make me four-fifths of a champion. Not bad for thirty-seven," he laughed.

Describing the solo athletic event he'd invented for himself, Hugh made it sound like a parody. But he seemed to take the idea of being four-fifths of a champion seriously—seriously enough to train for it. At the same time he left a little hole for himself to duck into, to escape from what anyone knew about him, using humor to hide his commitment to it.

There were so many things Hugh never talked about, it seemed odd that his father's death, the most crucial loss, was one he told almost readily. Perhaps I'd said something about fathers and sons that made him think I'd be sympathetic, and I was, although I could do no more than listen. Or maybe it was the perfect summer night, the blank slate of talking to a new person, the wine, the beer—although Hugh showed no signs of tipsiness. By that night in Cambridge, Hugh's life had more than doubled in years since his father's death and he knew or was beginning to know nothing would ever happen to change the effect it had had on him. So maybe the retelling allowed him to feel a flash of hope that it might change, somehow, that confession might have some kind of mysterious force, if it were done under the right circumstances, even if you didn't quite believe in it.

The women had come back to the table. Hugh and I were now talking sports. The last candle was guttering out and we were all sitting in the still darker dark. Debby touched Hugh's bare knee and said, "It's time we should go, Hugh." He interrupted himself and said, with a laugh, a hearty one, "Why, just because we can't see anything?"

Later, after he and Debby had left, I retold Hugh's story to Kate, and hearing it again in my own voice it sounded as if Hugh had been explaining the reason behind some signature characteristic, like if he walked with a limp or had a patch over one eye. Whatever motivated the moment, it was something he never did again. His confession might even have contained a touch of pride, describing the grave incident he'd survived. Or revealing a crime he'd committed. And gotten away with, although he lived with the knowledge of what he'd done. However it had happened, his father's death wasn't a neutral, natural event. His son was implicated. Besides losing his father, Hugh had also lost an essential innocence. His life had become, in some irrevocable way, more than his responsibility—it was his own fault.

2.

There is a timelessness to that night on the patio in a rundown corner of Cambridge, sitting under the rowan tree, listening to the voice in the dark. When I hear it again I think that was Hugh at his best, his most accessible and humorous, his closest to "normal," and I wonder if his life was already at its peak that night, or even past it. After a career which had never really begun during his twenties and through more than half his next decade, Hugh might have felt the job at the "flagship" public television station in Boston was just what he'd been waiting for. After a long delay he'd crossed the starting line and now his career would really begin.

The way he got the job was an accident, not something he'd been looking for or the product of his ambition, and a serendipitous event can often feel like a blessing, even if you don't really believe in such things. Hugh and Debby had been jogging by the reservoir in Cambridge when they met Kate, fellow runners greeting each other, of the same age and social milieu, and a chance comment led to the discovery—small world!—that Debby and Kate had a common friend. It was just the kind of coincidence Hugh would re-interpret through the laws of probability to show that it wasn't so unlikely at all, given the relatively small number of people in a certain age group with shared histories at a relatively small number of universities, living in a relatively small number of urban communities. Within those limits it wasn't so surprising at all, it was even statistically probable that already overlapping paths would cross in a new "coincidence." Nevertheless, what felt like serendipity had led to coincidence, carrying its own magic, a sense that this is the way things were meant to be, this is how mysterious forces are revealed, and by the end of their jog around the reservoir, Kate was telling Hugh to call the executive producer of the show she was working on. He did, they met, and hit it off instantly. After the interview, Donald thanked Kate for recommending Hugh and said, "I don't know what he'll do for us but I've got to have him around." Voila!

After the meeting with Donald it must have seemed to Hugh that he had finally met someone in a "responsible position" who appreciated him and his talents. He knew he was an unusual person with well above average skills but an odd résumé, so his rightful place was...where? Doing what? Was there a name for it? A consultant or guru, a philosopher/jester, the kind of mind certain discriminating people would want to have around so they could tap into its grasp of a subject whenever they needed to.

Hugh's insights might be quirky, but they were often original, and the truth could take strange forms, as Donald appreciated in his own idiosyncratic way. The actual work wasn't quite so exalted; Hugh researched the subjects for shows and wrote up summaries of the two opposing arguments with supporting material. The ungovernable quality of his powerful brain was evident in doing this work because he never knew where to stop. His summaries went on for pages and might delve into a digression on a fine point, becoming finer and finer in Hugh's helpless pursuit of a definitive truth. Helpless because he knew what he was doing—his self-awareness was acute—but he was helpless not to go on, following every tributary, every trickle, back to its source. On he went, unstoppably, aware that the mounting qualifications were smothering clarity, and might soon reach absurdity; yet it wasn't absurd it was logical, and if there were any conclusive, irreducible truths to be discovered this was the only way they'd be found, even if the footnotes and sidebars canceled each other or led off in new directions that threatened to pile yet another library on top of the subject. The other problem Hugh had was dividing his research into two opposing arguments. Some facts could be used on both sides, or didn't support either but indicated a third or fourth aspect and showed how arbitrarily drawn the two sides were. So his summaries were full of distracting detours which expressed the contradictions in the material as well as in his own mind. Nevertheless, for the first time Hugh had found a job that seemed at least approximately matched to his talents. Kate and the other producers who supervised Hugh's research found ways to restrict him, or sometimes just pulled the notes he'd written out of his hands and worked from them. To protect his pride, Hugh played the naughty boy whose misdeed was doing too much too well, a role that suited him. In his excess he recognized his own way of thinking, fearlessly juxtaposing contradictions and exposing illogic and specious argument, and it reaffirmed that even though he was working in television he wasn't of it, he was still his own man, chasing the truth in a world of generalizations and misconceptions, bias and ignorance.

Hugh's previous job—the place he'd been working when he met Kate—was at a tire shop, so he went from breaking tires off rims with a heavy steel rod while power wrenches shrieked as they spun lug nuts off wheels to a job sitting at a desk. He was no longer totally anonymous and irrelevant. His thoughts about issues of national significance—the economy, foreign policy, bills before Congress and cases in the courts—were listened to. For a while he enjoyed an aura, as if he was Jefferson's plowman wiser than a philosopher or a socialist's idealized man of the people admitted to the councils of power, although in fact he was as educated as anyone working on the show. All this could only have given Hugh a terrific lift, made him feel as if his life had finally slipped into a groove that was at least something like where it belonged (if it belonged anywhere), and in this new, elevated mood he might have been able to tell the critical story of his youth to someone he barely knew. Perhaps for the first time he felt it was behind him, that some chasm had been crossed and now he had a position that would let him silently say to his father's ghost, "I'm sorry for what happened—please forgive me, and go away."

3.

Hugh went to the University of Michigan after high school. I pictured him as the bright son of a working class family, like some kids I grew up with, and probably got this impression because Kate had heard from Donald that after his father's death Hugh's mother married a plumber. His stepfather was a man Hugh didn't get along with—no surprise there—and may even have fought with physically. He never mentioned his stepfather and I didn't ask. Hugh didn't encourage personal questions. Donald had heard a few details, but not much. Besides a natural reticence, Hugh might have wanted to retain a certain power, to control what people knew about him. The past had wounded him and could be used to hurt him again. He seemed to feel contempt for the history imposed on him and refused to be defined by it, at least in ways other people might assume if they knew something specific. Yet all this doesn't add up to the whole mystery of his relationship to his own past. He had more than one secret chamber in his soul. The way he hid ordinary facts but suddenly opened a door into himself created a checkerboard portrait of light and dark. For the first several years I knew him I pictured him growing up in a two family house in Detroit, or a bungalow in one of the inner suburbs, his taciturn father coming home in industrial grays, playing for the company athletic teams. Then one day when Hugh and I were playing tennis he mentioned that his father had once been the amateur tennis champ of Long Island. "Long Island? I thought you lived in Detroit."

"Most of the time," Hugh said.

"What was he doing—what did he do when you lived on Long Island?"

"He was an engineer."

The pictures were suddenly scrambled. The man in industrial grays who was vaguely modeled on my childhood friend Tommy's father, a plumber himself, vanished and in his place was...who? It was a man I couldn't see clearly. He was middle class and worked in an office. I couldn't quite picture him sliding into second base, not in his white shirt and tie. Yet the new image wasn't vivid enough to blot out the original one and that was how I automatically saw him. Maybe he was an engineer who worked in a factory or plant, not an office. Hugh didn't say.

"And he was amateur champ?" I said, picking up the other thread to keep the conversation going.

"Yeah," Hugh said. "But he never taught me the game."

Just like that a new psychological view opened up and in the next moment the shutters came down.

"You never played with him once? He didn't take you out to some court to hit a few balls?"

Hugh gave a short shake of his head but that was it. He wasn't taking any more questions. To keep pressing him in this mood would drive him into stone silence and might change our friendship. He would think I saw him not as a friend—an equal, an unequal equal—but an object of study or merely nosy curiosity, one who might not respect the tacit pledge of omertà at the core of the male bond for any issue touching one's pride.

Hugh and I really were unequal equals. It wasn't that my life didn't interest him; he might have liked to know certain things but didn't want to ask questions. He rarely asked personal questions of anyone, perhaps because he didn't want to be asked anything about himself in return. In the delicate balance of our friendship there was also a sense that even if he was the superior athlete and had the more powerful brain he was not an equal in worth, in self-esteem, in professional status, so he had no right to ask anything personal. It wasn't simply because on society's scales he didn't register. There was something else, a deeper scale he weighed himself on. When you asked a friend a personal question, you were putting yourself in debt to him. You didn't simply owe him a reciprocal piece of knowledge about yourself; a quantity of trust was also exchanged, and you now owed him that too for having asked him to confide in you. Hugh didn't want to be in anyone's debt and I couldn't imagine him asking anyone a personal question.

4.

At this point Hugh still had a story, even a rather conventional one, which may be why I was thinking of calling whatever it was I was writing about him *Four-fifths of a Champion*, or alternatively,

The Virtual Parricide. The latter sounds a little too hip, too fashionable, with a melodramatic overtone which doesn't fit Hugh. But *Four-fifths of a Champion* has an ironic yet positive spin and also a touch of irreverence which feels right. The hint that it's a sports story is also apt because Hugh was first and always, before anything else, an athlete, a physical person. After he was done playing organized school sports—basketball, baseball, track and field—he continued running, cycling, swimming, rope-jumping, lifting weights, and doing exercises of his own invention. Besides also doing ungodly numbers of sit-ups, push-ups, and pull-ups, he played pick-up basketball and casual tennis. He couldn't imagine himself without sports and physical culture. As it was for full-time professional athletes and models and dancers, cultivating his body was a daily activity, probably in clinical terms an obsession. Hugh was also a student of sport, always fascinated by the games and tournaments man had invented to test himself in—who were the best and what were the limits of human ability. He could flip open his copy of the *Guinness Book of Records* and start reading at random, his curiosity about the extremes of achievement always piqued. Amused too, by the weird and ingenious ways people found to excel, to set themselves apart, to carve their initials on history's tree.

Four-fifths of a Champion was Hugh's title too, the label he put on himself, the distinction he diffidently aspired to. A champion stands alone on a pedestal. The four-fifths champ stands lower down, a step toward the mass who can't even compete. Hugh would immediately see this in terms of statistics. If you fall one-fifth short, 20%, you are nearer the top than the bottom but you are also approaching the point where the bell curve swells out and down toward mediocrity. So calling himself four-fifths of a champion has to be a joke. Yet it's his own joke, one disguising a high and earnest purpose. At the age when Hugh conceived this solo event, in his mid to late thirties, his goal—besides competing as a runner—was to achieve an experience. Completing a mile in five minutes meant that he could run at a champion's pace, run like Bill Rodgers for at least one of the twenty-six miles of a marathon. It was only one, but it would give him some sense of what it was like to run that hard, although it would also be a profoundly humbling experience. What exhausted him was a feat a champ could repeat twenty-five more times without losing pace. So Hugh, who was always computing things in his head, knew just where four-fifths of a crown would put him in the hierarchy of excellence.

Perhaps Hugh's solo event also appealed to him because running a mile in four minutes had been the biggest track event of his youth, a high water mark in athletics when Roger Bannister broke the "barrier" in 1954, and Hugh may have wanted to get into that line of champions. But it did seem to be an odd choice. Hugh didn't have the right physique for the distance, carrying 155 or so pounds on a 5'10" or 5'11" frame. He was built like a middleweight boxer, not a long distance runner. As usual, he might have been hardheaded about it, regarding the handicap as part of the event. Or it allowed him to rationalize his time: If I weighed twenty-five or thirty pounds less, he could say, then maybe I really could have been a champion distance runner. But Hugh knew the difference between himself and a champion, and he had it confirmed when he actually took a run with Bill Rodgers. It was arranged by mutual friends, and Rodgers was past his prime by that time, but the experience gave Hugh a physical feeling, not just a metrical one, for the difference between him and an athlete who not long before had been the best distance runner in the world. Hugh may have been in the 99.9th percentile of cardiovascular condition himself, but the pace Rodgers casually set made conversation uncomfortable for Hugh. Yet Rodgers chattered on naturally while they ran. Before their fun run together, Hugh might have secretly thought he could (almost) stay with Rodgers, but when he described the experience he couldn't keep his wonder at the real champion's ability out of his voice.

The dreamers who watch sports events on TV and think with a little practice or training they could do that too, or could have once when they were younger, were protected by their fantasy from acknowledging that superior humans—when they are doing what makes them superior—are not like ordinary ones. They are different by orders of magnitude, on a separate graph, in another realm. The serious students of the sport, on the other hand, can have the opposite response and be so boggled by the chasm between the ordinarily talented and the very best that they undervalue themselves. In his notebooks, Hugh quoted an eighteenth century English writer describing the experience:

"Illustrious examples engross, prejudice and intimidate. They engross our attention and so prevent a due inspection of ourselves; they prejudice our judgment in favor of their abilities, and so lessen the sense of our own; and they intimidate us with the splendor of their renown, and thus under diffidence bury our strength."

The man who wrote this, Edward Young, was "a man of genius" himself, according to his friend Samuel Johnson. Hugh's own comment on Young's observation was written below the quotation in his spare scrawl: "Great men are a great burden to us all."

5.

There were several great men, superlative achievers like Richard Feynman, Larry Bird, Immanuel Kant, and Sigmund Freud (every team has to have a flawed member) who figured in Hugh's mental life. From one angle it seems strange that a self-sufficient individualist like Hugh would have heroes but there's another reason for admiring heroes besides the childish one of wanting a parent or strongman or god to protect you or merge yourself with. If you believe in something greater than yourself, or the potential for it, and what you believe in is somehow manifested by someone else's life, then your admiration for the ideal or principle comes to life, it's embodied in a real person, someone who shows what is possible. Or, as in the case of Freud, the hero stands for what one might have revered but abominates, embodying a corrupted form of the peak of human endeavor. The ideal and its shadow—its dark side—exist, sometimes together. Feynman, Bird, Kant, and Freud along with Hugh would make an interesting team and I can't resist thinking of them on the basketball court. Bird is at center—or wherever he wants to be, really—and Hugh would be the only other one who knew the game, and possibly the only other one with any athletic ability. Even if he was only three- or four-fifths of Larry Bird at his very best, he would be feeding Bird the ball if he touched it at all. Feynman might try to get into it in his playful way, clowning around till he lost control of the ball, kicking it, switching to soccer; Kant and Freud would be baffled by the sport. Trying to encourage them would only irritate them and offend their senses of dignity. The opponent might be the Washington Generals, those old foils of the Harlem Globetrotters, solid players, four-fifths champions themselves.

So, did he do it? Did Hugh run his five-minute mile? I don't know. I think he came close, because the one time he mentioned his progress he was only a few seconds short, or long of the goal. We didn't know each other well then, so I never heard. Later, when I did know him well, if I'd asked about the old, personal challenge, he'd have made a joke to deflect the question. Whatever the outcome, whether he ran it in 4:59:99 and that was it, or if it was never more than a personal best, maybe 5:04, is mute history. Over the years Hugh kept setting other ambitious physical goals, besides the routine daily ones, so the idea that he might be four-fifths of a champion is something I see as a running private joke, one that he fulfilled in different ways at different times, in other solo competitions. Whatever he said about his continuing private decathlon was expressed tersely, with a dismissive laugh, and at most he might answer one follow up question before changing the subject. Since he was more likely to talk about what he had failed to do than what he had done, it was hard to add up his achievements and get the right sum.

So in the end, as attractive as the title is, *Four-fifths of a Champion* is insufficient. It's a quip and although Hugh's life in the greater scheme of things may be no more than that, it's unfair to portray him so narrowly, as a fraction instead of the whole—or if not the whole the striving, incomplete person he struggled with being.

6.

The way we started playing tennis required a go-between. Neither of us could quite ask the other directly. It seems stupid now, but that's the way it was. Hugh wasn't going to ask me because besides his natural reticence he was the superior athlete, so it was my place to ask him. But he was working with Kate, so if I invited him to play and he said no it might be awkward. I didn't ask Kate to ask him for me, though it might have sounded to her as if I was hinting just by mentioning it. In the end it probably wasn't a decision at all, just a spontaneous comment in her candid manner telling Hugh if he was looking for another partner I'd be willing to play with him.

"Sounds fine," Hugh said, although he didn't sound all that eager. I could understand that. It just confirmed our positions in the athletic pecking order and if Hugh had sounded eager it would have been out of character. When he agreed to do something he often sounded vaguely reluctant, as if he was under an obligation not to disappoint people and that a portion of his free will had been sacrificed to this principle.

Our tennis playing didn't seem to have a very promising start but as time went on, racquet sports became the thread or glue in our friendship. In this sense our friendship was primarily physical, and conducted outdoors, like kids playing in the street. We rarely met just to have a beer and talk, or did any other activity together, like going to a movie or sports event. Hugh's company was demanding. Even when he was jokey, he always arrived with some idea or reaction to the news or what he'd been reading that was brimming and seething in his mind, and especially as we got to know each other better he felt I was an audience he could unload his mental burden on.

It took a while for us to develop our particular rhythm and ritual of playing tennis, and later squash, together. Although Hugh was the better player, neither of us was very skilled. We'd both learned the game late, in our thirties, when the motor neurons don't want to bother to learn new lessons. Besides that, neither of us was really motivated to learn the game. What Hugh wanted to do was hit an ideal ground stroke. It was an esthetic goal as much as athletic, like executing a perfect dance step, and people sometimes paused to watch when we warmed up because Hugh looked so good on the court. Besides his proportioned physique, his form was classic, right out of Vic Braden's book. We might hit for an hour before playing a game, just for the pleasure of feeling a well struck ball on the strings of the racquet. Our games, especially on my side of the net, included plenty of hacks and mis-hits, but sometimes stroking the ball back and forth in those long rehearsals we looked like real players. Over time we got better and played the game well enough, almost well enough, to begin to feel it from the inside, or from the edge of the inside.

We usually played on the courts behind Harvard Stadium. The Har-Tru surface was as smooth as the felt on a billiard table, and on the best days the sun warmed us and a breeze blew from the Charles River on my right, Hugh's left. We never changed ends because it wasted time and I always brought my sunglasses and visor so I could see facing the sun. Hugh had little interest in any of the shots besides ground strokes. He never looked fluid serving. Maybe he had too much muscle, and maybe he didn't want to let himself go either. Once he left the comfort of the baseline, he looked uncomfortable, like someone whose self-consciousness makes them awkward on the dance floor. Hitting overheads or volleying also risked being embarrassed. He never rushed to the net except to chase a short shot and since I rarely executed a real drop shot, they were often accidents. When he was pulled to the net by one of these, Hugh looked like someone who realizes too late he's the butt of a joke. A joke not in fun either, but profoundly unfair, a trap meant to mock his goodwill. To protect himself from these embarrassments, Hugh was a fatalist at the net. Whatever happened was such a fluke there was no meaningful difference in outcomes between trying and not trying. Trying made you look as if you didn't get the joke, and not trying subverted the spirit of playing any sport at all.

Hugh's formal, orthodox approach to the game liberated me. I didn't have to worry if I looked bad because Hugh was both the protector of Form and the alpha dog on the tennis court. Losing face for him really hurt but I was the younger brother, less strong and fit, so I had the freedom to look bad without damaging my self-image.

This was the core psychology between us on the court, although there were variations. What I wanted most from the game was to get outdoors, get a good workout and have fun hitting the ball. Hugh didn't need tennis as exercise; by the time we played he had already run up and down the steps all the way around Harvard Stadium, and if that wasn't enough he'd do a hundred rope jumps at the top of each set of stairs. Plus chin-ups, sit-ups, push-ups, and chair-steps and weightlifting, and whatever else he'd done at home. So for him tennis was dessert. That's what it became for both of us, a treat we enjoyed together, could only enjoy together.

It wasn't long after we started playing that Hugh's job ended and he was unemployed. I worked for myself, on my own schedule, so we both could squander one long afternoon a week whacking a ball. Sometimes it felt as if we were playing our lives away, just for the hell of it, as if there was nothing better to do. There *was* nothing better. We were physical beings, sun-worshippers who would also play in the rain until we were slipping and falling on the court and the heavy ball spewed out a rooster tail after it was smacked over the net. While we played, we banished time. In our best sessions we also banished the Darwinian reality of sport and competition, the inequality of triumphal outcomes. This was a game we could both win, as long as winning wasn't the goal.

7.

Work and love is all we have, Chekhov said. Freud said the same thing, and no doubt someone earlier than either of them said it too, more than once, because it's a pretty obvious thought and must have passed through many minds.

Hugh's job in television had ended with a whimper when the series of shows was done; the funding ran out and wasn't renewed. No one else offered Hugh a job at the station. This wasn't unusual, programs came and went, there were always more people than jobs in television and Hugh was hardly the type to put himself forward. Quite the reverse; he put himself back. Most people in television are ambitious and, no matter how cynically they talk, they believe in what they're doing because they believe in their own careers, even if the shows they're working on are only vehicles. The way Hugh questioned everything down to its roots, then challenged the roots too, the soil, the air, the sunshine, was unsettling. It was a sensibility out of place in television where everyone was, one way or another, showing themselves off. That's what people do in academia too, the successful ones, including even the philosophers, who may talk sincerely at times about the meaning of meaning but when it comes to writing and publishing and promoting themselves are just as skillful and calculating as anyone sitting in front of a camera with a professionally earnest smile on his or her face. So the job which had teased Hugh with the possibility that he had found a niche to perch in, to be able to use more of his abilities than required by breaking truck tires off rims, had floated out from under him with the same tidal motion with which it had so recently buoyed him up. Donald explained to him, in the mixture of English and Russian delivered in Mr. Magoo's voice which he used to keep the world at arm's length, that there was no more money for the show, no prospect of renewal, no budget for hiring uniquely gifted philosopher-mechanics, and that he too was now scrambling to find a job at the station.

Since Hugh rarely reported things that happened to him until some cushion of time had passed and he could mention them offhandedly, it was a while before he told me he'd been cut loose. If he had begun to believe he might finally have a real career—something he would never have said point blank—that hope was quashed. His new, briefly enlarged self as a television researcher had joined the major league baseball or basketball player, the professor, the writer, and whoever else lay on his personal pile of jettisoned possible selves. We didn't really talk about how he felt or what he was going to do. Most of the rest of the staff had lost their jobs too, including Kate, so Hugh was just one of the many sloughed off. Nevertheless, that was also the point. He wasn't special after all, no matter how much Donald appreciated him. Or he was special but it gave him no role, no added protection. He wasn't going to be strolling around the station like Einstein at Princeton, an ornamental point of light hovering over the landscape, or however he saw himself in private reveries. The other significant change he did talk about, eventually, and soon obsessively, was in his emotional life.

Hugh and Debby had met when they were still kids, just out of college, working at one of those social service agencies which drew the hopeful, unblemished college kids into the funky cities to make a new world. Fifteen years later, incredibly enough, they were still in the same relationship, prisoners of love and loyalty, and of their evolved history too, even if in recent years it had stalled. She was attractive and smart and, at a glance—despite Hugh's own male attractiveness—it looked like a mystery why she had stayed with him so long, stuck together in the vestibule of their lives. But she loved him. She understood him too, and she admired and forgave him for being himself. She was also nearing forty years old. If she was going to have children, it was time. To think of Hugh with children, his own children, as any kind of conventional father...it was hard to picture it. It wasn't just his lack of a career or steady income or their cramped, two room apartment in a decrepit building in Cambridge, it was also his critical attitude toward any defined place in society. When I went up the narrow back stairs toward their home, it was possible to imagine I was climbing up to a garret where a princess was held against her will. The living room was so tight you could reach across from the couch without standing up to adjust the black and white TV perched on a brick-and-board bookcase jammed with books. The kitchen was too small to hold a table to eat on and the bedroom was just barely bigger than the double bed filling it. To add a baby to this apartment would have meant living like the masses behind the Iron Curtain. More than that, Hugh's inability to become whomever or whatever he was going to be in his one and only life made it obvious that he wasn't ready to replicate himself in the form of another human being. He seemed more like someone in his twenties than nearly forty, and he still scorned everything middle class, starting with parenthood and the cult of the child current among enlightened parents. Could Debby herself imagine Hugh as a father? Not just because of their circumstances but also because of his history with his own father. If Hugh had a child would it resent him, especially if it was a son? Would she be burdening that child, her child, with all Hugh's bad history, and his rigid opinions, as well as their pinched material life? In practical, worldly terms—Darwinian terms—Debby could do better. Yet she was so in love, or attached, or devoted to Hugh, or so neurotically unable to imagine him without her, or her without him, that she couldn't leave him. Only he could push her out. Which is what, after all those years, he finally did. Perhaps in some kind of self-sacrificing, abnegating way, he was throwing their relationship on the pyre to release her, as if to say Yes, you can do better than me. More likely it was simply his response to the intolerable. Hugh had to do something to change his paralyzed life. So he got a girlfriend. Or, more accurately, he responded to a woman who made it obvious she wanted him, physically. She wasn't what Hugh really wanted at all but the infidelity broke the emotional, the psychological impasse. Debby moved out and almost as soon as she did, he wanted her back.

It was already too late. Debby had been thrown out of jail and her new freedom was exhilarating. There was no way she was going back to the cramped, Soviet-style apartment, to Hugh's obsessions and preoccupations, his suffocating categorical imperatives. Once the spell broke she could see the negative image of the man she had lived with for fifteen years. She may have felt sorry for him, it probably hurt her terribly, but there was no going back. To protect herself, she moved away, out of town, putting distance between them, refusing to call or write.

When I saw Hugh on the tennis court, all other subjects were now a prologue to his lament for Debby. For several weeks, his grief went into his creative attempts to communicate with her, to remind her who he was and the depth of the love she was missing.

He did this by making audio tapes, complex aural collages he concocted from parts of dubbed songs, radio jingles, quotations, combined with his own layered, baroque verbal inventions. All his frustrated emotion and creativity went into these private Firesign Theater productions which he spent hours and days recording. Among the interwoven threads and multiple subtexts, the leitmotif was his undeservingness, the classic self-demeaning pose of the wretched, penitent lover. Except that Hugh meant it. It was too painful to hear the actual words or follow him as he described his Rube Goldberg audio contraptions, each one displaying such creative ways to say I'm sorry, I love you, I need you, what a fool am I, and the rest of the limited vocabulary of a crushed heart. I pictured Debby dropping these sad bombs of love into a wastebasket, their only sound a soft thud as they fell in the trash.

After all the years in the garret apartment, glued in place by their mutual history, suddenly things happened very fast. Debby had moved out during the summer, and in the fall, as Hugh and I were walking back from the tennis courts on one of those days when the weather is so perfect you feel immortal, he said seemingly out of nowhere, "Debby got married." I almost said, "To who—you?" but checked myself. Had she been having a secret affair too? No, it was some guy she'd just met, and in the same speeded-up tempo the news soon came that she was pregnant. Pregnant? Was Debby trying to put something irrevocable—not just another man but a child—between them so there was no way ever of coming back to Hugh? It seemed so. He was in agony. After all those years locked together he'd gotten to the point where he couldn't live with her. Now he couldn't live without her. For a man who loathed cliches, Hugh had fallen into one of the oldest ones, and he described his emotions as if he could hear the laugh track in the background. What he felt for Debby now was like a wave which kept crashing and breaking around him. He drowned every day in grief. That she had found a man so different from him too seemed to negate the meaning of who he was and all the years he had spent with her. The new guy, her husband, had a conventional career, wore a coat and tie to work, and—unthinkable as it all was—somehow the worst of it was his nebbishness. He wasn't even in shape! Hadn't the temple of Hugh's body been a place he and Debby both worshipped? Not narcissistically but esthetically, for the raw health and vitality of his strength. Yet, if she had found a man as much of a physical culturist as Hugh, a marathoner, a cyclist, an ironman, a tennis pro—or worse, a mathematician, a physicist, a writer, anyone he compared himself to in his imagination—he'd have been just as dismayed. But he couldn't see that. He couldn't see that whoever replaced him would cause him agony, an agony which the details would always make worse, whether the guy was a couch potato or Olympic gold medalist. Either way, Hugh felt nullified. Debby had been his. They'd been together nearly twenty years. Twenty years! (The number had swollen with his grief.) How could that be so easily thrown away? He was blind to how hard it had been for her to leave him, he forgot that he had to do everything but physically remove her from the apartment—carry her down the stairs in his arms—that she hadn't left quickly in anger but in her own slow agony of torn up years.

When we met to play tennis, all our conversation about sports or politics or books was a distracted prologue to Hugh's blues. If she could marry a man so unlike Hugh, what had all those years meant? Nothing! If I agreed with him by saying I'd noticed women didn't seem to care about a man's physique as much as men did, he'd jump over that, as if he agreed it was superficial, to get to the real sticking point. It wasn't the guy's shape, it was how conventional Debby's sudden new life was (he never used the word "bourgeois"). Hadn't Hugh's ethics, his belief that we were required to reject the blandishments and exploitations of the gross national product, hadn't that meant anything? Because that was the whole point of Hugh's existence. (He didn't actually say that either.) How could she have betrayed it—with her heart, her soul, her life?

He soon got to that final resting place for the bereft lover, a seat by the grave of their long affair. No wonder Debby had left him, Hugh moaned. He was so unworthy, so useless. He deserved to be wretched. He kept repeating what had become an obituary for his youth, the long prologue to an adulthood which had not yet arrived, a transformation which Debby had fulfilled for herself, but only by leaving him. He didn't say this directly, but it could be heard in the background. The way she started her new life so decisively felt like a further rebuke to what he thought they had shared, as if her respect for him and what he believed was insincere, even a charade, and she'd just been waiting to make her escape. That was nonsense, of course—waiting for fifteen years?— but in the turmoil of his own mind, these thoughts multiplied themselves endlessly. The rebuke was to *something*, if not to his ideas, then to him as a person, a man without a career or direction. Yet it didn't matter—or it merely doubled the rebuke—because Hugh really was his ideas. He might have denied it so he wouldn't appear to believe in anything, but he was an idealist—a jilted one— who credits the abstract over the concrete, and only truly believes what he can't see.

However Hugh looked at it, Debby's fresh new form as housewife and mother was a wildly disorienting experience, and as tedious as he could be I understood his anguish. How could he have lived all those years so close to a woman who secretly had the soul of a housewife? If Debby hadn't truly believed in him, then no one did. No one could. Yet, at the moments when his emotion cleared or was drained by exhaustion, he could see that Debby's new life wasn't that far away from their life together. She was a warm, nurturing woman with all these dammed up desires to be a mother and enjoy the comforts of a more conventional life, everything denied to her by living with him. This view of Debby wasn't so much charitable and generous as it was an involuntary insight which he expressed as a confession, with self-flagellation. He was worthless, so of course she had left him, and alone in bed before dawn he sometimes appeared to himself in the third person, unprotected by any vanity, a proud, stubborn man stuck in the ruts of what he had nurtured, and his proud integrity was a nullity.

8.

I always wondered why Hugh hadn't gone on to graduate school. He was the perfect student in so many ways, the kind who enjoyed reading books on abstruse subjects by thinkers like Bertrand Russell and Wittgenstein and Schrödinger and Feynman. Unlike most of us, Hugh remembered what he had read. A lot of it, anyway, and he remembered in detail, not just a hazy impression of a writer's argument or ideas. Besides recalling what he'd read and studied in college the way Red Sox fans recite their team's history, Hugh also imprinted sports stats like a devout sabermetrician. These gifts, along with his playfulness, might have made him a good teacher. He enjoyed mental games, conundrums, and tricks to solve them, but when he tackled a moral question—How should one live?—he became serious, however jokey and playful he sounded, and couldn't trim or adjust or compromise. To turn the pursuit of truth into a career was perverse, even if failing to do it meant you were refusing to grow up and face the adult problem of surviving while maintaining some kind of integrity. But what if you didn't believe in the product of the intellectual life—books and monographs written in such a way that they could be published by academic publishers? Then the question about whether you were compromising your ideals wasn't even the issue. You didn't believe in the commodity the academic industry produced and consumed. You weren't playing the game. Hugh instinctively knew that his iconoclasm and lack of political skills doomed any career in an institution. Or any effort to put his ideas into a salable form, especially when one of his reigning ideas was not to market himself in any way.

He also wanted something more or other than a "career," whatever it might turn out to be. This vagueness was part of the problem. He couldn't exactly define what he saw himself doing, yet the idea of pursuing a career made him laugh. That was what everyone did and whatever or whomever he was, he was not everyone else.

Underlying it all, there was another reason why Hugh couldn't imagine a career as an intellectual. He was the wrong physical type. If a man is a superior athlete and a superior intellectual, which attribute defines his primary sense of himself? This is the kind of question Hugh would have answered by making some wisecrack about the relative value of philosophers versus shortstops. But seriously, Hugh, if you could be either which would you be? Maybe he hadn't pursued playing professional baseball because he knew that despite his athletic ability there was a hole in his game and he could only go so far, that even if he made the majors he would top out as a middling or marginal player and he demanded excellence of himself. Four-fifths of a champ wasn't enough. Maybe he also felt—here's that self-negating conflict again—what he did with his life had to be a mental activity so he couldn't really devote himself to a sport. That left him stuck in between. A jock with a brain, or a brain in a jock? Neurologists say we don't really make decisions, they are formed in our mind by forces we aren't quite aware of, then some other part of our brain makes up a story afterwards so the decision we think we made fits with our "personal narrative." Perhaps Hugh hadn't been able to make up a story about why he did what he did. Or perhaps he tried out many stories but none of the plausible narratives he constructed could stand up to the interrogation he put everything through that entered his mind. His scalding honesty—or helpless affinity for the reductive—seemed to prevent him from taking the refuge in fiction available to the rest of us. In the end, paradoxically, for someone so stubborn and willful, it could seem as if Hugh was waiting for some force to reveal itself, to take him in hand, and lead him to his proper destination.

In the meantime, during this mysteriously long prologue to what one day would become his real life, his identity was always partly defined as a man who could have played with the big guys. In his forties he went out one morning to the Harvard athletic field and threw a softball farther than the then-current throw in the *Guinness Book of Records*. Could Wittgenstein match that? Men are strong and women are beautiful, and Hugh's original physical form defined him in a way he couldn't help but embrace. As an intellectual, a philosopher, a writer, he always felt like a changeling, as if there was an element in that identity which was not entirely authentic or had been layered over another deeper self. He could joke with guys like a jock, he was a natural at flirting with girls, but the human type Hugh could never identify himself with was the hyper-cephalic klutz whose athletic IQ made him a physical moron. Hugh was rooted in the physical world, strong before he was smart, a handy man who knew the vernacular of the locker room and the back seat, present in the same here and now everyone else lived in, hyper-aware instead of lost in space. As much as his talents made him exceptional, and as little of Nabokov's despised vulgar *poshlost* as there was in him, Hugh shared a high percentage of the traits we call normal. He liked beer and a hamburg, his heart lifted to pop tunes, he threw Frisbees, teased little kids, joked with guys, flirted with girls, and "How you doin', babes?" was his ur-greeting to the world.

9.

Hugh had saved a lot of money, by his standards, during the year he worked in television. The salary was higher than he ever would have asked for and because he lived so frugally the money piled up in the bank. When the job vanished he didn't feel any pressure to find a new one. Like Thoreau he valued time more than money, and used his leisure to improve his body and mind. Because he was so handy and competent, people asked him to fix things, and not wanting to disappoint them he usually said yes. He also usually refused to take any money. People often misunderstood this exchange, logically since the world's currency was money, not favors, which as the name indicates are something we see as bonuses of friendship, not a medium of formal exchange. Hugh didn't explain his system of values to people so one could say any misunderstanding was his fault, except that it was out of character, impossible, really, for him to explain himself, so the whole situation had something foreordained about it. If he did enough favors for someone they usually found some way to compensate him. So he did have a small trickle of income. Then, at some point, he began working part time for a carpenter. He hated the work and any excuse, like tennis or squash, was enough to make him pass it up. His revenge on a job he disliked so much was refusing to learn the trade of carpentry. It was a futile protest since it was impossible for someone as observant as Hugh not to learn what he was doing with his own hands. But his comment made me think about his attitude and I realized that despite the chronic frustration his life was settling into, I never heard him curse his situation. I never heard him curse anything. Searching my memory for the sound of his voice using an obscenity, I only hear one when he is quoting someone else. He wasn't a prude, not in the least; he enjoyed a little light lewdness ("Please come and sit on my face"), but his speech wasn't sprinkled with casual curses or obscenities. He was good-humored, not testy, and except for the big things the world didn't rub his nerves raw. No epithets either, even describing in high temper the politicians and public officials whose deceit and demagoguery drove him so crazy. People were always themselves, not their race or ethnicity. Hugh may have loathed certain traits and behavior but he wasn't vindictive or vengeful. Instead there was a restraint, a tact, a decorum in his character. He was that antiquated male type, a gentleman: civil, patient, gracious. Of course, how he behaved as an intimate partner may have been different, since his private code could be tyrannical.

His discretion in showing his physical prowess had the same restrained character. Mostly it was all performed out of public view but at odd times in surprising ways he might show off his strength. One of the guys he worked with called him "the strongest carpenter in Boston" after he had been hired especially to help carry a cast iron bathtub down four flights of stairs in a Back Bay building. They did it, two guys on the downstairs end, Hugh solo on top, his rare combination of hand, arm and leg strength suiting him for the job of bending forward and descending while holding so much weight with his hands. He told me about it later, repeating the comment about himself ironically, because by now his situation had become so deeply ironic in nearly every respect that incidents like this seemed to amaze him too: how had his life led to this kind of accomplishment? It was baffling, to him most of all. His telling me this incident was a reminder, one I only partly appreciated at the time, that he saw himself so differently from the person people assumed him to be. The childhood projection of the person he would someday become still existed as a conscious part of him, and that was someone who could never be summarized as "the strongest carpenter in Boston."

In using his strength Hugh was the opposite of the show off or bully. He withdrew self-consciously when he felt he was being watched, and he despised bullying in any form, physical or verbal. Malcolm Lowry wrote that he wanted to be strong to protect the weak. Hugh would have agreed, but I think for him it went to something deeper. His constant exercising may have had a narcissistic element in it but it was impossible to imagine him oiled and preening like a bodybuilder; instead it sometimes seemed that he was mortifying the flesh like a medieval monk who had to punish himself so he could be forgiven. Except that Hugh really enjoyed his physical culture. Maybe that was the effect of the endorphins, the natural opioids flooding through him during exercise. Perhaps it all worked together, the mortification and the pleasurable internal painkillers and the pride in being strong and fit. Which comes back to the desire to be strong to protect the weak, among whom might be, first, oneself. Hugh might have needed to protect himself by being so strong he wouldn't have to fight. He abhorred violence. He quit playing pick-up games of basketball at the Y because he couldn't stand the guys who threw elbows and played dirty. He couldn't play dirty himself, and he couldn't risk a fight because he didn't want to lose and to win meant hurting someone, a nauseating thought as well as taboo by his code.

Besides what happened with his father, had there been other incidents in his adolescence when he hurt, or thought he hurt someone? Had he fought with his stepfather, as Kate had heard? Because of his sensitivity, it would only have taken one incident to make him afraid of his own, or of anyone's strength, and if his mother had blamed him, even just insinuated that he'd contributed to her husband's death it would have stayed with him forever. That, besides conflict with his stepfather, might explain why he was so estranged from her too.

10.

Hugh meant it to be funny. We were on our way to play tennis at the Harvard courts and he was describing his phone call the night before to his mother. "You called her?" I said, surprised. "How long's it been since you talked to her? Did she knew who it was?" I laughed.

"A while. Five years, maybe."

The 'maybe' tacked on to the number didn't convince me; I think he knew exactly how long it had been.

"What was it like—talking to her after all that time?"

"I wanted to let her know she'd been a good mother," Hugh said, by way of answering my question. "I tried to think of something that would make her think she'd done a good job raising me. So I told her I knew how to use a fork."

"A fork?"

"I didn't use my fingers when I ate, I knew how to use the proper utensils, I didn't embarrass myself when I ate in front of other people because when I was young I was taught how to use a fork."

We were laughing.

"You told her you knew how to use a *fork*?"

He wasn't even saying he'd been taught how to use the right fork, as if he'd been brought up with society manners. Just a fork, a utensil, instead of his fingers. Had she been offended? As usual, I couldn't get Hugh to embellish the little he'd said.

It certainly sounded as if there was something perverse in his comment, as if he meant to hurt her. If calling her after so many years of silence and then talking about table manners was meant as a joke, a parody of the mother-son relationship, it was one that might make his mother wonder how Hugh could have cared so little about her. But I had to keep in mind that his mother, he said, was a flirt (like him), not a serious person (unlike him), and it was possible that this was the way they had always communicated, by teasing each other, that she was irreverent too, so there might be real affection in it. Perhaps it was the only way Hugh could communicate with his mother.

The few things he had said about his past always referred to his father. His mother never figured as a source of conflict or guilt or anger or any other strong emotion. She sounded gay and frivolous, someone he could blame at most for choosing a second husband he could not get along with. (A first one too, for that matter.) Or for being no more than gay and frivolous, a kind of airhead. One of the few things he told me about her was that she took books away from him when he was a kid—snatched them right out of his hands. "You should be out playing!" she scolded him. This sounded unbelievable. Hugh was such an habitual, avid reader, so dependent on reading for his private dialogue with the realm of ideas, that I assumed if his father was the athlete his mother must have been the one encouraging his intellectual side. Again I wondered if he had grown up feeling he was some kind of changeling, absurdly misplaced with a mother who grabbed books from his hands and a father who had no time for him, resenting his only son and competitive heir.

Hugh liked women. He liked women socially, romantically, and sexually, and his problems in relationships arose from his frustrations with himself, and his place in the professional and social order, and from the anomalies of life itself, not with the gender of women. Yet he was uncomfortable with feminists. He had been an adolescent during the '50s when boys were boys and girls girls. His mother's model was quite the opposite of a feminist who demanded liberation. Besides that—and this went deeper—he resented women portraying themselves as victims. The cult of victimhood was repugnant to him. He didn't blame blacks for portraying themselves as victims because their battle had been with slavery and nothing was more wrong than enslaving another person. But the women Hugh had known were a pale shade of victim compared to the African-American experience. Women had some genuine complaints but it sometimes seemed to him they were piggybacking, adopting the role of victim because it had a certain currency. At the same time, Hugh was well aware of the place of women in most cultures historically and was the last man one could imagine forcing himself on a woman either sexually or physically. But he lived in a subset of American culture where many women had jobs more prestigious and better paying than he'd ever had, so he objected to the claim of victimhood when so much had already changed. To him it sounded absurd, as if they were claiming a right to a kind of fulfillment no one was guaranteed. Finally, although he wouldn't say it, he was almost proprietarily sensitive to claims of victimhood because he felt he was a victim himself, a psychological victim. As a white male there was no social remedy. Events were to blame; one might even say the cause or culprit was life itself. There was no solution except to change everything.

11.

When I asked Hugh if he wanted to play squash he said yes eagerly. He had an old racquet he'd bought at a flea market but had never played, so when we ducked through the low door into the enclosed indoor court our roles were reversed. I'd only played a few times but it was enough to get past the klutz phase when the combination of the nearly dead ball and the long slender racquet with its stingy sweet spot made you hit spastically or even swing and miss completely. Everything you knew about bouncing balls and hitting objects out of the air felt wrong. Hugh got through the initiation quickly, embarrassed at times but also curious about the odd characteristics of the game. After we'd played a few times and he should have reached the point where his superior athleticism equalled and then passed my skill, he was still routinely losing. At times he lapsed back into something resembling the klutz phase of learning, with a personal dollop of self-loathing added, and began whiffing wildly and hurling himself around the court. It was dangerous and unsportsmanlike. With his usual scholarship he'd read the rules of the game and some of its history and learned that sportsmanlike behavior was supposed to be an essential part of the game. Two players armed with long wooden racquets in a small enclosed space meant the possibilities for intimidation were handy. Restraint and a certain awareness of your opponent's location were assumed; if you couldn't swing at a ball without hitting him you called a let which was always honored. So just like his occasional uncontrolled play on the tennis court, which had begun after he lost Debby, frustration was threatening to ruin squash. Finally, during one session, I intentionally muffed a few points and gave him a victory. He must have been receptive in just the right way, because a switch was flicked and his energy changed from negative to positive. He suddenly liked this guy Hugh who wasn't, it turned out, a bad guy at all, and had a rather natural ability to play squash racquets. He maintained that attitude for the rest of our session and brought it back to the court a week later. After that, to my amazement, I couldn't win. Hugh owned me. I'd assumed I could turn it on and off and win a game now and then if I wanted to, but once Hugh got his attitude straight, his natural superiority made him unbeatable. I even succumbed to a dose of the self-loathing that lay in wait for anyone playing a sport badly, and reverted to some fairly spastic play. Then that passed and our squash games took on a comfortable equilibrium. Hugh dominated winning but I was competitive, and some of the points went on long enough that we felt as if we ourselves had become part of the strange physics of using long racquets to hit a bounceless ball off the inside walls of a small polyhedron. The physics moved from our bodies into our brains, elevating us into a zone I had certainly never experienced before. During the extended points when we both hit the ball well, anticipating caroms and moving the other guy around with well-placed shots until one of us finally smashed a winner or dropped a finesse shot into a corner, and did it all at a speed that pushed both of us to our limit, we were enacting some kind of Platonic ideal of The Game. These moments might occur only once or twice each time we played, but they sometimes lasted for several long points in a row, and it was exhilarating and exhausting. It was the magic of sport; by playing both with and against another person, you could achieve a physical experience way beyond anything you could do alone. In the midst of those points when your body was hurling itself around the court in a strenuous *pas de deux*, you wanted to win the point more than almost anything. But only almost, because most of all you wanted the extreme dance to go on, and on, and on. Squash sessions were booked in forty minute intervals and we always played three if a court was available. Squash was famous for the cardiovascular workout it could give a player and I certainly felt it even if Hugh never seemed to get anything more than mentally tired from playing. When we stopped for a drink I stood over the fountain as if I'd just crossed the Sahara and Hugh took a few quick mouthfuls. Then we ducked back through the low door and one of us was serving again. The sessions eventually fit themselves into our larger routine, alternating with tennis when it got warm outside again.

The strange caroms and underlying perversity of squash seemed to fit Hugh's personality, although there was a definite limit to how good he was going to get starting in his forties and only playing once a week with one less talented partner. Like distance running, squash wasn't the best sport for his physique either, since he carried more muscle than could be applied effectively to the ball. When I bumped into him on the court—a few collisions were inevitable—he simply didn't move. It was like running into a statue, something metal or stone instead of flesh, and although I hardly needed to be reminded of the fact, it gave me a physical sense of how strong he was. I was a guy in decent shape who liked to play a vigorous game, and Hugh was in his own category, off the bell curve, a freak.

12.

"I destroyed all his poetry," Naomi said. "He told me to, if anything happened to him, so I did. I didn't look at anything. But I still have a box of his notebooks and some clippings. Do you want them?"

It sounded almost like pleading: Please take these and relieve my burden.

I said yes, of course, I'd be glad to have them—not sure I wanted the burden either.

"Most of them are blank anyway," Naomi said with a slight laugh, as if Hugh had played a joke on her, on all of us.

"Really?" I said, laughing too. Perfect. The terminally blocked writer has a collection of notebooks—and they're all blank! I could hear Hugh laughing too. What can I say, babes, nothing to say, too much to say.

It wasn't until several months later that I had the right conjunction of time and mood to dip into them. The image that came to mind as I stood over the box was of a treasure chest. I was a pirate, opening the spoils of a raid. But when I picked up the first notebook the pirate was gone and I was a kind of spiritual relative going through his things—things too private, and trivial, for anyone else to want to deal with.

Under the first notebook I picked up was a Joan Didion book, *Salvador*, which I hadn't read. I assume Hugh did since he liked Didion, shared much of her politics, and liked her spare, quick, cinematic style. He also recognized that as much as he shared her worldview, she and her husband John Gregory Dunne lived in another universe, one completely alien to Hugh, the New York/Hollywood hip, artsy jetsetters. If Hugh had really known Didion and Dunne, he'd have been uncomfortably aware of the social inequality between them—they were rich and well-known and he was poor and anonymous—even if a large part of their sensibilities would have met in a place where they revered and abominated the same things. There was something else Hugh shared with Dunne in a very different way. Despite his achievements and acclaim, Dunne's life was nearly as shot through with frustration and a sense of inadequacy as Hugh's. So much for the rewards awaiting the successful and famous, or semi-famous, writer. One might even say that as a writer Dunne was four-fifths of a champion. Except the title or honor meant something quite different in the separate spheres inhabited by Dunne and by Hugh. Dunne, and Didion even more so, wherever they stood, wherever you placed them on the literary bell curve, were both players; they were in the game, with credentials and contracts and money and meetings and agents and lawyers and openings and parties and reviews. Most of all they had colleagues, they were part of the club. All that leavened frustration, made it social instead of hermetic. They also had each other.

I set *Salvador* aside and picked up the "Harvard" brand ring-bound 6x9 notebook (bought at the Coop in Harvard Square). It had no date. I'd chosen it first because it looked like one of the older ones, but I soon discover that nothing has dates, not the notebooks nor the entries. How like Hugh—how maddening! Inside is a page of Hugh's semi-legible left-handed scrawl. Ambidextrous, like many gifted athletes (including Larry Bird) he handled a fork (Hi, Mom!) and wrote with his left, but threw a ball and played sports right-handed. The notes are from his reading of several books on creativity: *The Art and Science of Creativity, The Universal Traveler,* and five or six others, mostly notes on blocks to creativity. An apt place to start. Categories include "Perceptual Blocks, "Cultural and Environmental Blocks," "Emotional Blocks," "Intellectual and Expressive Blocks." Also notes about problem solving, with several headings for "Exercises." Already the outline of so much of Hugh's thinking emerges, all of it driven by his restless urge for self-improvement. And of course the inability to fulfill the improved self. Most poignant is a heading, "Basic Expectations of Modern Man." He lists four:

1) To be engaged in creative work
2) To have an imaginative life-style
3) To have a complete love and sex life
4) To be in control

These sound almost as reductively hopeful, and obvious, as any self-help handbook, and I'm briefly embarrassed for Hugh. Then I remind myself that all kinds of moronic incongruous thoughts can be found in a private notebook. Or inside our own heads.

There are notes from Robert McKim's book *Experiences in Visual Thinking* with exercises to sharpen the senses. There is a paper clip holding together seven carefully cut out pieces of paper—a square, five triangles and a parallelogram. They make up the tangram, an ancient Chinese puzzle that can be formed into different shapes. Hugh seems to be trying to find what is behind the kind of ordinary thinking we take for granted. Besides wanting to know how his brain works, he also wants to know how else it might work and how it might work better. Finding out requires effort, from injunctions as simple as, "Try to dream productively," (which sounds impossible and silly) to "Changing graphic languages implies changing mental operations," to which he adds: "Is this true?" Behind it all is the urge to exercise his mind the way he does with his body.

I had gone through several notebooks before I came to what I was really looking for, some thought of Hugh's own rather than quotations or lists. From internal evidence I figured out it was written when he was still trying to rid himself of the ghost of Debby and the long prologue of years with her that had led to nothing, to her absence.

"Where do all those desperate people go," Hugh wrote. "A woman who will be forced to leave her home because she owes $88. Another woman, perhaps 60, had a judgment against her reduced from $2000 to $1000. She will be removed from her home in ten days. 'You should be happy,' the judge says, 'you just made $1000.' I rode my bike slowly through several of Cambridge's ugliest streets. Behind a Chinese restaurant was a small subterranean kitchen. Windows at street level were dirty, broken. Noises from the gloom within could be heard. The noises mingled with Chinese restaurant smells. Busy hands holding grilled prawns with cilantro and ginger sauce."

13.

After nearly an hour of hitting we'd just started playing a game when a couple kids from the Harvard tennis team walked out on the court next to us, a signal that we were about to be bumped by the rest of the players. We finished the game and packed up. Hugh was in a glum mood, it was affecting his play, and I was ready to call it a day and go home. He wanted to play on, making an effort to be stoic and show he could be a good sport even though his life had collapsed, so we walked over to the courts behind the business school. They weren't as new or well-kept and several were empty.

It had taken us a while to get to this point where we played less to win than to enjoy the game. The goal more than ever was to hit the ball well and if you did but the other guy won the point, fine, although at the end of the day Hugh expected to win more games than he lost. Occasionally, one of my winning shots might be rewarded by the contemptuous sniff athletes flicked at each other in grudging tribute, but neither of us used any gamesmanship and we often played points over because a shot on the line was too close to call. We'd end up Alphonse-and-Gastoning each other. "In!" I'd call Hugh's shot. "Naw, way out," he'd call back. "It was in, man!" "Play it over." A beautifully executed shot, if it was close, was always good. Always. How we played the game was determined by Hugh's complex attitude toward winning and losing but it coincided closely enough with mine. At the first level, like any athlete, he hated losing. Mostly, with me as his opponent, he didn't. But if I won with guile or a fluke, like a drop shot, Hugh could slide into a funk, because then the game was imitating life, defeating him even though he had prettier ground strokes, knew the game better, was the superior athlete. If Hugh was in a self-castigating mood, I sometimes adjusted my playing and didn't try to win as much as I tried to keep the ball in play. When Hugh's game was on, I didn't have to do anything but play hard and he would win almost every set.

This mutual attitude we'd evolved toward the game could be fragile because at the same time that we'd gotten more comfortable with each other on the tennis court, Hugh had begun to relax the hold on his moods. That might not have mattered—it might have been the normal progress of familiarity making us more tolerant of each other's quirks—if the rest of Hugh's life hadn't been falling apart at the same time. But tennis, in another of the several analogies with sex, can reveal how you feel about yourself no matter how you try to disguise it, and on this beautiful autumn afternoon, in the leafy sanctuary of the Harvard Business School grounds, Hugh began having a kind of nervous breakdown. Perhaps being bumped from the better courts was one insult too many to bear because when we resume playing I can see that he's losing the struggle against his demon. All the frustrations of his life are seeping out of him like a foul gas. After a shot or two goes awry he gives up trying to control his rage; now he's trying to hit the ball as hard as he can. His shots aren't just flying long over the baseline, they're like wild pitches. He hits one over my head on a line and the ball impales itself in the wire squares of the chain link fence surrounding the courts. Swinging madly again, he mis-hits, the ball caroms off the racquet frame and shoots up in the air like a pop-up and flies over the fence. On the next shot Hugh whiffs almost spastically and stands staring at the empty space the racquet passed through. I try to hit some of his cannonades back but finally ask Hugh if he wants to quit. "This is just a bad day," I say, making an excuse for him. "No, no, I'm okay," he says, affecting stoicism. He's not okay, he's having a tantrum and I'm getting pissed off at him. We're too old for this. At the end of another love game which I've won without hitting any winners, all the points defaulted because of his whiffs or line drives out of court, I walk over to the gear by the fence and pack up. Despite all the encouragement we usually throw at each other over the net—the opposite of gamesmanship, trying to make each other better players instead of getting into the other guy's head to screw up his game—today reminds me of everything that's become wrong with our tennis. It's a burden to play with Hugh. I always feel as if I've got to carry his mood around the court with me. This can be liberating because it relieves me of fretting about my own bad shots, but today it reminds me that Hugh is becoming dysfunctional. The old wood racquet he insists on using is like a crutch, but instead of enabling him in some way it's a reminder that he is crippled. It has begun to feel as if he wants to be crippled, that he's in love with or dependent on his disability. This is a glib analysis, I'm aware, and I feel sorry for him, but what the hell, I've got my own life too; we're supposed to be grown-ups and I feel like a babysitter.

Hugh's life has slid into a very bad place. I can barely talk to him anymore. His diatribes against the government, the corporate oligarchy we live under, the values of our material society, the complacent stupidity of the human race, the futility of his own life, his worthlessness, have congealed into a toxic mass in his brain and to relieve the pressure, the poison, he emits a stream of exasperation, an arraignment of existence naming all these outrages. His knowledge of examples is impressive, even overwhelming, but it's also intolerably boring to listen to, like a hammer striking an anvil over and over again. Yes, yes, I agree lamely, but what can anyone do, which is also his response to how useless his own life is. His ranting has become his theme song, turning conversation into unstoppable monologues delivered in a hushed, strained, confidential voice. It may all be literally true, like the fact that everyone dies, but it's also unhealthy, it's no way to live, and walking back across the river to Cambridge with him, I begin seething myself with frustration, angry to have wasted so much time with such a self-involved nut. I'm seething and he's so angry at himself, at me too I can feel, just for being there, for not being as miserable as him, that finally he can't talk either. We're like kids yet again, in another way, kids who lose their temper and fight, call each other names, misbehave, because they haven't learned civility yet.

Hugh's misbehavior cuts him deeply for several reasons, not least because it's so much a part of his code to be civil. It reaches deeper than civility too, all the way down to the elements of Kantian philosophy he abides by, and we're both aware he is failing himself in this deeper way too. We say goodbye briefly, embarrassed, and shortly after I get home Hugh calls to apologize "for being such an asshole." His rare, almost unprecedented use of a vulgar epithet gives his apology a large pathetic weight and he goes on to explain how he has felt so useless and down. He's got enough distance from his self-loathing to characterize it, but he doesn't describe his state of mind as a mood, as the emotional weather, because to him it isn't temporary or changeable, it's the way things really are. The world is fallen, venal, and corrupt, not worth living in, and he is worthless. He is caught in a cyclical, self-reinforcing solipsism. This is clinical depression, I realize, which means it should be treated in a clinic, not at home, not by maniacal exercising, by whacking a tennis ball as if it was Kissinger's face (or Hugh's own), by brooding solitarily, and for company listening to late-night talk radio shows with their call-in volunteer casts of the ignorant, the indignant, and the wounded, while doing push-ups and sit-ups. But Hugh wasn't going to go to a clinic. Not that it would have helped anyway. He wouldn't take drugs and he wouldn't have tried the "talking cure" even if he had the money to see a shrink or a therapist. I didn't believe in those cures either, not for him anyway. What he needed—and he knew it himself, he ached for it—was a woman and a career. He needed a role and position in life, a function, something to do, and he needed someone to love, a woman to put his arms around, and without either he was at the bottom of a well with no way to climb out.

I accepted his apology, whatever that means, but also decided we needed to find different partners. I didn't want that experience again, standing on the court like a punching bag while my friend melted down.

14.

Among the many things that made Hugh different from other people was that he had a code he believed in and lived by. It was thoroughly worked out in his mind and expanded itself out to include everyone, all humanity. In his reticent way, by hints and dropped comments, he had disclosed how deeply it had seeped into his being, and I was aware that while he was melting down on the tennis court he was also betraying himself and his beliefs.

The categorical imperative was the defining principle. It was the scripture codifying his preoccupation with the broader underlying ideal, the concept of justice. Immanuel Kant's categorical imperative is the thinking man's version of the Golden Rule, the left brain's rational restatement of the command ascribed to Jesus of Nazareth, Do unto others as you would have them do unto you. Kant's version of the concept said a person could use reason—reason, not emotion—to figure out how he should act and that what he did had to be something everyone could do in the same situation. Your actions had to pass the test of universality. If you took this seriously, down to its root, like Hugh did, it meant you couldn't act for material gain and be consistent with this philosophy. Not if your gain was someone else's loss. The great monster of guilt over his father's death may not have come up from the deep by the time Hugh was eighteen or twenty and reading Kant for the first time, but he seized the ideas with both his reason and his emotion, even if he didn't entirely understand why. They appealed enormously to a young man's idealism, and once you peeled away the dense layers of Kant's metaphysics, you revealed the skeleton of a code one could live by. It simply required that people not do anything that everyone else couldn't do. Kant called this strict duty: you were bound by strict duty to act by this principle. There were no exceptions for individual inclinations. At the next level were imperfect duties, as Kant called them, which were flexible and allowed for individual interpretation. Helping others, what we call "being a good person" was a personal choice, not an obligation, and it couldn't be strictly defined. Virtue was a choice, justice was not. Above all, you did not take advantage of anyone. By adhering at a minimum to strict duty you were acting to create a livable world. Besides this practical effect, there was a loftier philosophical implication which was expressed by Germaine de Stael in her commentary on Kant: Doing your duty by choice is the proof of the independence of man. It's what can give a human being significance.

Since de Stael and Kant, many sages had challenged the concept of free will and claimed to show it was a delusion. Hugh had read the arguments, and they were convincing. After all, this was the age of Kafka, Beckett, atomic bombs, and rock 'n' roll, not Goethe and Mozart. What we thought were choices were responses to the actions of forces we weren't aware of. Who knew what his brain was really up to? The twentieth and twenty-first century thinkers had waded deeper into the cerebral morass of how we knew what we knew—what we thought we knew—and what we assumed about ourselves and the world. The new ways of deconstructing certainties could make Kant seem almost quaint, but for Hugh—when he stepped outside his head into the world we all had to live in—the concept of strict duty continued to feel like a revelation to him. It was a simple, logical argument that explained how he instinctively felt. That this became a compulsion, a code he must live by, also seemed to deny freedom of choice, yet Hugh always felt the choice had been made in his mind, that he had been persuaded by logic. So the sense of compulsion came from the fact that Kant's argument described what he felt in his gut. And was confirmed in his head.

The next step for Hugh, which came soon after he discovered Kant, was to find a political philosophy that fit with the ethical one. He read Saint-Simon and Proudhon, and later, more critically, Marx. It was obvious. The answer was socialism.

15.

I found a new tennis partner, a couple of them, and abruptly I was playing a different game. Tennis lite, tennis unburdened. There might have been a little gamesmanship about line calls and lets, but not much, and I no longer had to worry about the psychological state of the guy on the other side of the net. If he loathed himself because of a poor shot or his marriage sucked or his job was a make-work sham, it was his problem. He kept it to himself and if it undermined both his self-esteem and his game, then all I had to do was play a steady, conservative game and I'd win, without guilt. Actually, the guy I began playing with regularly was pretty steady himself, with a nice fluid serve-and-volley game and a basic mastery of all the shots. The game of tennis, not just the pleasant exercise of smacking the ball, appeared on the court and it was a welcome surprise. Gamesmanship was much easier to deal with than therapy, and the partners I found were decent guys who brought unmixed motives onto the court. Instead of lugging six tennis cans full of water from home like Gunga Din to irrigate the three hour plus sessions Hugh and I had indulged in, I jogged over, played a quick couple sets at mid-day, jogged home and had lunch. Cliff, the guy I'd begun playing with weekly, was an engineer working for a consulting firm and thought it was amusing that an education at MIT had led him to design components for sewage treatment plants. "It's not what you write in your yearbook," he laughed. "'Hope for an exciting career in deep shit.'" He had a wife and two young kids and knew as well as Hugh did, or I do, that man seems to be adrift in an echoless universe, that a pure blue sky is a special effect created by photons bouncing off the atmosphere, and that if there is any justice in life it's not distributed according to virtue but follows the same arc as the socio-economic curve. The rich live well, the poor get screwed, and if you're lucky you can hide out quite comfortably in the middle class, with a small thorn in your conscience over the size of your carbon footprint. Cliff also seemed amused by the knowledge that no matter what condition our species lives in, we exist under several layers of delusions. No kind of wisdom can trump these ironies, so all one can do is go to school, get a job, get married, have kids, and sneak off for an hour of tennis at lunch. The rest is just noise interfering with the narrow but clear signal of attainable happiness.

16.

While the biggest change in my life was a new tennis partner, Hugh's life had been going through convulsions. He had spent most of his young adulthood enjoying the happy accident of having found the right woman in Debby, and now that that chance had been withdrawn (fate did not reward ingratitude was one way of looking at it) he was discovering what it was like to find the wrong one. He probably had no choice but to find the wrong one since he was still grieving so miserably for Debby.

The object of his desire, named Denise, was a slim, almost cute, unhealthy looking woman who lived in the building next door. As usual he didn't mention her until the relationship, such as it was, had been going on for a while. I'd seen her once, before the break in our tennis playing, glimpsed across the narrow alley and small fenced yard that separated her building from Hugh's. He had met her, said hello, flirted lightly, and was soon to slide into her arms. Or she into his. If Debby was the salt of the earth, Denise was the salt in his wound. Life had damaged her in some way and although she was inarticulate, or mysterious, in telling Hugh about her emotional scars she seemed adept at using Hugh's terrific need for affection to get things. Or maybe not adept, just not averse. Or maybe, in her wanness, she didn't care enough to repel his attention. Hugh's own description of what she was like and what they did together was as sketchy as what she had told him about herself. She was a watercolor, an unfinished one. They had sex together, at least once in a while, but he said she lacked passion, or didn't seem to enjoy it. That disconcerted him. He was such a physical man and in his current condition his desire raged, so he couldn't imagine that if she felt even the palest attraction to him she wouldn't want to express it in bed. As high as his desire mounted he was, from his own passing and allusive descriptions, gentle with women, a playful and creative lover, but from the one glance I'd had of Denise, slender and undernourished, like a plant that needs sunlight and water, she looked too depleted for passion.

Hugh was still working now and then as a carpenter, or carpenter's helper, determined as ever not to learn the trade while he was doing it, and had been acquiring a collection of tools. With the same obsessive passion that had gone into recording cassettes for Debby, he fixed up Denise's apartment, which was just as shabby as his, repaired her car and bicycle, and bought her a color TV. "What the hell are you doing, Hugh?" I said when he told me about buying her a brand new television. "You've got that shitty old black and white set. You don't have the money for that kind of gift. Besides it sounds like you don't even see that much of her. She's taking advantage of you!" He shrugged. He knew it was a demented act. It was Debby he wanted to give something to, abase himself in front of, not this stand-in. His attitude was so fatalistic it was as if somewhere all this was written. Which was bullshit. He didn't believe in such things. Like an artist with a new muse, when he found Denise he also continued making cassettes, at least one anyway, to express what he felt for her. I asked him what she said about it. "Nothing." Nothing at all? "No." Maybe that was her technique to cool him down. Ignore it. I could imagine how strange and possibly even scary she'd think it was. She, a sip of skim milk, provoking this eruption of hot magma in her next door neighbor.

During the period leading up to when our tennis sessions halted, Hugh's description of himself as useless became chronic. He said it vehemently, as if confessing it would drive this devil out of him and a voice would shout back, "You're okay, babes, and don't believe anyone else, including yourself, because you're okay with me!" I said something like that myself in a jokey, ironic timbre, but he shook off even the most qualified compliment. He denounced himself in the tone demanded of the capitalist-roaders and reactionary pigs by the Red Guards in Mao's Cultural Revolution, as if scourging himself would remake him in a new mold. Not to change his wrongheaded ideology—which wasn't wrong, he never blamed his ideas or ideals for his troubles—but to alter his entire psychology so he wasn't constantly punished for being himself in a world which had no use for him, even rewrite the past so it could become retroactively a journey from somewhere to a meaningful present, instead of this maddening incoherence. Perhaps there was some way—if he were cleansed by confession as a means of showing his sincerity—for the materials of his life to be rendered hospitable and nourishing instead of forcing him to tread back and forth over the same ground, committing the same unintentional sins against love, and against whatever purpose he should have found for his existence.

Life may be a trite writer, as Nabokov said (although the first twenty years of his own life were written by an author as fondly gifted as himself), but it can also be a comedian, and into this deepening trough of Hugh's depression it introduced a new, semi-outrageous character.

17.

Ofra shot over Hugh's wallow of depression on the wings of her own several manias: the familiar neuroticisms of a smart, savvy, not-so-nice, thirty-something, self-described New York Jewish girl heightened by hormones and her own frustrated ambitions. That's what I gleaned long after the fact. Initially, when he first met Ofra, Hugh's attention was still fixed on the wan Denise whom he described again and again in the same scanty words like a Homeric epithet, as if his conjuring her up would stir her emotions and make her respond to his passion. By this time it was obvious Denise wanted nothing from Hugh, not even the free color TV, which she kept only because she was too frail to carry it back to his apartment and Hugh wouldn't take it back himself. (Such an odd symbol to be standing for him and his needy attraction to her; another example of how skewed his life had become.) While Denise had seemed barely to notice the TV, her repaired car, the improvements to her apartment, or even Hugh himself, Ofra's sight, by sudden contrast, was filled by Hugh. She wanted to consume him. He was the meal she'd been starving for. She leaped over the cracks in his self-esteem to grab his body. To her it wasn't a useless or futile or absurd exercise machine; it was an incredibly strong, graceful, elegant, sexy male. He was like a big cat, so light on his feet, so feral in bed. I heard all this much later, when our racquet sports had hesitantly resumed, and Hugh described her gushing briefly, in shorthand, with a tone of wonderment, as if she was a little crazy, and that anyone's attraction to him was a mystery, especially this kind of drooling (although it was the way he talked about Denise). Ofra made him uncomfortable and self-conscious but nevertheless he was unable not to follow her into bed. What he wanted from Denise was impossible but what Ofra wanted from him was simple. She wanted his body, the one temple he could worship in every day, doing his workouts, chair-steps and chin-ups, sit-ups and push-ups, weight-lifting, rope jumping, running, cycling, swimming, climbing the stadium steps, all the endorphins jacking up his dead spirit so he was a kind of hyperkinetic zombie. Ofra wanted him physically almost as much as he needed himself physically, so the temple of his body was a place they could meet, each for their own purposes, of course. Not that she didn't care about his mind and spirit too. Hugh's original brand of braininess, his iconoclasm, even his bitterness, appealed to her too, seconding her view of how strange and shitty life was. But, shitty as it was, buried by the outhouse, right down there next to the organs of filth, were the ones of pleasure and ecstasy.

Whenever he spoke about her, Hugh sounded baffled and even stunned that someone, a not unattractive woman—although Ofra was big, a real armful—would want him so avidly and so uncritically. It was also the first time he'd been with a woman who appreciated his body as much as he did. Her delight in his strength and the way it turned her on was a dose of positive feedback at a time when he needed praise as much as a god. She exulted in his strength, girlishly wanting to see what he could do with it.

Besides Ofra erupting into his life, there was another significant addition. Hugh had begun doing workouts with a guy who competed in Iron Man events. Ron could cycle fifty or a hundred miles, swim a couple miles, then run a full marathon. "I couldn't do it," Hugh admitted, describing a workout. "I can do it physically but I haven't the metabolism. Ron can go without eating. At the end of a run someone stepped in front of me and I almost knocked her out of the way I was so irritated," he said. "My legs were fine but it was just because I was so hungry." He had found someone just as maniacal as he was but who had even more stamina. "He lifts weights every day—doesn't take days off in between!" Hugh said, in the same tone of amazement I might describe his regimen to someone else. Ron had a no-show or barely-show job in the Brookline city government and sometimes he worked out eight hours a day. As a physical culturist he equalled and in some ways even exceeded Hugh, but he was also unathletic—couldn't hit a ball, had no hand-eye coordination—so Hugh's athletic self-esteem found a niche of its own, a way to raise him above Ron.

During that long tortured winter after the meltdown, I never even considered going into a cramped squash court with Hugh. I couldn't risk getting hit by his big lethal racquet in case he lost it again, but when the weather warmed up in the spring we started playing tennis again. Not in the regular routine like before, but occasionally, almost tentatively, and it was obvious that Hugh was slowly lifting himself up, or being lifted up, from the deepest trough of depression. Ofra was part of it, certainly, as ambivalent as Hugh was about his incomplete relationship with her. It was nice to be worshipped, a novelty, even if it made him feel silly at times. Ironman Ron had no life of the mind but for the first time Hugh had a companion who could match his zeal for physical culture. It also gave him some perspective on his obsession; Ron's monomania made Hugh feel a little closer to normal. So in that sense their training sessions were therapy, and Ofra was therapy too. Like Ron she was such a blunt force she altered Hugh's dead end trajectory and blocked his view of himself, at least momentarily allowing him to enjoy what he looked like in her mirror instead of his own dark and distorted one. Much of his soul may have been opaque to her, but her personality shoved its way into his head, either taunting him out of the doldrums or matching him whine for whine. Her complaint against life—instead of philosophical and moral and twisted around a gnarled solitary self—was direct and obscene, and it demanded a remedy now. For Ofra, before anything else with Hugh, there was always the physical stuff. They played together like sexy kids. She sat cross legged on Hugh's back while he did push-ups. He and Ron played this game together, his girl on his back while he did push-ups matching Hugh with Ofra aboard, and although Ron's girl was smaller than Ofra, Hugh could do more. Riding up and down on his back, feeling him lift and drop beneath her in a mime of coition, Ofra squealed with delight like a bawdy cheerleader. How could Hugh not enjoy finally having an audience who appreciated his vaunting strength, his amazing physical feats. It excited her sexually in a way she'd never felt before. Him neither. "She says she's my groupie," Hugh said, between sets at the tennis courts, with a sardonic laugh. He was in an extra-sardonic mood that day. Before I arrived, he'd run the Harvard Stadium steps, up each concrete stairway, all the way around. At the top of each set of stairs he did a hundred rope jumps. (In his notebooks he'd scribbled, "Running the stadium has become too easy.") When he got done some guy came up to him and introduced himself as an assistant coach for the Harvard varsity rowing team. They talked for a few minutes; the guy couldn't believe how old Hugh was (he had to ask point blank for this statistic and got a number rounded down to the nearest decade). He asked Hugh if he would like to come and work out with the crew, thinking a man twice their age exceeding them would push the young rowers harder than any conventional coach could do. The coach said he could get him some tickets to events and hinted at favors using athletic facilities. Hugh refused of course. He didn't want to be displayed like a freak. "You should have said yes, Hugh," I told him. "It might lead to something, you know?" With his combination of physical and mental prowess he might become a figure, a kind of guru, to the Harvard athletic teams. But I knew, even while he was telling me about the chance meeting, he wouldn't accept the guy's offer. Hugh had a need to be known, but to be known as the person he truly was, and as ambivalent as he felt at times toward his own self he always knew who he was not. He was both more and other than his physical achievements, and as soon as he sensed he was being regarded as a freak or a curiosity he would clam up and vanish.

Ofra cared nothing for Hugh's touchiness about being seen as a freak. Of course he was a freak! That's who she was fucking well fucking, for chrissake! Hallelujah! Hugh was the physical and sexual specimen she had always craved—one of the pleasures, the passions, she had to experience to the limit—so she was also deaf to his rants castigating himself. When he said, as he often did, quoting Groucho Marx, that he would never join a club that would include him as a member, she just laughed. "You're already in Groucho's club, baby—you were born in it!" And when he described himself as useless, Ofra squinted and sneered at him and said seriously, no joking around, "You're a little fucked up, Hugh, but one thing you are not is useless!" An off-the-charts stud with brains couldn't be useless. He was there to throw your arms around, to lift you up like a doll and carry you into bed. What was less useless than that?! She was a lifetime neurotic who'd tried all the therapies, knew all the psychological jargon, and when Hugh denounced himself she heard the familiar complaint of the depressed. "You just need to get focused, Hugh. You didn't invent the problem!" Ofra wasn't going to let anyone trump her when it came to being neurotic. That was her native territory.

Hugh's acid views of materialism, social convention, political venality, and the self-delusion of the human animal were to Ofra no more than commonplace truth, the obvious facts of life, and instead of thinking he was obsessed she thought this was just the way an intelligent, sensitive guy with so much physical intensity would express himself. Hugh wasn't normal—who wanted normal?—but to get hung up on a philosopher-airhead like Kant meant he was also a dreamer with a serious case of arrested development because anyone in their right mind could see all that categorical imperative shit was insane. Just try to live like that—you get run over! Ofra's answer for getting him pointed toward a goal or started in some kind of career was just as automatic: "Just do something, Hugh. Anything. Who the hell cares what it is?" Ofra's own life had been a series of stops and starts, lurches and lunges, whose main coherence was a cyclic re-invention of her needy self—which she admitted—so Hugh didn't even really hear her advice. It was just noise. Not that it mattered since he wasn't going to take anyone's advice, anyway. That was another of his problems, arrogance, Ofra told him, not accusingly but as if it was fact, like his shoe size. He may have said he was useless, but secretly he thought he was better than everyone else. Hugh smiled at her analysis. She was a relentless therapist. Their relationship was the opposite of the traditional talking cure where the doctor sits listening, barely saying a word and the patient monologues. In their reversal of roles, Ofra spritzed unstoppably while Hugh made wisecracks. At some point she told Hugh she had discovered what his real problem was—he was denying his own identity. It was poisoning him at his core. He needed to acknowledge it and until he did he'd be paralyzed. That was the real root of his problem. Like so many other things that had happened to Hugh in the past twenty plus years, since the time he was a student and before any of the possible lives laid out before him had been quashed, her verdict was something he could only treat as a joke. She was probably, possibly, right but certainly not in the way she interpreted it. Not for him, anyway.

18.

A writer Hugh liked was Peter De Vries. He loved the anecdote about De Vries having lunch with New Yorker editor Harold Ross to talk about a job at the magazine. Ross asked De Vries if he knew anything about South America. "No, but I can do a gorilla," said De Vries. "We need someone who's been to Rio," Ross answered. "We don't need a gorilla." De Vries' gorilla was in the spirit of Hugh telling his mother she had raised him right because he knew how to use a fork. The archness of De Vries' writing was amusing but could also be irritating, making you feel the banter was a way of keeping you off. Just like Hugh. At other times, also like Hugh, it felt excessively diffident. The undertone sounded as if the author felt he was failing some standard he set for himself, a standard so lofty and so different from what he was writing it couldn't be mentioned.

Hugh's affinity with De Vries went deeper than the jokes and nonsense. Walking back from the tennis courts, Hugh made a comment that seemed to invite me to ask if he knew anything about his father's background. "Did your father ever talk about his own parents or family?" I asked. He said no. "Did you know your grandparents?" No, again. He shook off all my questions, saying no to the questions themselves, so I dropped it. Then one day in a used book store I picked up De Vries' novel *The Vale of Laughter*. There it was, on the first page, something Hugh might have said himself. "What nationality I am I cannot say. My father would never tell me, always clamming up when the subject was broached. So I guess it is some race held in low esteem, which he deemed it just as well to keep from his offspring...." De Vries' arch tone wasn't quite right for Hugh but the content was dead on, and I thought of it another time when he volunteered a biographical fact, or rumor, about his father.

"My mother thought he was Jewish," Hugh said with a laugh.

"She thought—you mean she didn't actually know?"

Hugh answered my question his own way, by quoting his mother:

"She said, 'His name is Sam, that's usually a Jewish name, isn't it?'"

Hugh laughed again. He thought this was funny, sardonically funny.

"Like Sam Clemens," I said. Then I asked seriously:

"*Was* she just kidding? She must have known something about his family." I was curious to know more too, even if it was only to know that Hugh himself really knew so little about his own background. But once again he had said all he wanted or was willing to say, and that was the last time we ever talked about it. Jokey Hugh quoting his flirty mother. Maybe no one in his family ever gave a straight answer. Maybe his father was silent as stone about his history. Instead of having something to hide it could have bored him. He could have been the classic taciturn male, the independent agent, the athlete sprung from the fact of his own being who was what he did and apart from his function had no other self, none of interest to him anyway. But it was hard to believe Hugh didn't know more than what he'd revealed. When he was a boy he must have wondered about where he came from; his parents would really have had to stonewall him if he knew nothing at all about family history. So I assumed he knew more than he was willing to say, even if he didn't know many specifics.

However much or little he knew, there was no doubt Hugh's father had wounded him and perhaps part of the wound was not telling his son about his own origins, as if Hugh wasn't worthy to inherit his father's personal history, or was so insignificant it wasn't worth his father's trouble to pass it on. Another possibility is that his father told Hugh about his family history in such a grudging, reluctant, or indifferent manner that Hugh decided he would refuse to hear, refuse to remember where Sam, and Sam's son, had come from. In any of those cases, despite the harm to Hugh's sense of himself, his feigned or genuine ignorance of his own origins fit with the attitude he took toward everyone's family history and ethnicity, the attitude consistent with his philosophy.

We were all made of the same stuff and for Hugh the question of ethnicity or race was irrelevant to his identity, to his self, his soul, his being. An ethnic identification was tribal, a sign of an undeveloped mind, an affront to reason. The backwardness of identifying yourself by your tribe was reflected by the make up of the human genome. All humans, all races and kinds, shared 99.9% of the same basic genes. But wasn't the flip side of that the more important message? Genes were so potent that the narrowest individual slice, whatever it was that made us different, counted for more than the long dull normal string we all had in common. For Hugh the argument had been settled long ago: the philosophical mind had to bow before reason and reason said we were morally all the same stuff. Since Hugh was a connoisseur of the exceptional in everything, an example himself of an almost freakish superiority among the mass, he was always aware of the tension between what we all shared and what made a few individuals special. He loved to cite Thomas Huxley quoting what his gardener said to him when Huxley commented that the differences among human beings were very small: "They are very small, Mr. Huxley," the gardener agreed, "but the differences between us are also very great." The unstated social difference between gardener and master also resonated profoundly with Hugh.

Whether by adoption or inheritance, Hugh possessed a quality that kept bias out of his manner or speech. He never used the terms of race or ethnicity to describe anyone. He didn't use epithets or call people bigots or fascists or assholes, no matter how much they offended him. He strictly avoided the fallacy of the *ad hominem* argument. Gender he talked about, since he noticed women as women, although they were never girls or chicks, and he was always aware of the desire some people had to play the victim. He also assessed physical traits, especially athleticism, but regarding the person he seemed to have completely internalized the spirit of Robert Burns' poem, "A Man's a Man for a' That," although he never expressed it romantically. It was a way to avoid the logical fallacy and it was also a demand of the categorical imperative. If your acts had to pass the test of universality then race and ethnicity and even culture were obviously no more to be considered than they were in applying the Golden Rule of Jesus of Nazareth, an authority he never referred to, no doubt because of his deep scorn for religion. He mentioned once, glancingly, the ideas of John Rawls which included a compelling thought experiment that appealed to Hugh: imagine creating a world you will live in yourself but you don't know anything about the person you will be—your social or economic position, your physical or mental talents, your gender or ethnicity, nothing. You must decide from behind a "veil of ignorance" how privileges and assets will be distributed in this new world before you know whom you will be. If that were the situation at the starting line, says Rawls, wouldn't you naturally prefer a just world with everyone equal, so whomever you turned out to be you'd get a fair portion, the same as everyone else?

From his own physical appearance, dark hair and eyes, regular features, a large, strong symmetrical head, Hugh could have been most anyone ethnically, or no one, a true everyman in having many genetic strands combined in his person. Intellectually, however, the people he admired were the questioners, the iconoclasts, the doubters and wiseguys, the mental gymnasts and tricksters, like Richard Feynman, who could stand for them all, the skeptics who rolled bombs under the bed and for whom nothing was sacred except the next question. Hugh admired the thinkers who accepted a state of profound doubt and fought back against the uncertainty of life not by creating a God to believe in but by trying to fill themselves up with as much knowledge as possible.

Since many of the people who thought in this way—scientists, writers, intellectuals—were Jewish, it was easy to see why Ofra decided Hugh was at least partly Jewish, especially if he had told her his mother's comment about his father named "Sam." However she came to the conclusion, it became obvious to Ofra that the root of Hugh's problem was his refusal to embrace or at least accept his ethnic identity. Hugh just laughed. Ofra was serious and her project to give him his missing identity and fatten up what she saw as his undernourished sense of self quickly became a new field of combat for them. For Hugh it was all too trite to take seriously but he couldn't laugh off her passionate and tangled feelings about her own identity. Ofra had redefined herself when she embraced her Jewishness and forsook all ambivalence about her own ambivalence, a renaissance or even conversion that also led her to fiercely embrace the idea of Israel. When she urged this on Hugh too she pushed him past his sense of humor. "I think Israel is a mistake," he told her, and seen through the lens of the categorical imperative it couldn't be otherwise. It had nothing to do with anyone's ancestors. It was absurd to think so. To correct an historical wrong like the Diaspora or a more recent one like the Holocaust by moving Arabs from their homes so Jews could move in was not something that could be done everywhere. The principle underlying it was tribal or national, not universal.

Ofra heard Hugh's argument as another symptom of denying his own ethnic identity—he was hostile to Israel because he didn't want to be Jewish. This accusation frustrated Hugh; he had nothing against anyone based on ethnicity or background, and meant what he said. Israel was a bad idea, it had nothing to do with Jews or history. That was their argument; his argument was that you couldn't uproot people from where they lived and move them around based on claims of ancient texts. Or for any reason. It was unjust. He tried levity, quoting Mark Twain, "Every square foot of earth has been stolen from someone," but Ofra wasn't listening.

Neither was Hugh. He had gotten no further explaining his code to Ofra than a capsule "Kant for Dummies" description of the cat-imp, as he called it, and when she sniffed what was coming she held her nose and mocked it. This was a conversation with two dead ends. Hugh made it worse because he was so reluctant to explain himself. What he believed was sifted and molded into a coherent system of thought from many thinkers and to try to describe it to someone whose mind was blocked by a zealous nationalism—well, that was one of the human fallacies banned by his philosophy. To describe it in the face of Ofra's hostility meant all subtlety was lost, and he just sounded like someone who'd never grown up since college, someone who really believed all the idealistic fodder of dormitory bull sessions.

Hugh's reluctance to defend his philosophy went another step deeper too. He didn't like explaining himself on any subject or situation, and his natural privacy had been intensified by experiences he couldn't explain clearly or logically to anyone. If he was a mystery to himself, if his life had turned out to be a form of existence he couldn't understand or explain, he certainly didn't want anyone else to understand it, to sort out the events and non-events and in the process possibly create a story showing he was not the hero of his own life. Or create their story of his life, which Ofra was doing. It would necessarily be some kind of fiction, not his own story, the one he couldn't write himself. He had begun to need the mysterious, the inexplicable reason or non-reason for how his life had turned out.

Most of this remained in the mute chamber of Hugh's private thoughts since the relationship with Ofra wasn't that deep. Despite all the talk about identity, there were several levels of Hugh she didn't understand, even if she had seized the physical and sexual one with both arms. Keeping a part of himself in the dark confirmed his ownership of his mystery and although to be so utterly misunderstood by Ofra was frustrating, it also did more to reinforce his identity than adopting the ethnicity she urged on him could have done.

So their relationship lurched from sex to psych talk and from psych talk back to sex, and as one activity became more and more frustrating, the other was as easy and pleasing as if they were a pair of bonobos. Wet with her sweat, Hugh parried her arguments in his strained, exasperated voice while Ofra sang the opera of loss and restoration and how it could fill an empty soul like Hugh's (as if it has filled yours, he never got angry enough to say, except in a way so convoluted she didn't hear it). He didn't lose his temper but in the arena of argument Hugh was as tireless as he was doing push-ups, and would never concede a millimeter of his position in the spirit of finding ground for agreement. How could you agree to something that was wrong? The best he could do was re-state your argument in his terms, a way of showing he understood without agreeing, and Ofra tried a variation on the technique with him.

"Okay, you might not be a Jew but you're Jew-ish," she said, still arguing, and Hugh, still arguing too, agreed.

"I might not be Greek but I'm Greek-ish," he laughed. "I might not be a good man but I'm good-ish. I might not be someone but I'm someone-ish."

19.

Hugh had the two volumes of Richard Feynman's *Lectures on Physics* on the bookshelf beside his ancient black and white television set, and had read the physicist's popular books too. Hugh idealized Feynman—to the extent he would let himself indulge in boyish admiration for someone—as a natural enemy of bad thinking, puffed up authority, and acceptance of all the unexamined notions that were complacently accepted as facts. Hearing him talk about Feynman, repeating quotations and quips that expressed his irreverent spirit, I began to see Hugh as the anti-

Feynman, a similar human particle but with the opposite charge. Feynman's electrical charge was positive, a plus sign, while Hugh's was negative, a minus.

All the famous Feynman anecdotes gave Hugh great pleasure to recall: Feynman cracking safes at Los Alamos to get classified papers he wasn't cleared to see (even if he'd written them himself), then leaving thank-you notes in the re-closed safes. Feynman asked by a hostess whether he wanted lemon or milk in his tea and replying, "Both!" (eliciting her response: "Surely you're joking, Mr. Feynman!" which he used as a book title). Feynman dipping the rubber O-ring into his glass of ice water to show how the Space Shuttle *Challenger* might have blown up. It was irreverence in action, a leap from the trivial to the momentous, a blend of skepticism and wonder, a quality that could be carried into any arena of life like a torch revealing surprises and misconceptions of all kinds, as well as hypocrisy, prejudice, and fawning before authority, all obscuring the truth. Hugh had seen Richard Feynman once in person, coming out of a Harvard building, and waved a greeting. With his typical ready friendliness Feynman waved back, Hugh reported to me, laughing at how much pleasure he took in this fleeting exchange, the two particles flying by each other. Seeing him in motion, however, Hugh was disappointed to notice how unathletic Feynman was. As much as Hugh admired him and his scintillant mind, it was impossible for him to identify wholeheartedly with a man who lacked physical grace. So there was a gap, even a chasm between him and Feynman. It interfered only slightly with the desire to identify with another person, someone you feel is like you in spirit, who shares your essence, but due to a wobble in fortune's spin is a total success in life while you are unfulfilled and unappreciated. To contemplate Feynman as a potential semi-equal, Hugh could set his physical excellence beside Feynman's immense mental gift and, at least in his imagination, meet as a roughly equivalent particle. Feynman was five-fifths of a champ to be sure, almost beyond any rating, and Hugh at this point had slipped off the bell curve entirely, so he was aware that expressing any identification with the Nobel Prize winner risked committing a presumptuous absurdity. It was only a shared affinity for knowing the truth and an irreverent attitude that allowed the two particles to occupy the same field, even briefly.

Yet Hugh's disappointment when he saw Feynman's physical awkwardness in person was revealing. If Mephistopheles had appeared at that moment and offered Hugh a chance to swap lives with Feynman, with the condition that they change bodies too, would Hugh have made the deal? (Forget how silly the question is.) Hugh considers the offer briefly, then shakes his head. No? Really? Yes, because the one thing Hugh knows about himself, and knows it so automatically I doubt he ever thought about it as a discrete quality, is that he was an athlete. He was an athlete before he was anything else. He didn't value his brain any the less but his brain lived in a body of a certain quality and type, and he could not imagine himself otherwise. Athletes rank themselves and each other by how good they are at their sport. They are judged on their talent, their ability to perform. Nothing else matters. They calculate this hierarchy as automatically and mercilessly and coldheartedly and mockingly as physicists rank each other's brains. If Hugh had been unable to give up the naive ideals of his youth, it was partly because he was still the athlete who had to win whatever event he entered. Because he couldn't do it—and perhaps this was how he came to terms with those ideals—he changed the rules or the game or nested the game in a larger one, so large no one could win, and the concept of winning was redefined so it could be finessed or outfoxed. Nevertheless, a mind as sharp as Hugh's was aware that no matter how old and mellow and wise one became, one never outgrew this reflexive act of ranking; it was always there, always potent, always disabling, no matter what game you played on yourself to defang it.

The physical difference between the two oppositely charged human particles called Richard and Hugh has nothing to do with the similarities of their spirit or soul or mindset. There isn't any single word that captures this essence of who we are individually, the metaphysical seed from which our personality and character and nature and values sprouts and blooms, the self, the soul, the spirit, the totality of genome and culture and history, so I'll call it the *vzeoogby*, a personal signature of one self as unique as an email address. There are many ways in which Richard Feynman and Hugh anti-Feynman shared a similar vzeoogby. In Feynman's letters, published under the affably in-your-face title, *Perfectly Reasonable Deviations From the Beaten Track*, there is an exchange which illuminates Feynman's opinion about the meaning of being Jewish which reads like an elaboration of Hugh's own attitude. A writer named Tina Levitan wrote to Feynman asking for a biographical sketch to put in her book, *The Laureates: Jewish Winners of the Nobel Prize.* Feynman wrote back and said that it would not be appropriate to include him in her book "for several reasons, one of which is that at the age of thirteen I was converted to non-Jewish religious views." She replied that her book would include both professing Jews and, "also those of Jewish origins for the simple reason that they usually have inherited their valuable heredity elements and talents from their people." Feynman demurred again, saying, "It is quite certain that many things are inherited but it is evil and dangerous to maintain, in these days of little knowledge of these matters, that there is a true Jewish race or specific Jewish hereditary character. Many races as well as cultural influences of men of all kinds have mixed into any man. To select for approbation the peculiar elements that come from some supposedly Jewish heredity is to open the door to all kinds of nonsense on racial theory."

In his opinion of religion and ethnicity as moral or quality-of-the-mind determinants, Feynman could be speaking for Hugh.

Another example of their similar vzeoogbys was expressed in Feynman's letter resigning from the National Academy of Sciences. "To be a member of a group, of which an important activity is to choose others deemed worthy of membership in the self-esteemed group, bothers me. The care with which we select 'those worthy of the honor' of joining the Academy feels to me like a form of self-praise. How can we say only the best must be allowed in to join those who are already in, without also silently proclaiming that we who are in must be very good indeed. Of course I believe I am very good indeed, but that is a private matter and I cannot publicly admit that I do so, to such an extent that I have the nerve to decide that this man, or that, is not worthy of joining my elite club."

This is the flip side of Groucho Marx's quip about never joining any club that would have him as a member.

For both Richard Feynman and Hugh anti-Feynman skepticism was more than an attitude, it was an article of faith, the only means of approaching the truth. Throughout his letters, Feynman urges people to make up their own minds ("don't believe me," he tells one correspondent) and says about his own field, "In physics the truth is rarely perfectly clear, and that is certainly universally the case in human affairs. Hence, what is not surrounded by uncertainty cannot be the truth." Hugh had the scientist's cast of mind and was unable to take any comfort from believing in superstition. Feynman couldn't take any comfort from superstition or religion or mythology either—they were alien to the way his mind worked—but that didn't mean he lacked a sense of wonder which gave him joy and delight in existence. But the source of this wonder, and its nourishment, is where the shared vzeoogby divides, underlining how differently the two men were cultivated as children:

"My father, a businessman, had a great interest in science," Feynman wrote. "Wherever we went there were always new wonders to hear about; the mountains, the forests, the sea. Before I could talk he was already interesting me in mathematical designs made with blocks. So I have always been a scientist. I have always enjoyed it, and thank him for this great gift to me." *This great gift to me.* Throughout the letters, Feynman's references to his father are always profoundly appreciative of his encouragement and they always express love, an uncomplicated love and gratitude for his father's attention. Replying to another correspondent who complains about dull textbooks, Feynman once again remembers his father's gift to him: "Don't despair of standard dull textbooks. Just close the book once in a while and think what they just said in your own terms as a revelation of the spirit and wonder of nature. The books give you facts but your own imagination can supply life. My father taught me to do that when I was a little boy on his knee and he read the Encyclopedia Britannica to me! He would stop every once in a while and say—now what does that really mean?"

Now what does that really mean? There's a phrase that could be emblazoned on a monument to Feynman. But here is a fact that almost makes me weep for my friend Hugh: it could be emblazoned over his life too. The difference is that Hugh had to discover this question for himself and instead of first hearing it in the doting voice of a loving father and associating it with a sense of wonder for nature, the question for Hugh interrogated his own life. It challenged his existence down to its root. It demanded he justify why he was here. The father who wouldn't teach him to play tennis and the mother who took books from his hand may have combined, however carelessly or thoughtlessly, to give—or at least contribute to giving—their human particle's vzeoogby a negative charge.

The "great gift" of his father's encouraging interest in science not only took root in Feynman, it also became a model. To a former student who said he wasn't working on any worthwhile problems in physics, Feynman wrote, "No problem is too small or too trivial if we can really do something about it. You say you are a nameless man. You are not to your wife and to your child. You will not long remain so to your immediate colleagues if you can answer their simple questions when they come into your office. You are not nameless to me. Do not remain nameless to yourself— it is too sad a way to be. Know your place in the world and evaluate yourself fairly, not in terms of the naive ideals of your own youth nor in terms of what you erroneously imagine your teacher's ideals are." When you read this advice lifted out of the context of the whole book of letters, where Feynman's spirit is felt on every page and opposite this excerpt you see a photo of a happy, tuxedoed Feynman dancing with his pretty wife at the Nobel Prize ceremonies, you feel how much context is everything. Or nearly so. Feynman's despondent correspondent is sitting in some dreary office at a university in Japan, confessing the humble nature of the problems in physics his life is given to solving. The even more purely desolate anti-Feynman human particle called Hugh has no office, no position, no wife or child or colleagues, not to mention no Nobel Prize. He has no problems at all to solve. If Hugh knows his place in the world and evaluates himself fairly, as Feynman recommends to his former student, might he not say, like him, that he is nameless? Useless? Is that because he is evaluating himself by "the naive ideals of his youth"? Has he failed to grow up? Perhaps his goal to be four-fifths of a champion was an attempt to be realistic, although it was always expressed as a joke, as such an ironic ambition that even if he had run a five-minute mile at age 40 he wouldn't have bragged about the achievement to anyone, except perhaps to mention it, with a laugh, to his tennis partner.

Throughout the letters, Feynman extols the personal pursuit of some study or activity that will excite wonder. "Work hard to find something that fascinates you. When you find it you will know your lifework....While looking for what fascinates you, don't entirely neglect the possibility that it may be found outside of physics. The man happy in his work is not the narrow specialist, nor the well-rounded man, but the man who is doing what he loves to do. You must fall in love with some activity."

Feynman is a wise man because he is good at describing what he knows and doesn't try to describe what he doesn't know. If you don't fall in love with a subject, or don't have the talent to study a subject you love, your problem does not fall with the orbit of Feynman's wisdom. So he has no advice for the anti-Feynman. He doesn't know what it's like inside Hugh's mind and, self-protectively, has no inclination to try to imagine it. Hugh, by comparison, has spent a lot of time imagining what it would be like to be Richard Feynman. Reading Feynman's books, the ones for the popular market, he has often felt as if he was, or could be Feynman because their attitudes and senses of humor are so close. But reading Feynman's writing about his subject, his *Lectures on Physics*, Hugh has instead felt the difference between them. It jars him awake, out of any possible fantasy, like taking the fun run with Bill Rodgers. Hugh has understood much of the physics and math, but despite that, reading Feynman as a physicist instead of just a companionable raconteur has reminded Hugh forcefully that he couldn't have originated any of what he was reading. His knowledge of physics must always be second hand. In baseball terms, he would not make the team. If he showed up with his glove and spikes, ready to play, they would make fun of him. The snickers and cracks would start as soon as he walked out on the field and the other players saw he was a klutz. Instead of feeling his organ of wonder expanded by the thrill of playing a physical game, he'd feel defensive and awkward, ill-made for life on a diamond. So Hugh's limits playing Feynman's game remind him again of the imbalance between them as human particles. Feynman has a casual, utilitarian attitude toward his physical being, while Hugh is self-consciously aware of his body all the time. Paradoxically, however, Feynman seems barely to notice what he's missing. If he envies athletes, he never says so. Yet Hugh is reminded every day of what he's missing. So, once again, the anti-Feynman feels a strong attraction to the Feynman and the Feynman feels no pull at all towards its opposite. This imbalance skews the whole relationship between them. There is no mutual relationship, there is only an attraction felt by one for the other. Since the Feynman particle doesn't seem to be bothered by its lack of athletic ability, it wouldn't feel any particular envy or attraction toward the anti-Feynman and its unusual physical attributes, certainly nothing to balance in force the attraction Hugh feels toward Feynman's creative comprehension of particle physics, quantum electrodynamics, and all the rest of the mental exercises he can perform so deftly and pleasurably and with such originality.

What was the nature of what I've been calling the "electrical charge" of the two human particles? As long as it's just a metaphor I feel comfortable enough with the terms. But when I try to be more specific, to put it literally, it all feels simplistic. Feynman/yes, anti-Feynman/no, positive/negative, life force/death wish. I resist writing the shorthand because of what it leaves out, but sometimes I can't avoid ending up there. With Feynman it's easy, he's upbeat, he faces each day with a smile, although you know he's much more complicated than that. For Hugh, the new day presents a problem, one he must struggle with, one he can't solve. Yet you couldn't be around Hugh without feeling his abnormal energy, both physical and mental. As low as his moods got, he still seemed to brim, or seethe, with this vital force. Even his denunciations of himself had a fierce vigor. He didn't need much sleep, he didn't nod off, he was always alert. He seemed to be living at a higher energy level than most people, even when he was heavily depressed. Nor could you say, with a reductive glibness, that he was "bipolar," the fashionable disorder of our times, because his physical and mental exertions were a daily constant. He didn't binge on exercise and then collapse. He stuck to a routine and the number of calories he burned every day didn't fluctuate much but stayed within a narrow range. Were his mental and physical routines routine or driven? It was hard to say because his routine was so extraordinary, but at times it seemed as if his own strength was turned against him, as if he was trying to use himself up physically and mentally so he might be sublimated into another state of being.

20.

At some point, after a few months, Hugh got tired of Ofra's attention. The sex and the way she enjoyed him physically weren't worth the friction, the constant resistance to her attempts to redefine him. These were his reasons, anyway, when his interest wearied, and he told her he wanted to stop seeing her. That was when he learned it was not going to be easy. What Hugh assumed was just an arrangement, a sweaty and noisy one with its continuing parody of therapy, turned out to have become an obsession for Ofra. Maybe it only rose to the intensity of an obsession when Hugh tried to get away from her, but there was no way to gauge the quality of her feelings because the more he backed off the tighter she held on. Hugh realized too late that he had become the meat in a sandwich of obsession—that was how it felt and the awkwardness of the metaphor felt uncomfortably right too. Ofra wanted him and he wanted Denise. Sex and the parody of psych therapy with Ofra had been a not unhealthy distraction but when he was home alone he still kept glancing out the window at Denise's apartment across the narrow alley and helplessly watched her coming and going. He was unable to kill the fixation which had grown out of his even deeper preoccupation with Debby, which also wouldn't die. Now Ofra's neediness was pressing him from the other side. By becoming an object of someone else's crazed desire, Hugh felt the emotion from both sides and it had the effect of inoculating him against his own disease. As Ofra's behavior became more manic, his own dogged attraction to Denise began to dwindle. When he caught himself looking out the window to see if she was there, he thought of Ofra, and if he happened to glimpse Denise, the stab of desire was blunted by embarrassment. Instead of tracking Denise's movements, now his days were warped by trying to avoid Ofra. She came to his door and if he wouldn't answer she'd bang on it, looking around hopefully to see if anyone was noticing. Sometimes when he went out or came back from a day of work, she'd be there on the doorstep, and instead of sheepish she'd be aggressive. "Where the hell were you, Hugh? I've been here for hours!" It wasn't true, nothing Ofra said was true anymore. She lied automatically, not for any purpose but wantonly, just to get back at the truth, because it hurt her. The truth was that Hugh was no longer interested in her, not even sexually, and that had been the one thing they had in common, besides their estrangement from middle class culture.

At first the whole thing was funny. Her outrageous pursuit seemed of a piece with her trying to get him to accept his inner Jew, a refusal she now claimed was part of his trying to escape from her (itself another sign of his illness); but it was a dark humor, and not so funny if you were the butt of the joke. One afternoon when we met to play tennis Hugh was quiet and preoccupied, almost distant, and on our way back to Cambridge, crossing over the bridge with the traffic noise making it hard to talk, Hugh said Ofra had petitioned a court to get an injunction against him. "What? An injunction?" I almost shouted. "What for?"

"Harassment," Hugh said, shaking his head so his Einsteinian head of wiry hair trembled.

It had gone beyond being funny.

Because Hugh had so little public identity, he felt as if the threatened injunction against him had become his face. This was who he was, a replica of Kafka's Josef K., guilty because he'd been accused and had no way to prove the negative—that he had *not* been harassing Ofra, had in fact been trying to avoid her, to escape from her, and that in her own twisted obsession she interpreted his avoidance as harassment. In Ofra's wild mind, because he knew how much she needed him, he was harassing her by his absence. That was her logic. Not to the court but to Hugh, complaining about what he had done to her. Grudgingly, Hugh had to admire her tactic. It had a contrariness like his own. But Ofra was also willing to lie, something Hugh couldn't do, and however deranged she might feel by Hugh's rejection she was still sane and cunning enough to invent conventional incidents alleging what he'd done to support her petition to the court.

"She's been calling me, she left notes for me, stuffed into the door jamb. Then she swore out a complaint saying *I* kept calling *her* and left notes in *her* mailbox...." Hugh said in his tense, whispery voice, as we walked through Cambridge. I couldn't believe her petition to the court wouldn't be thrown out. Wouldn't they see Hugh was a non-threatening, non-violent man with a hypertrophied conscience? That Ofra was overwrought and vengeful? Hugh didn't respond to my encouraging scenario. He just shook his head as if this was another inexplicable way fate had abused him. He didn't answer when I asked if he'd had any contact with the court, if there would be a hearing so he could show up and testify. It might not help his case, I realized thinking about it. The court might believe her instead of him. She was good at playing the victim and I could imagine Hugh, almost mute with fury, denying the charges in a taut, barely audible voice, his crown of unruly dark hair quivering. He might make a very plausible stalker and misogynist.

He walked me almost all the way back to my apartment and we stood on the corner, Hugh holding on to his bike. "I guess you could talk to a lawyer," I said, knowing he wouldn't.

Hugh shook his head. A lawyer, a doctor, an Indian chief. Who could help him.

Although he refused the role of victim vehemently, that's who he was, and to have reality turned on its head, on his head, to be turned into that most obnoxious kind of person, the one who imposes himself on someone else, left him speechless and witless. I didn't remind him of the perversely doubled irony of his own "harassment" of Denise. Some months before he'd confessed to me that his attachment to her had become a little crazy, describing how he watched her window from his, monitored her coming and going, arranged to cross paths out front in the street, left romantic notes under her door. He had continued to give her gifts she didn't ask for or want like a fresh-baked tart, or repaired the tire on her bike when she left it locked on the street. There was also the color TV. So we both knew if he had been guilty of harassing anyone it wasn't Ofra but Denise, and if Denise had sworn out the complaint against him it would have been true, he would have been guilty, and because of that fact, he was incapable of defending himself from Ofra's bogus complaint.

The next time I saw Hugh, he had another surprise—Ofra's request had been granted. The court issued an injunction enjoining Hugh from any contact with her for ninety days or six months or whatever on penalty of arrest, fine, imprisonment, etc. Incredible. But what if *she* contacted *him* now—what then? Hugh just shook his head with a resigned smile. Fate indeed had a sense of humor, and although it was absurd, you had to admit it could be a real wit too.

Later I wondered if there was a side of Hugh I hadn't seen. In other words, was I wrong in some crucial way about him? Was he misrepresenting his behavior toward Ofra? He was obsessed by his own several demons, but I couldn't believe he would tell a conventional lie. A deep psychological one, yes. Like anyone else, he could lie to himself, both aware of it and unaware at the same time. But he'd already confessed his obsession with Denise and described in humiliating detail the gifts, the cassette tape, all the unwanted gestures of help, so I believed in this case he was the victim, not the perp. After centuries of abuse, women were getting some justice, and sometimes it was at the expense of the innocent, or the semi-guilty, male.

The one sure effect of the court injunction against Hugh was to knock all the passion out of him. The injustice of it, the ease with which a false charge could become who you officially were, made him feel obliterated. He was having a pale version of the experience of living in a ghetto or a totalitarian society. No violence had been done to him, he wasn't afraid or terrorized, but he still felt he had lost control over his identity. Ofra had wanted to redefine him—well, she'd succeeded, and it all happened so easily, as if it was normal, as if Kafka had never showed the world this perversion of the individual by officialdom—and on top of all that it had happened in Cambridge, the People's Republic of Cambridge! What they did was justified by their power to do it, not by right, and it drummed in Hugh's head that it all happened in the most ordinary way, while people passed by in the street, no visible harm done to anyone. He who lived by strict duty and had a court and judge presiding in his head day and night was being commanded to live by injunction! How could a court in enlightened Cambridge issue a piece of paper that was a lie, yet to the world stated the truth? The piece of paper with its official seal that came by registered mail lay open on the tiny table in his kitchen while he lifted weights till his arms were rubber. Then he rode over and ran the Harvard Stadium steps, and afterward rode his bike out to Walden Pond and swam around it. When he got home and rode his bike up the sidewalk, head down with weariness, he nearly ran into Denise coming out the front door of her building. Their eyes touched but he felt no spark from the wan, expressionless face. She made him think of a translucent single-celled creature, and he felt sorry for her and even sorrier for himself.

When I saw Hugh the next time his shock at being hauled into the legal machinery had softened to irritation, and soon he learned that like so much in our wonderfully free society the injunction against him had virtually no meaning at all. If it weren't for his embarrassment over the whole thing, it would have been just another tree falling unheard in the forest. His sense that he was being oppressed and redefined by the state was a chimera all blown up by his reaction; in fact it was a trivial farce and the only one who cared in the least about it was him. If he quit caring, the injunction would be no more than another unread, unnoticed official document. The Cambridge court enjoined him to have no contact with Ofra, to abstain from phoning or writing her or approaching closer than a hundred feet from her residence—but it said nothing about her acts or movements. Within days of getting the injunction against him, Ofra had approached within a hundred feet of Hugh's residence, had called him and laughed into the phone, had sat at the top of the stairs to his apartment waiting for him to come home and giggled as he came up the stairs carrying his bike, a sound meant to turn them both into children who were going to do something naughty together, no matter what the court said. It was as if the court had enjoined her too, and this was their rebellion. How could a piece of paper keep them apart, any more than another piece of paper with very different words on it could keep people together when a marriage had soured. Mocking the power of pieces of paper became a game to her, and Hugh could only laugh when he found a note in his mailbox, signed with a heart symbol, saying, "Please come over and fuck me tonight!" In *1984* Orwell used sex as a form of rebellion against Big Brother, Hugh recalled, and now he and Ofra were doing the same thing. The farce of the injunction had become liberating to both of them and his carnal interest in her was re-spiked by the extra thrill of rebellion. Lying in bed with Ofra, Hugh felt that his life was imitating art. It was also a comment on the dizzying, maddening, overstimulated and soul-squandering culture he lived in that neither the injunction nor their transgression meant anything at all.

Ofra's craziness was still saving Hugh from his own, and he knew it without wanting to acknowledge it, even knew according to his damnable Kantian ethics that perhaps he owed her something. Her churning provocations had pulled him an inch or two back from his own obsessions and forced him at least to stick his head up out of his trough of depression. She was a kind of reality check (the kind of slangy pop expression Hugh never used) whose zaniness forced him to think more clearly. He had let himself become her playmate again, despite resenting the way she had managed to use the court as a pimp. He kept hearing Peggy Lee singing that dumb song "Que Sera Sera," taking him back to the fifties and high school, back to the time before all his choices turned into dead ends. The song gleefully mocked him as he rode his bike over to Ofra's to fuck her—mocked again by his need—gliding unimpeded through the invisible shield the court erected around her apartment, the one he'd been forbidden to penetrate in the Law versus Hugh Lewis. The craziest part of their relationship was happening after the legal system had intervened, after he had consoled himself that even if he was branded a nuisance by the court at least now she'd leave him alone. Instead, after Ofra had repeatedly broken the court injunction meant to protect her from Hugh by abducting him back into her bed, he learned the real lesson: it can be just as exhausting to ride the forces that rush in when you let go as it is to try to take control and bend the world to your will.

21.

From Hugh's notebooks:
Modern woman sitting on a man's penis. "This is just so intelligent and extremely fun I might add."

22.

This period of Hugh's life had a peculiar quality of suspension, as if it was a prologue and something was about to happen. That was an illusion, and the sense of imminence was probably nothing more than another way of perceiving how temporary the current state of affairs was. Somehow it was appropriate that during this spell of transience, Hugh and I went to a movie together, the only time we ever did.

We had met to play tennis, despite a threat of rain. We started hitting and the rain soon began, but we didn't quit till the ball was sodden and we were slipping on the wet court, every stroke sending the heavy ball with its rooster tail of water spraying over the net. Walking back through Harvard Square we passed a sign for a theater showing a "Renoir Orgy," as they called it, to help students get through finals. The off-and-on rain was starting to get serious and when we ducked under the marquee for cover and I saw the poster I said, "Hey—it's one of the great movies, 'Boudu Saved From Drowning'." Hugh hadn't seen it, or even heard of it, and there was only ten minutes or so till the next show. What the hell. The afternoon was shot anyway. Coincidence was pointing its finger. Hugh shrugged and said yes. It was only when we got inside the theater that I wondered if this was really such a good idea. I remembered Hugh telling me about the story he'd written in college about a man who, following the logical end to a philosophical argument, kills himself. It sounded like a young man's story, the kind inspired by reading Dostoyevsky or the existentialists, more true to an idea than to experience, but the deeper truth in it seemed to be in Hugh's ambivalence about his own existence. Boudu himself was a suicide. He tried to be, anyway. At the start of the movie, on a beautiful day when Parisians are enjoying themselves on the riverbank, he throws himself off a bridge into the Seine. By chance, a bookseller sees him from his shop window, abandons his customers, and runs to save him. Boudu, an eye-rolling, unkempt tramp played as a philosophical clown by Michel Simon, berates the bookseller, saying, "If my life which I tried to throw away is so important to you then fine, now it's yours—and you've got to take care of it too!" So Boudu becomes a leech on the bookseller's life, eating his food, sleeping in his bed, offending his customers, trying to make love to his wife and daughter. Instead of making Hugh depressed or feeling offended that I was sending him some kind of message, he loved it and we laughed so loud we drew the attention of the few undergrads around us. Boudu regarded the life force as the nonpareil joke, a nasty trick played on man by nature. Anyone whose life afflicted them was crazy not to slough it off, and if someone was foolish enough to try to save it, it was tough luck for them if they succeeded, because now it was theirs and its original owner was free. What was mordant in real life was funny on the screen. When the movie ended the rain had passed, and Hugh and I emerged into a damp sunny Cambridge, laughing and light-hearted, semi-permeably saturated with Michel Simon's eye-rolling Boudu.

As we walked up Mass. Ave., the merry mood dissipated into silence. We were both thoughtful and subdued, and had only walked a couple blocks when Hugh took a side street, angling down toward his apartment rather than accompanying me further. Hugh wasn't Boudu and I didn't want him to think I was so insensitive to his predicament that I thought it was funny. I remembered a comment I'd read by John Updike saying that if all of us had a button on our bodies we could push when we ardently, urgently preferred oblivion to life, there'd be no one left on earth. We all wanted to escape, at times. I wished I'd remembered the comment earlier, so I could have mentioned it to Hugh, to make the temptation Renoir had portrayed universal. I realized that wouldn't have worked either. There was really nothing to say, and neither of us ever mentioned the movie again.

23.

In his relationship with what he believed, as I mentioned before, Hugh was the opposite of an evangelist. He kept it to himself, mostly, and what he particularly didn't talk about was his commitment to it. Perhaps that was a means of keeping its potency intact by not exposing it to the wisecracks and misapprehension of casual conversation (aware of his own jesting reaction when anyone told him what they believed in), and it might also have been a result of his not wanting what was dear to him to be known, not wanting to be vulnerable, especially when so much of his anguished life was already in public domain. Faith in anything made a person look credulous and after the experience of the twentieth century Big Ideas bore the guilt of crimes against humanity. Yet occasionally, in his tirades against bad ideas or denouncing behavior that could in no way be universalized, Hugh would refer to the principle behind it, so what he believed wasn't a secret. If you asked him a question about ideas or philosophy, he would give you an answer, unlike personal questions. Most people didn't ask questions of that sort, but if they did Hugh enjoyed the exchange. His responses were often gnomic, a little obscure, or expressed as conundrums or jokes, which made him particularly good around children. He savored puzzles and brain teasers, perhaps because so much of himself and his life seemed puzzling to him, or maybe simply because his mind was comfortable with mathematics and numbers games, and riddles and questions felt closer to the truth than answers or solutions. Whatever the reason, the heavyweight brain teasers of math like the Reimann hypothesis and Poincare conjecture, just words to me, fascinated Hugh. The relationship was almost personal to him. For example, math wizards said there was a formula for predicting the occurrence of prime numbers, they just didn't know what it was. That was the kind of statement Hugh could lie down and stretch out in. There was an explanation for Hugh's life, he just didn't know what it was. No one else did either. We all ran up against the problem of the knower knowing him- or herself but this was qualitatively different. It had to do with narrative coherence and at its root was feeling, not reason. Hugh's own account of the way this process works to create meaning where none may exist appeared in his notebooks, on another subject which at its conclusion veered back toward his own problem. He wrote:

"A call-in television show. A bearded man, wire rim glasses, a jacket that had 'Philosopher' in medium-sized letters written over the breast pocket. [What kind of show was Hugh watching—it sounds like a satire made by The Onion!] Another man, longish hair, straight, flaxen, falls over his left eye. They listen to a viewer, a caller. The viewer explains how it makes him feel better to believe in God. The flaxen-haired man amplifies what the caller said, describing other good feelings associated with belief in god. The philosopher objects that many ideas make you 'feel good.' I'm disappointed in the philosopher. I think there is a profound fallacy embraced in the proposition that in order to feel good one believes in god. This fallacy is visited by Pascal in his Cosmic wager. He says it's a can't-lose bet to believe in god. The fallacy is this. Belief must <u>precede</u> good feelings and wise bets. We <u>believe</u> because we feel something is true. The linkage between beliefs and feelings is anything, and happiness or unhappiness is utterly contingent. It could, for instance, make me very unhappy to discover the existence of certain kinds of gods. The philosopher mugged playfully while the caller talked. I expected a brilliant dismissal of the very old hat idea. I detest the willfulness implicit in the fallacy, while I appreciate the necessity of willfulness in the creation of a comprehensible world."

Hugh's conclusion curves back toward his own situation. Pascal and the caller both already believe in God before they "decide" to make a bet that he exists, a bet they "can't lose" which makes both of them feel better. This is willfulness, an insult to reason. But Hugh can accept the necessity of this kind of willfulness if we do it to create a comprehensible world. The willed world must be some kind of fiction. The creation of a comprehensible world—your own "story"—depends on first believing or feeling the world is comprehensible, or could be, which in turn is dependent on your own life making some kind of sense. Hugh's doesn't. He doesn't feel or believe it does, and isn't able to create a comprehensible story by an act of will. He can try but the effort fails because belief has to precede the act of will, the decision to create a comprehensible story, and in Hugh's case there is no prior belief. So for him, it's a can't-win bet.

Nevertheless, as unable as Hugh is to create a plausible narrative for his life, he still can't avoid feeling a moral responsibility. The paradox is inescapable. It seems unfair for Hugh to be tortured by this sense of responsibility when his life is so incomprehensible to him. As he says in his notebooks, "Is it possible to grasp life as other than a progress. A life is knowable to the extent it makes sense." You can't understand your life except as a fiction, a story you believe in in some way, which he was unable to do. So to feel responsible for that life—that it carries the burden of moral significance despite its incoherence—was the weight he had to carry through each day.

24.

The compulsive sense of responsibility Hugh felt leads back to Kant's strict duty, one stepping stone he could always put his foot on, even if it never indicated where to step next, because it confirmed that his feeling was connected to a universal ideal.

Kant said all we knew was phenomena, that our experience and our ideas didn't conform to an external reality separate from our minds but had to conform to the structure of our minds themselves.   This fit with Darwinian evolution, yet to be discovered when Kant offered his own "Copernican revolution in philosophy" as he called it, which in its evolved form said that our minds were products of the world they were "selected" to operate in (to use the language of evolution). Everything outside experience was unknowable; it was all in what Kant called the realm of noumena, but going further into metaphysics than the skeptical Scot David Hume, who said our brains contained nothing but perceptions, Kant insisted on the existence of this unknowable world of noumena; he said its existence was necessary. Yet any attempt to know what he called "things-in-themselves," anything beyond actual human experience, would fail. It had to be taken on something like faith, whatever one called it. Despite the metaphysical temptation this formula succumbs to, it is based on a revolutionary thought which moves reality from out there somewhere to inside our heads (while asserting something still somehow exists out there simply because we need it, we will it). It's a kind of parallel train of thought to Hugh's belief-precedes-placing-your-bet and the question of whether you think the world is comprehensible or not: it is if you think it is, if your "story" about it makes sense. There is something "out there" beyond experience, if you think it is there.

Hugh reduced Kant's three great problems of metaphysics—God, immortality, and freedom—to the last one. In his view the first two were products of the human imagination—fictions, which you could believe in or not—but the last posed the question of how to live which was inescapable for everyone. We were not mere sense organs taking in data about the physical world. We were sentient beings, actors with a certain freedom. If we weren't, if we refused to accept this shining and tarnished fact, then we merely shifted an additional burden on someone else. One person's dereliction didn't lessen the moral burden of being human, it just increased it for someone else. (Which is why Hugh's personal burden was so heavy.) To argue that we had no choice, that choice was an illusion, was a device to avoid the burden of being human, even if you could show that choice was an illusion. The psychology of decision-making and the neurology of how a brain worked were infant sciences and each incremental discovery showed how deceived we were about how we made decisions, about everything our brains did. (So was evolutionary psychology which aimed its light from another direction.) Yet no matter how deep our deception, there could be no "free" society without "freedom" of choice, which meant each human became a moral agent even if whatever he or she did was all but determined. This kind of paradox was the shape truth assumed and if you were honest you accepted it's knotty form instead of using it as an excuse. The margin of freedom might be slim but it was also huge, just as Huxley's gardener had said about the differences between human beings.

It was impossible to talk about what it meant to be human without ending up in the thickets of moral philosophy, which itself was a proof of our nature, and Hugh carried the burden around the way a camel carries its hump. But instead of life-giving fat, sustenance for a journey or famine, Hugh's hump was more like a tumor stealing nourishment from its host. He might have wanted to slough it off, as much as it defined him, but he couldn't. He was a powerless and useless person in his own estimation, but often felt that if he didn't know the truth and shine a light on it, however dim, it would cease to exist anywhere in the human mind. He knew this was nonsense—solipsistic, self-centered nonsense—but was unable not to feel it as fact. It was his counterweight to oblivion, on some days his only one. The proof of its existence was his inability not to feel it.

25.

The burlesque of obsession he had played out with Ofra worked its final, lethal effect on whatever was left of Hugh's misbegotten passion for Denise, and one autumn day after we finished playing several hours of tennis (tentatively, considerately) in glorious sunshine, he said, "Public service announcement—I no longer love that woman." His self-mocking way of declaring it, as if officially, but without using her name, made me say, "What?" Had I heard right? Yes. All desire had gone. "It's very embarrassing," Hugh said. He thanked me and Kate for putting up with him, listening to him. I told him he shouldn't be embarrassed, no one could help who they fell for. "She was never right for you," I said lamely—who was right for him?—but from the little he'd said about her that was descriptive instead of obsessed, it sounded as if she was a serious academic who'd dosed herself with EST therapy—Christ Almighty!—and she sounded humorless. (Ofra was funny and liked sex!) Granted, the image I had of Denise was formed almost entirely by Hugh's words but when he described her to Kate one night over dinner, she said, "I don't think you like her at all, Hugh. It sounds like you hate her." Perfect, Hugh. Fall for a woman you hate so when she rejects you, you can hate the guy she rejects too. ("My great gift is that I am a man that a woman need not be embarrassed to hate," he'd written in his notebook.)

All this was unfair to Denise and whomever she really was, but she had her own friends and our concern was Hugh; in his life she was barely a walk-on, more like a walk-through. By now he seemed to realize he'd loved some artifact of his imagination—the old, indestructible ghost of Debby—not the actual woman living next door.

I quashed the impulse to ask if he'd gotten the color TV back.

26.

From Hugh's notebooks:

Postcards from the edge. Two bees conversing. First bee: "Boy I sure could use a weapon of some sort. Something light and strong. Maybe poison-tipped. Something I could carry around." Second bee: "You know if enough of us really needed it, really really wanted something like that, hell, in 3-4 million years we'd have it."

27.

There could be something reassuring for Hugh about expanding his view beyond the quaintly human one (a reflexive process his mind did on its own), since if you took a long enough look, we were all useless. Hugh simply had a less cluttered view of the arbitrariness of human affairs and consciousness than most everyone else. In his notebooks, he copied out several quotations from David Raup's *Extinction: Bad Genes or Bad Luck*, which illustrated the odds of nature: "If flying reptiles had not evolved, no anatomist or physiologist would question their absence."

I picture a cartoon strip of Hugh and a pterodactyl eyeing each other quizzically. "What are you doing here?" Hugh's caption asks; then in the next panel the pterodactyl asks him the same thing. There's a third panel where the two of them stare at each other silently and in the last one Hugh laughs. The pterodactyl is right, the question applies equally to himself. Hugh returned again and again to this theme of randomness, as if contending against the human tendency Raup also described:

"With each change in fauna and flora, the global biota becomes a little more contemporary. Because we have a vantage point at one end of the time sequence, the changes give an impression of a directed sequence leading to where we are. In other words, progress. But this impression would exist even if the evolutionary sequence were totally chaotic."

Hugh underlined the last line. He doesn't comment that this impression which we interpret as progress might also lead to the next point about human nature—that we're the ones who create meaning. We create it out of whatever's at hand, facts and illusions cobbled together along a narrative string ending at our vantage point. It's strange that Hugh who loved puzzles so much couldn't absorb in his bones the notion that life itself is a game whose meaning is a fiction we make up. Or rather he does feel it and resents it. He resents it because to play life as a game is to treat it as a kind of competition he doesn't want. He wants a game played by rules so the virtuous win. He can see all the "postmodern" levels of illusion and fiction as analytically as anyone, but he is unable to take into himself the kozmik fact that we're all using the same available materials to make up the Game of Life, and although it's a game whose rules were not designed with us in mind—were not designed in any way that we know of—yet we keep spinning the wheel so the game is all about us (that part he scorned and decried). The attitude that it's a game mocks the imperatives of strict duty too, forcing Hugh to defend a formal belief system, at least in his mind, and as I mentioned before potentially exposing him to the ridicule dumped on those with faith in less rigorous beliefs.

Immediately I have to qualify this once again and say Hugh does take it in that life is a game, but with only half of himself and the other half—the heavier half—remains deadly serious, an ethicist if not a moralist, insisting the game is real—there is no other experience!—and if we refuse to face facts which would force us to admit that our lives are false to the values we sentimentally deceive ourselves into believing, and never act upon them except symbolically, then there truly is no meaning to what we are doing here. All we have left is the game. With undeserving winners and arbitrarily deprived losers. In imitation of nature, of course.

28.

The high priest of randomness in evolution, or at least the most publicly visible one, was Stephen Jay Gould, who stood in about the same relation to Hugh as Bill Rodgers did. Each was a champion in a field of endeavor Hugh venerated. Instead of taking a run together, he and the Harvard paleontologist occasionally went to baseball games together, and Hugh also did odd jobs fixing things in Gould's house in Cambridge. Gould had grown up a Yankee fan in New York so when the Yanks came to Boston he invited Hugh to come along to the games. At Fenway Park, the same place Ted Williams once played, Gould described his theory of why there would never be a .400 hitter again—the rising average in ability of all players had also lowered the peaks of the most exceptional ones. Hugh shared Gould's fascination with excellence in the human species and how it was achieved and measured, and as a stats freak himself he appreciated Gould's argument, as well as the statistical analysis backing it up.

The dynamics of Hugh's relationship with Gould were complex. With an amateur's interest in science, Hugh was once again cast in the role of four-fifths of a champion, always looking up at the real players like Gould, aware that the gap between them was a chasm. Yet physically the imbalance between them was equally vast, like Hugh's with Feynman. Gould was a typical nebbish, the brain who couldn't throw a ball, and "Hey, babes," was not a language he spoke naturally. Yet he had a formidable mental discipline, equal to any athlete's. When he got cancer he handled the disease with an impressive combination of courage and intelligence. Hugh described to me more than once Gould's excusing himself in mid-conversation to go get sick in the bathroom, then returning a moment later to resume talking as if nothing was wrong. He had a skeptical, scientific mind but had no doubts about himself. Like the contrast with Feynman, when paired with the positively charged Gould, Hugh seemed to be the negatively charged anti-particle. In this case, however, Hugh got close enough to see how different their two human particles were in another way that surprised and dismayed him. It happened because of Gould's reaction to *Sociobiology*, written by his colleague at Harvard, biologist E. O. Wilson. The book, which turned out to be seminal, suggested that natural selection might favor genes which adapted organisms to succeed in their societies, as social beings, besides as reproductive individuals. It sounds harmless enough but at the time it looked to some critics as if it was an argument to support traditional white male dominance, even take us back to moral horrors like the eugenics movement of the early twentieth century. If society itself was a product of natural selection, might it imply that racism and sexism were the inevitable result of evolution? If so, sociobiology could be used as a rationale for all the ugly old prejudices, now dressed up in new clothes and claiming that culture with its racist and sexist biases wasn't man-made but natural, a product of biology. So the critics said, anyway, and the most prominent one was Gould. It became a fight for whose interpretation of Darwinian evolution would dominate. Hugh strenuously agreed with Gould's position, but as the controversy flamed on the critics began to accuse Wilson personally—as a white, Southern male perhaps he carried a bias for reaching such a conclusion. Hugh saw the questioning of Wilson's motives and background as using the ad hominem argument, a logical fallacy, the oldest of all bad arguments. Besides that, the pettiness shown toward Wilson by some of his Harvard colleagues, including Gould—shunning him on campus, refusing to speak to him—violated Hugh's code of civility. As the drama was played out in the press, I noticed that when Gould's name came up in conversation there was a note of irritation in Hugh's voice, as if his renowned acquaintance's behavior had become one more thing disappointing him.

29.

The subject of civility had grown large in Hugh's mind because of his own struggles to maintain a minimal civil attitude when every day felt like another defeat. I could see the effort he was making on those days when we arranged to meet on the tennis court. My main substitute partner had been promoted to a new job in his company's suburban office and he could no longer walk to the courts for a couple quick sets at lunch, so getting Hugh back in the routine of my life was doubly welcome. He was obviously trying hard to control his moods, at least on the court, and despite how difficult his company could be, I realized how much I'd missed our idiosyncratic racquet sports. It meant hearing his complaints about how flawed the world was, with endless examples from daily life and the news broadcasts, which were yet another form of fiction or ritually distorted reality that stuck to Hugh's brain like sucking eels. But he was up out of the deepest trough of depression by a degree or two, and functional now, with some thanks to Ofra despite the craziness of those months, and the court injunction against him on his indelible record, if anyone cared to look. All that seemed to have been erased when she abruptly left Cambridge for Israel, taking their history with her. The opera was over and Hugh was suddenly irrelevant. For months, that's what he'd wanted but now that he really was irrelevant to Ofra, along with everyone else, the vacuum was chilling. It felt as if everyone had fled to Israel, to some place they hoped would fulfill them, while he was left in the same place, alone.

A different kind of darkness hung over him now. Before he'd had his own personal cloud; now it seemed as if the lights in the whole world had been dimmed. He was past forty, well into his fifth decade, and the sense that he was useless seemed more firmly set, as if he no longer believed some angel of fate or backhand stroke of good luck would rescue him. It would have to be an accident, some target hit without aiming for it, Zen style, or without even drawing the bow. Because it was evident there would be no career. Not if it was left up to him. He no longer imagined any phone calls from Donald asking him to work in TV again. His long relationship with Debby had become marriage and fatherhood for someone else, and looking back over the wreckage of his collisions with Denise and Ofra he wondered if a woman would ever love him again. Once Hugh had had almost a cockiness, he had been a man of strong mind and body, which along with his wit and talent must have made him seem, to his young self anyway, invincible. With his abundant gifts how could he fail? Especially since he didn't want material success, he wanted personal fulfillment. He assumed the material success would follow naturally. He assumed the love too.

A few years before, jogging with Kate through the leafy, mansioned streets of upscale Cambridge, Hugh told her he'd always assumed he would live in a house like the ones they were running past, like Julia Child's and John Kenneth Galbraith's. She was surprised he'd had such conventional daydreams. He seemed so naturally austere in his lifestyle, with a carbon footprint the size of an indigenous Amazonian's. It was impossible to imagine Hugh living the life of a Cambridge grandee; you could more likely see him in a monk's cell or perched on top of a pillar in the desert than on Brattle or Francis Street. It was a clue that the person he imagined he might be was far from the one we knew. That person assumed he'd become an important writer or thinker. He'd produce something the world couldn't ignore. And it would have to express the truth! That was paramount. Instead, he hadn't brought forth anything, or if he had it lay hidden, known only to him. Only once had he mentioned anything he'd written, the story ending in suicide he'd won a prize for in college. It had made me uncomfortable to hear it. More and more the plot seemed too prescient, even deterministic, as if the theme of self-destruction had always been the most natural story line for him to follow. He didn't make that connection himself, not out loud. It was just an incident from his youth, about a prize he had won. Another false promise.

As the clock ticked on and his potential evaporated like unburned fuel, he seemed to begin regarding me as an example of what he would now gladly settle for. I had something that at least resembled a career, and probably even more important than that, I had a good marriage. If that wasn't two out of two it was one and a half out of a possible two. For someone who regarded himself as having zero that was a huge score. The fact that I'd had a not-so-good marriage before gave Hugh even more hope. It meant one's emotional relationships didn't always, inevitably, helplessly, follow the same pattern. You weren't the same man to all women, doomed to play the same role every time. At any moment you might find someone, even if you'd given up hope there was any career or position, any other function in the world for you besides surviving.

To be as intelligent as Hugh was and as baffled by the way things had happened made him an even more captive student of psychology, a covert, ambivalent one. But instead of providing any kind of explanation, the loathed subject only seemed to reduce him to a diagnosis. A specious one. The thought of Freud was always handy to taunt him—Freud the self-anointed pioneer, the inspired innovator, the fraud, the quack. He was also a conundrum himself. How could anyone claim to be inventing a new science and lock up his notes, deny people access to his research? Okay, maybe that was his followers who'd done that, but a pathology ran through the whole enterprise. What kind of scientist works in the dark? Obviously he had something to hide, something embarrassing or falsified or both. (Just like his patients!) Look at him compared to Feynman, who did all his tricks right out in the open. Instead of suspicious and wary he threw back the curtain, he opened his mind and all its resources up to you.

Hugh's problem with Freud was more personal than his disgust for the doctor's deceptions. The theory that Sophocles' ancient tragedy about Oedipus killing his father and marrying his mother was the primal allegory of all male psychology was too close to Hugh's own family history for him to dismiss. The Oedipus complex might not be universally true, or it might have been true most especially for Freud himself with his own elderly father and young attractive mother, but it was close enough to the truth for Hugh that he had to have his own answer to the meaning Freud ascribed to the story. Had he truly wanted to kill his father— so badly that his death wasn't simply a physical event—just as Hugh had felt when it happened? What about his flirtatious mother? Was he really attracted to her? Seriously? As a sexual rival to his father? Was that what was behind their conflict? A note in one of Hugh's notebooks shows his awareness of his problem. "Is it necessary that seeing (Oedipus knows mother) must give rise to not seeing (branches in the eyes) in order to stagger on." Was it necessary to blind yourself to your own deepest desires so you could live? Did the very knowledge he thought he was seeking have to be suppressed?

With his reflexively skeptical mind, Hugh couldn't believe he believed it. Yet how did you know what you really believed? Maybe he was refusing to believe it (score another for the fraudulent doc). This was part of the indelible legacy of the Freudian world view. It might be fake but how did you know? You couldn't, not if your own mind couldn't be trusted. Yet in clearheaded moments Hugh felt as if this was merely the diseased version of a healthy skepticism. In this more confident mood he recoiled from psychology for explaining him so tritely, for the feeling it gave him of having been violated or invaded by its solipsisms, stuck on the end of Freud's pin, a tool or weapon used in bad faith.

Psychology had moved on since Freud, his "discoveries" now irrelevant to science. Where he lived on was in popular culture and in the literary world, and that was the way Hugh had experienced him. Reading Freud at an early age had cracked him open and replaced whatever story he might have told about his deepest and most troubling feelings with someone else's version of what they meant. Hugh was imprinted with a certain story and he couldn't erase it. The meaning Freud assigned to the Oedipus allegory could only be conjecturally true, like any fiction, yet Hugh couldn't come up with a more plausible description of what he'd felt toward his father, what he might have felt toward his mother, and most telling of all, for the meaning of the consequences—what actually happened, and his guilt.

That was his emotional response to Freud. His other response, to Freud's betrayal of reason and ethics, to his manipulation of the scientific method, also led into emotion, a very different one. Once Hugh learned that Freud had fabricated his research—indeed that his whole project was a kind of epical fiction—he was jolted. It contradicted, it sabotaged, it satirized the goal of trying to find the truth. How could you not want to know the truth? Why else ask the questions? Because you wanted to win. Win what? The game of life. But wasn't knowing the truth incomparably more significant than merely winning? Not to everyone, apparently, and if the truth wasn't knowable maybe winning was the only definite goal.

Hugh's tortured attitude was partly relieved by reading Frederick Crews' critical essays which laid out Freud's machinations. When the ambitious young doctor realized that his seduction theory was shaky, it suddenly looked as if his whole career would self-destruct, his dream of eternal fame blown away. Freud had already written papers saying he'd discovered evidence of infantile sexual abuse buried in his patients' minds. What he hadn't realized, or cared to acknowledge, was that his technique during "treatment" of describing the event the patient was unable to remember meant, lo and behold, he could find it in anyone. Why? Because when the patient was struggling to remember a seduction so traumatic that they couldn't express it in words, Freud supplied the words himself. But how did he know what the patient was trying to express? By intuition. He *knew* they'd been seduced, even if they didn't, and were denying it. In other words, he found what was he was looking for. It was the oldest mistake in science.

Perhaps he was earnest, perhaps he didn't appreciate just how domineering his role was. However it happened, he finally realized that he was "discovering" the same infantile sexual experience in nearly everyone he examined. His subjects had all been molested! Yet he still didn't have one single statement by a patient describing such a seduction themselves, in their own words. What he did next, either cunningly or deceiving himself yet again, was to make a bold U-turn. He announced he'd made a mistake, that the seduction theory was wrong. In the paper he wrote to save himself and his theory, he said his patients had only *fantasized* that they were seduced. What his patients had resisted recalling was not a *real* event but the *fantasy* of one. And the fact that all the patients he'd treated had had the same fantasy of seduction as a child showed that this experience was universal! The core flaw in his research was its crowning virtue! The new theory became the foundation of his psychoanalytical edifice: We all feel sexual attraction to a parent or adult as an infant, strong enough to create fantasies of seduction which for some people later cause neurotic symptoms, and all these impulses live in a part of our mind of which we're unconscious. It was a perfect closed circle based at no point on anyone's actual experience.

What Freud's contemporaries noticed was the allegation that even babies were sexual creatures and the late Victorian middle class was so shocked it didn't notice the absurdities that lay strewn around the circle of fantasy. When Hugh read this what shocked him, besides the fact that it was all sprung from Freud's own mind with no external evidence of any kind, was the discovery that Freud was a pioneer in a way very different from his reputation. By imposing his own fantasies on his patients and then explaining their behavior according to these fantasies, Freud had invented or perfected a kind of mind control. Here was an original form of what would become the nefarious tool of totalitarian states, a technique for invading the sanctuary of the mind to replace its individual purpose with something else. If the subject disagreed with this new purpose he or she was insane because it was based on a higher truth than their own. Freud insisted just as vigorously as any totalitarian tyrant that patients who resisted his diagnosis were denying the truth of psychoanalysis. He knew their secret fantasies, they didn't, and the proof was in their denial.

This twist on Freud made him in Hugh's interpretation the dark prince of 20th century totalitarianism. He only described it to me once but there was awe in his voice, as if this innovation was too big, too monstrous even for Freud's ego. That it was inadvertent, or had wafted through the air into Freud's own fantasizing brain, and wafted from him like airborne spores into malign political minds made no difference. It was only more evidence that no one knew his own mind, including Freud. We were now far from intentions and will power. We were drowned in the psychological murk of the century of technological nightmares where everyone had "lost" their mind, where even Freud could not say with any assurance whether he believed what he had written, or if he had done it just to save his career.

This clarifying view of Freud provided some breathing space for Hugh, but the residual struggle with his psychoanalytic "fictions" continued. They were someone else's story—a story Hugh did not want told about him—but they still lived in his mind, they were part of his experience and the culture around him, and he could never deny them and Freud's malign authority enough to make it all vanish. Sometimes before dawn, during the slow rise toward consciousness, Hugh had a vision of whom he really was that seemed to confirm his semi-permeable self. During this vulnerable transition, when the glue that binds a self together dissolves or hasn't yet congealed, he experienced himself in the third person, the way someone else—everyone else!—saw him. The hypnopompic experience could linger into wakefulness so during the first minutes, even the first hour of the day he still felt this semi-permeable or diffused quality, as if he was somehow less than the sum of his parts. Missing was the glue, the conscious healthy sensation of a self, the ego Freud had so much of he could lie to the whole world and let himself get away with it (aided by cocaine stimulating his dopamine receptors, those hardeners of the glue). It was the kind of act Hugh's temperament, reinforced by his philosophy, denied to him. Thus he was forced into the perversity of envying his nemesis for a trait he despised.

30.

From Hugh's notebooks:

"He had no explanation for himself though an explanation seemed called for."

31.

Whether all this is true, or just my misconception of someone I thought I knew well but instead misunderstood richly, can't be known. As his moods ratcheted downwards, Hugh sometimes opened himself up so candidly it was embarrassing, but he may not have spoken of other things equally significant to whomever he was. Memory is also unreliable, we all know that too, both his and mine. Not only in the sense that one gets it wrong or twists it or leaves gaps, suppresses and deceives, but in a much more commonplace way—memory simply fails to record what happens the way a disinterested camera would. So it isn't just because of dark "Freudian" reasons, but for prosaic ones about the way the mind works that you can't see everything in the past, and even if you could, even if there were some video cache of the whole of one's life, no one could watch it. Life would be spent watching life. There's an idea Hugh would have laughed at heartily, and in a way, with his acute self-consciousness, he did spend his life watching his life, missing a lot by seeing so much of his own response while it was happening.

One thing I knew for certain. The days we played tennis under a perfect, uncritical sun were an epitome of physical pleasure. I can only compare it to sex, the kind where both people want to pleasure each other. As the weather continued to warm up, we regained our old groove. Hugh was careful to control himself now and even when he got frustrated he didn't start spraying wild shots back over the net. I was careful too. If I sensed his frustration rising I might make it a goal to see if I could hit a ground stroke right to him. What the hell. I cared more about hitting a solid shot than winning this or that point. Mostly I wanted to play well, the same goal as ever. We were both playing better. The resignation Hugh felt about his life, the plateau of reduced expectations his days rolled over, seemed reflected in his approach to the game. It was rare when he couldn't control himself, and when he played within himself, as the coaches like to say, he nearly always beat me.

Hugh still denied and negated himself but not with the fresh vehemence of a revelation. Now it was a routine, no matter how earnest, like Rodney Dangerfield never getting respect. Although it wasn't played for laughs, it was straight, and most of the time Hugh's temper was now under the shadow, and the direction, of his tragic sense. Why fight the frustrations of life or racquet sports, or the fickleness of women, or anything else? Give in, submit, and enjoy this, the blessing of a perfect sunshiny day. We played, as I said, like lovers. We loved the aura of the game, we loved each other in some unspoken way that was being acted out on the court, and we loved the sensuous pleasure of feeling our bodies recreate the motions and postures of the adept players. The arcing swing and THOCK! of a serve, the body turned just like Vic Braden taught to prepare for a backhand. I can see Hugh's pivot and crouch, the lifted follow through; the glide to the net with a little half-step to set up the shot and the surprise that your legs had learned something from watching McEnroe that your brain never knew; the rally that went on for stroke after stroke with not one mis-hit, pulling each other laterally like a pair of yo-yos, turning and running as hard as you could, swinging with all that momentum, then turning again, then again, till someone hit a winner. Like lovers who have learned each other's bodies, we knew the other's strokes and had both raised our games to achieve, at moments, a consummation greater than either could reach on his own. After playing a point when we both felt the pleasure, there was almost no difference between winning and losing. Recalling it now, I see the categorical imperative played out on the baize-green geometry of the Har-Tru court, as if Hugh and I were displaying to the absent world how an abstraction might look acted out in the flesh. We were a flag showing the wind. During the breaks to drink water (we still never crossed over to switch courts) we talked sports; the admired players, the ones who did it right. We each knew the kinds of stories the other one liked and saved them up to tell. Although there could be something embarrassing about being a fan, sometimes we couldn't disguise our emotion. Hugh's first identity, as ever, was as an athlete and he could imagine what it was like to play with someone like Bird. "They say he doesn't have natural ability, that he plays smart and works hard—but why isn't the ability to work hard or use your head as much an ability as being able to jump?" Hugh was a fan but ever the analyst and as usual he liked observations that illustrated how people got things wrong, like the statistician who showed the fallacy of the "hot hand." His taste for the truth was greater than his desire for a more emotionally satisfying superstition, so it had to be sacrificed. But statistics could lie too. "Statistically, a seven foot person can't exist," he laughed, describing the curve of possible body heights that ran off the graph before hitting the seven foot mark.

Some things that actually happened were impossible, and that might have given Hugh a kind of hope.

32.

From Hugh's notebooks:
I practiced suffocating myself.
God I like being alive.
(God's only excuse is that he doesn't exist.)
I should be describing these dwindling days (and my unfortunate susceptibility to obliteration), but I'm too passive, demoralized, hopeful and suicidal to begin to touch everything with farewell. It is pathetically easy, unheroically simple to delight me, to move me to despairing happiness. A smell of summer poplar trees carried in warm damp air can be thrilling.

A lovely, horsey, knock-kneed woman 25-35 climbed the stadium steps. Two very deliberate steps at a time. A slight hesitation as she paused at each step. Four steps from the top, she waved at me. Meekly, vulnerably, sweetly, tenderly. Another woman I could love forever.

I am tortured by sexy women. I crossed the street to better observe a voluptuously large-assed woman. I quickly changed directions when an ethereal beauty and her dog proudly strode up the street. But the most maddeningly sexy woman was hitchhiking. She was dark haired and dark-complexioned. She wore skin-tight cutoff jeans and had on a translucent leotard top. She had no bra and her breasts were firm melon-like miracles with large, darkly vivid nipples. She was a gaudy sensual presence. I wanted her to know that she 'astonished' my heart. My gloriously unregenerate self wanted to speak. 'Are you talent?' No good. 'You must be an actress.' Not yet. 'A Rhodes Scholar, right?' No. 'Sister, what order are you in?' No. 'This must be a morality play and you're lust, right?' No. 'If I said you had a beautiful body, would you hold it against me?' What power resides in her perfect legs, breasts, hips, lips, tongue, toes, and.... 'Do you know whose body you're wearing? Es tu disponible?' Impatience and destruction. Innocence and violence. Her perfection was the illusion of availability.

I tried to listen and even to talk to a woman this Sunday. I couldn't stand listening to her so I asked her questions. There was a humorless willful, upscale pedestrianism in everything she said: group think or team think. Every whimsicality, every imagining, every reading of motive that I proffered was wrong. Hamlet was proof of my perversity and ignorance. "Don't you understand. Hamlet is flawed. He has a tragic flaw. He's sick. Reason can't heal his 'moral ambivalence' or you put in a normal person. I give up. I don't want to 'explain' Hamlet; he's my friend. And besides, Shakespeare wrote the thing for me and it's nobody else's business." The wider point I have achieved personhood and the proof: I am as given in my descriptions of things beyond the sympathetic imaginings of others. I am, in science' synonyms, wrong, incorrect, misinformed, crazy, unjustified.

33.

Since science is the only thing Hugh can finally believe in, for him to be wrong by its verdict is a modern damnation. There is something jarring about seeing Hugh as one who is damned. It sounds a little over the top, touching the melodramatic or the pre-scientific, the kind of thing both of us would laugh at. Damned? C'mon, babes, we're American guys.

It isn't a surprise is to find him identifying with Hamlet (even if it is a surprise that Shakespeare wrote it for him!), since the most important person in both their lives is a dead father. Hugh too is sick of life and doesn't see any way to get its rewards. (After tennis one day Hugh said he had too much time left, too much time to live.) He doesn't want sympathy because it only makes him feel pathetic and he needs no reminder of that. He can stand on his own two feet and stare in the mirror. He doesn't need you to hold it up for him. He doesn't need you to cheerlead him back to mental health. All this is the familiar blend of stoicism and self-pity, the advanced case, beyond tears. Hugh also doesn't say the obvious, that like Hamlet he is haunted by his father's ghost in a way that may be what has reduced him to inaction. However, Hamlet's problem is simpler. He only needs to avenge his father's death to quiet the ghost. Who is there for Hugh to avenge the loss of his father on—except himself? He needs to kill himself so he can get on with his life.

What extreme act of penance might substitute for the ultimate one?

Hugh also says he has got the world wrong. He accepts responsibility for that too. He is not a victim of his miscomprehension, he is a participant in it. He understood the world a certain way—because of beliefs he was taught, because of values the world praised—and because he misapplied those lessons, because he discovered too late or embraced too ardently the shining code the world buffed itself with, and missed the point that that was only an advertisement, a come-on, a fiction, not something to wrap your life around, he is at fault. He made the amateur's mistake of taking ideas seriously, of respecting them too much, of not perceiving them as commodities. Fungible like money, used daily in human commerce, but not finally real. You couldn't cash in your gold certificate for a lump of metal, and you weren't meant to act as if ideals could be lived by, only to agree you wished they could be, and then carry on like everyone else.

Hugh's estrangement from ordinary life connects him to another evictee, one sentenced to a kind of internal exile by forces he can't understand. Geoffrey Firmin, "the Consul" in Malcolm Lowry's novel *Under the Volcano* (a book Hugh had read) is stranded in Mexico, unable to act or do anything besides drink mescal while he struggles to comprehend the occult messages from the mystical forces afflicting him. The Consul can't explain to himself how this happened, not satisfactorily, although at one level he knows his problem is simply alcohol—he would rather drink than do anything else, including love a woman. But the Consul also denies that that's the real problem, or not all of it, not the essence, and there is another, deeper cause which he can't quite express. Hugh's drug of choice was his own endorphins, and he was certainly as addicted to extreme exercise as the Consul was to alcohol. Instead of destroying his body Hugh strengthens it every day, but both he and the Consul are addicts, and both are in love with their addiction and can't imagine life without it. They are also extreme critics of life whose pride makes them insist on the truth of their criticism, their rejection of life as it is, and their proud, stubborn, critical view won't let them compromise and make peace with what is merely possible. The Consul is somehow aware of this struggle and even relishes it in certain clairvoyant moments when he has "drunk himself sober." In this rare lucid mood, he can see that this is the cause below his addiction, and why his allegiance must be to it, not to any livable life. Hugh had moments alone, drunk on the endorphins of exercise, when he felt he had lived exactly as he should, and had done so by the only lights he could see clearly by, which was why his situation—if not his fate— was his "fault." But he didn't have as dark a side as Lowry's Consul, who was aware of how much he needed to lose to show he was right, and thus win, tragically. Lowry's intention in *Volcano* was to write a tragedy and the tragic element was his protagonist's knowing what he was doing and embracing his own fall as the inevitable consequence of refusing life on its terms, instead of his own. Hugh couldn't dramatize himself, his life wasn't tragic like the Consul's or farcical like Boudu's; Hugh's life wasn't anything. Not tragic, not comic, just a blank unable to be filled in. In the image I had begun to see standing for Hugh, he was a finely tuned engine with no transmission or wheels, running on a bench instead of propelling his life.

It wasn't a mystery either, not one with any satisfying solution which would fulfill the narrative and click shut. He was a man without a story, not because trauma had erased his memory of his identity or because a totalitarian state had suppressed his freedom to act or think or because he was such a pliant blob that he took the impression of what was around him and had no self of his own. There wasn't any narrative reason for his lacking a story. That's what he meant when he accused himself—in his notebooks, in his denunciations of himself—of being wrong. His eviction from the meaning of life was his fault, even if it wasn't intended, because that is the challenge of life as a free human being. You have to find something to do or someone to be while you're here. That's the game, the game we play once we've survived. It doesn't matter if all human endeavor is ultimately futile or that what we call meaning is a fiction. To live a complete life you have to find something you can believe in enough to do it or be it or play it. If you insist on pulling back the curtain and telling everyone what they're doing is a lie, a fiction, a fantastic construction with nothing behind it—well, then, that's what you'll end up with yourself: nothing.

Since the personal led inevitably into the social and political, Hugh couldn't help being an enemy of the culture, the state, all conventional society. As much as he loved baseball and girls and pop tunes and hot dogs, he ended up in our American gulag, which wasn't an archipelago of concentration and labor camps in the remotest part of a vast cold land but was sprinkled throughout the population among us, its prisoners frozen in their solo limbos.

Without a position or role, with nothing to connect him to the larger narrative around him, Hugh was invisible. He wasn't even seen as an exemplar of his own values, as someone who was paying a price for living according to what he believed in, because he lived without witnesses, without an audience, without an act to make his character manifest.

34.

From Hugh's notebooks:
    Alcohol can enhance the effect of drugs.
    1. Light meal (tea & toast) 1 hr. beforehand
    2. Three sickness pills
    3. 10 pills with spirits or wine
    4. Additional pills in pudding (eat rapidly)

Amobarbital	90 x 50mg
Butabarbital	100 x 30mg
Codeine	80 x 30mg
Diazapam (Valium)	100 x 5mg
Flurazepam	100 x 30mg
Glutethimide	40 x 500mg
Cloral Hydrate	20 x 500mg
Meprobamate	112 x 400
Methyprylon	50 x 300
Meperidine	72 x 50
Methadone	60 x 5
Phenobarbital	150 x 30
Secobarbital	45 x 100
Pentobarbital	30 x 100

35.

While Hugh was stuck in this private purgatory, making lethal lists and teasing himself with oblivion, an improbable thing happened—he met a new woman. Just as improbably, their meeting was a scene from a Truffaut romance, rosy-hued, with light surprised music enhancing their laughter and dialogue, soft-focus close-ups of wry, hopeful glances, and a lyrical interlude in which time passes longingly to set up a first tentative touch ending with the obligatory but tastefully composed scene of love-making. Hugh was still exercising as maniacally as ever and it was a vital sign that he hadn't entirely given up on himself that he could flirt—flirting was like a reflex for him—and meet women. It was also a sign that the compulsion to use his brain was still alive in more than one way because they met in an art museum. A few pages after the long list of lethal doses of barbiturates and sedatives in his notebooks, I came upon these ardent notes:

The DeCordova

Megan

The beginning. A walk. Food, wine, talk. A later visit, a kiss (Chekov's The Kiss). This could be everything. We made love and you were perfect. Everything. The beginning and the end.

The hopeless romantic, I said to myself reading it, smiling, wanting to toast Hugh with a beer, suppressing a thought about what "The beginning and the end" might mean. An echo of the Biblical formula for the kingdom of heaven on earth, maybe.

Megan was an even more unlikely mate than Denise or Ofra, and would turn out to be a real Tisiphone in her hapless role as the third of the Furies who accompanied Hugh on the long descent from Debby. Although the reference to Greek goddesses is casual ("Hey, babes"), and arch (like De Vries), it's appropriate that the Furies' role was to pursue and punish sinners, including those guilty of "self-cursing." With hair like snakes and eyes weeping blood, the Furies were also daughters of parricide, created when Cronus castrated his father Uranus and threw his testicles into the sea; the drops from his bleeding scrotum became the foam on the waves, which was then transformed into the Furies. In Aeschylus' telling the Furies pursue Orestes for killing his mother (to avenge her killing his father). He confesses, Athena forgives him, and changes the angry Furies into "the kindly ones," the Eumenides. This is too violent and melodramatic to fit Hugh's non-story, although it's shot through with the dread consequences of parricide. Unbelievably, it all ends well, but only through the intervention of gods. So the parallel is evocative, but ultimately goes no further than suggesting that Megan played the role of punishing Hugh for cursing himself. As it turned out, she did that very capably during her brief appearance in his life, and no gods intervened to save either of them from each other.

Several weeks after they met Hugh and Megan came to our apartment for dinner. Megan was big, almost as tall and broad-shouldered as Hugh, and well-proportioned, with handsome regular features and thick brown hair worn in a style that looked almost permed. She was wearing a dress—who still wore dresses?—and reminded me of a nurse in a 1940s Hollywood movie set during the war, brave, boisterous, and sure of her values, at least publicly, in conversation. In the kitchen beside her Hugh seemed to shrink, looking almost physically meek or subservient. It was weird to see him so altered by contrast and it heightened my sense that Megan was not entirely of this world (maybe she really was Tisiphone!). At the same time, she was quite ordinarily real, unshy, unself-conscious, a big strong person who assumed she belonged wherever she was, even if she seemed so out of place in our Cambridge kitchen.

Already the romantic glow between her and Hugh had cooled to room temperature. Megan's manner was as blunt as a hammer and instead of the spellbound enchantment they enjoyed when they met she and Hugh spent the evening knocking each other verbally with as much fluency as if they'd been married for years. In a way they had been, in other guises. Megan was recently sprung from an unhappy marriage to a husband who had constantly belittled her. Hugh had described this to me beforehand, a little warily but not without sympathy for her. Yet in Megan he had finally met the woman for whom men were the declared enemy, and her need to be appreciated and her equal need to get revenge matched in ardency Hugh's ache for affection shackled to his hostility to women playing the victim. It was like putting two big cats in a bag. Megan's mother, whom Hugh had met and charmed, took his side, blaming her daughter for her unhappy relations with men, so while Megan was fighting the battle between her ghosts and Hugh's she was also defending herself against her absent mom. All they could do was scrap and spar, and dinner was like an evening with Albee's George and Martha, except they didn't get drunk. Instead, Kate and I did, drinking too much to lighten, or deaden, the noise.

When I saw Hugh at the tennis court he talked almost unstoppably about their arguments. Megan, despite her healthy size and handsomeness, had all the grievances of a traditionally raised woman in the age of blooming feminism. Women were silently sacrificed, men were deaf and dumb conquerors. It was hard to imagine any man conquering Megan, except maybe one of Ayn Rand's cartoon protagonists, but I never saw her vulnerabilities, her secret heart. What Hugh described was a woman who felt she had been used, and used badly, and instead of being able to sympathize with her complaints he reacted to her claim of being a victim, and tried to win the argument instead of, say, agreeing with her and then claiming his own rights as a very different kind of victim. Which she, in turn, might have sympathized with, had it all come out in the spirit of sharing instead of competing. Who knows. In the event, it had quickly become all friction all the time, with the same themes recycled endlessly. When Hugh finally broke it off, drained by their dead end arguments, he immediately tried to get her back again—helplessly replaying the end of his union with Debby. His attempt to get Megan back did nothing but give her the chance to reject him again, and again, and again, in her need to drain her own well of resentment of men. The soap opera continued for another few months; Hugh wrote her poems and entreaties—the medium of audio tape cassettes had been exhausted—and he laid these tortured productions at the foot of his Muse who ridiculed him. She must have enjoyed it as a form of tribute because they kept seeing each other to end the already dead relationship yet again. Each time they met was the last, like Zeno's many last cigarettes which permitted him to keep on smoking although he had quit. Finally, when it seemed there could be no end because each time they met was The End, Megan moved to Los Angeles. "She's going to live with her sister. She said she needs to start a new life," Hugh told me. "I told her you can't start a new life by moving because you're still the same person. It's just a new form of deception."

Deception was a subject Hugh was expert on but the observation was so familiar it had lost any power to enlighten, especially since Hugh said it in his own interest, not Megan's. It had become sadly inevitable that whomever Hugh found to mate with would soon be stuck in the role of a Fury, with the relationship obsessive to at least one of them. In this case it had happened to both, so things were getting worse. Megan was wise to get out of town, even if it sounded like a trite device, a plot turn resorted to by a scriptwriter out of ideas. When Hugh described this denouement, neither of us had the stomach to mention that his previous romantic comedy had ended the same way. Ofra to Israel, Megan to L.A. That's the kind of non-hero Hugh had become—one an intimate had to separate herself from by a continent or an ocean.

When Megan flew west, Hugh got on his bike and rode out to Walden, fifteen miles on hazardous Route 2, with its narrow shoulders and angry traffic, wearing no helmet as usual. Then he swam around the pond and rode back home to lift weights, completing his ritual triathlon, scourging body and soul.

36.

From Hugh's notebooks:

Duck Sex Survey:

Question: How many times did you have sexual intercourse in the last month?

Ans: With ducks?

37.

Hugh had other friends he could confide in, but I was the one he described his physical accomplishments to, however briefly and cryptically, and also the one on whom he had shifted whatever ambitions he still had to write. I had a kind of shock of awareness of what this might have meant to him reading Janet Malcolm's description of what it meant to Gertrude Stein to have Alice Toklas approve of what she was writing. "Say yes," was the phrase Stein used for Toklas' approval. It was only one person, but that person was an intimate, the one who knew her most privately, and Toklas' validation of the difficult, complex, ambitious, and nearly unreadable novel Stein was trying to write was crucial to her carrying on with it. With Hugh it wasn't art that was being sustained but life, and life was the heavier burden to lift. My audience, along with a few others, helped remind Hugh there was someone who thought he was a valuable person, although it wasn't enough. Stein, by contrast, had someone to love her who encouraged her work too. There was the formula again, work and love. It kept reappearing in new ways.

I had begun to think of Hugh as too good for this world—flawed, yes, but also too good, too loyal to his impractical code—and when I told him so I added jokingly, "I'm serious!" in the same facetious, ironic tone of voice so he wouldn't think I was mocking him. Which I wasn't. I really did mean it. He didn't ask what I meant or solicit any elaboration because he was so diffident; instead his response was to tell me about a party at his friend Donald's house. He had gone to it only because he was already there doing some repairs, so Donald asked him to stay. A number of people from the television station were there, some Hugh had known before. He overheard one of them, the program manager, in a conversation comparing himself to Billy Budd. The guy was trying to illustrate how the pressures and politics of his job had squeezed him. He didn't spell out literally the parallel between himself and Melville's hero; it was enough just to use Billy Budd's name as a symbol of goodness brought down by malice, a man unable to defend himself because of his nature. Hugh could barely contain his fury that such a blandly comfortable manager could graft himself on to a creation like Billy Budd. To claim that in some vague way he was like the doomed sailor—provoked by the conflict between his naturally superior goodness and an envious malignant officer to commit a crime of passion by accident, and then forced by the same virtuous character to assent to society's destruction of him—to make that connection was an outrage, a travesty of what Melville was trying to say. The guy was a bureaucrat at a public television station! Who or what evil force was threatening him with destruction? On the guy went, in Hugh's telling, carried away by the imagined parallels between himself and Billy Budd, the paragon of a code resembling strict duty. Hugh's voice was a whisper of indignation, he stamped his foot for emphasis. His foot stamp was like the way his voice got softer with rage. He raised his right leg almost up to the height of his other knee and slowly pressed it down to the ground, as if he was pumping a bellows that would blow these outrageously mistaken notions so far away they'd never be heard again.

I'd rarely seen Hugh so wroth and finally realized how deeply this cut into him. To live by the categorical imperative wasn't a vanity one could trot out at a party over hors d'oeuvres and wine! Hadn't this manager noticed, while he was talking so glibly, that Billy Budd was silent, unable to speak in defense of himself because no matter how much he'd been provoked by Claggart he had done something *wrong*, he'd committed a crime? That he believed so much in his code that he died for it? Not willingly or proudly but unavoidably. Because if he truly believed in what he believed there was nothing he could say in defense of himself? Hadn't the guy noticed any of that, which was, after all, the whole point of the story? Not that there was a literal point, Melville was too subtle for that. But Billy's fate showed what Hugh was living, that about his life there had been some crucial misunderstanding, one which Hugh mysteriously had to suffer for, because he was his father's son or because he believed his ideals or because his life silently showed the complacency and hypocrisy of ordinary upscale middle class American life and he was unable to make the very compromises which the program manager was claiming turned *him* into Billy Budd. Or none of these was the reason Hugh's life was wrong, there was no reason, and because there was no reason he could not defend it, or explain it, and that if he had been arraigned for it—and this was the final, the capping parallel between himself and Billy Budd—Hugh would have stammered mutely and said nothing. There was nothing he could say in his own defense. Whatever it was he was guilty of was the truth.

To be too good for this world is not a job or something to do, and when applied to the problem of finding a woman to love it really does sound like a joke. (You wouldn't find any women who thought Hugh was too good.) The moral aura of Hugh's life might be something I could see and appreciate, but unless you were up very close it was barely visible. He did favors for people, he was infallibly polite and civil, he still did odd jobs and refused to take any payment—because he wouldn't take money, his friend Donald gave him a VCR so he could tape Celtics games, then it sat unopened in Hugh's apartment, an odd mate to the color TV he had given Denise—but all this was the Boy Scout stuff. Hugh didn't want money to be the reason or measure for every minor act of helping someone because his goal was to get along without exploiting anyone, a goal no one seemed to notice as an entry point to an alternate universe of values.

From Hugh's point of view what he did was logical, even inevitable, but he also couldn't avoid asking why he'd ended up in his late forties, nearly fifty now, living alone in a tiny apartment with nearly no money, reading obscure books and government papers, occasionally scribbling in his notebook, exercising maniacally, scourging himself physically and mentally, playing tennis and squash for pleasure, and sitting late at night with a bottle of beer and using his powerful mind to watch basketball or listen to the outraged callers on talk radio, alternately seething and smiling at their twisted idiocy, their ignorance, their raw need to be heard, aware that he was—no matter how different—a member of their fellowship of the miserable. It was the existence of a secular monk but instead of being a manifestation of a higher spirit in the midst of the busy world where everyone's thumb was jabbed in someone else's eye, he was nobody. Hugh knew the rationale for his situation could only sound like what you always heard from the losers. So even in the privacy of his own head he didn't try. But he heard the judgment anyway; he knew what another athlete would have said. Or his mother. Or, as I heard once, someone else even more significant.

It was a week or so before Christmas and we were playing squash at Harvard's Hemenway Gym near the law school. While we were taking a break so I could gulp water—as usual Hugh never needed more than a brief sip at the fountain even after playing two hours—he said, "I realized today was the anniversary to the day of my father's death and I thought if he was alive he wouldn't be very proud of the way I turned out."

I didn't have any answer for that, any more than Hugh did, and it was only later, in the evening when I remembered his comment, that a second thought hit me: Wait a second! Hugh told me his father died sliding into second base. What was he doing playing baseball in December?

38.

The longest entry in Hugh's notebooks was a passage from Italo Calvino's *If On a Winter's Night a Traveler.* "Ernes Marana dreamed of a literature made entirely of apocrypha, of false attributions, of imitations and counterfeits and pastiches. If this idea had succeeded in imposing itself, if a systematic uncertainty as to the identity of the writer had kept the reader from abandoning himself with trust—trust not so much in what was being told him as in the silent narrating voice—perhaps externally the edifice of literature would not have changed at all, but beneath, in the foundations, where the relationship between reader and text is established, something would have changed forever. Then Ernes Marana would no longer have felt himself abandoned by Ludmilla absorbed in her reading: between the book and her there would always be insinuated the shadow of mystification, and he, identifying himself with every mystification, would have affirmed his presence."

As a reading experience, this appealed to Hugh since he too identified with every mystification and could feel his presence affirmed in the text. In 19th century, pre-modern terms all Calvino is saying is that Ernes is jealous of Ludmilla's absorption in her book instead of paying attention to him. But the author adds a more contemporary mystification to the traditional device of a "real" person's jealousy for a fictional one to portray a world in which the foundation of plausibility—our trust in the "silent narrating voice"—stands for belief itself, and once shaken nothing can be trusted, nothing is true. This doubt starts by undermining the voice narrating a story about characters in a book, and extends all the way to us. Reader and author, all of us are fictions, and everyone's sense of him or herself is a mystification—unreliable and contingent—because no narrating voice can be trusted.

Even that "fact" is a fiction (all men are liars), yet the subterranean message is clear; it mocks Hugh's perpetual involuntary search for what is true, worth believing in. The mystifications make him reel. He has an appetite for absolutes yet none will stay in his stomach. So he engages in a kind of intellectual bulimia, ingesting some thinker's ideas until he is stuffed, then he throws it all up. How much nourishment does he get from these meals? Yet he keeps going back, like a dog or an addict, for more.

39.

At some point during this long slow descent—or stasis, with no movement at all—Hugh quit paying rent on his apartment. It might have been a classic passive-aggressive gesture, like Bartleby the Scrivener's "preferring" not to work, a refusal to play the game by the rules, and partly it could have been a strike against the privileges of private property. Initially I saw it as a sign of Hugh's frustration with his situation, his terrible need for some kind of change. Even if it meant things had to get worse, at least they would be different. The apartment was rent-controlled, a prize in

Cambridge despite its cramped dinginess, and he'd lived there for more than twenty-five years, back to when he and Debby moved east together, so it was a richly symbolic home as well as the cheap, convenient place he lived in. Instead of having any trouble with his landlord, they got along fine. With his typical handiness and generosity (once again, the categorical imperative in prosy operation), Hugh was always fixing things in the building without telling the landlord, even buying the materials himself, and had become a kind of unofficial super of the four dilapidated units. So the landlord was mystified when Hugh quit paying rent. He called Hugh and asked if he meant to move out. "No," Hugh told him. "I just decided not to pay rent anymore."

"But if you don't pay the rent, I'll have to evict you," the landlord said.

"Okay," Hugh said.

"But I don't want to do that," the guy said. What the hell was his strange tenant up to?

"Okay," Hugh repeated, as if it was also fine with him if the landlord didn't evict him.

"But I'm gonna have to, if you don't pay the rent!" said the landlord.

No, you don't have to, Hugh didn't say. That was the part the landlord had to figure out for himself. An obvious weakness, or arrogance, in Hugh, was that he didn't explain his philosophy to the landlord, who wasn't a complete idiot and could easily have understood Kant's dictum, even if his tenant's allegiance to it was mystifying. However, for some reason (I hear the shrink murmuring "low self-esteem, feelings of inadequacy, an obvious narcissist"), Hugh wasn't able to describe the rationale behind his action. Maybe he was afraid any explanation would not, could not, do justice to the whole philosophy it was distilled from and that he would just sound contrary (which he was) or nuts (he was always in touch with reality), or silly, childish, and petulant.

For a long time nothing happened. It took quite a while to evict a tenant in The People's Republic of Cambridge and the landlord kept entreating Hugh, almost begging him, to pay before he filed the papers to evict him. But Hugh was firm. Once he'd made a decision it became an act in the past, irrevocable.

As usual, Hugh had waited till long after the process began before he even mentioned it. We were walking out of the Hemenway gym one afternoon when Hugh said quite casually, "I'm being evicted."

"Evicted? How can they do that?"

"I haven't paid rent for more than a year."

"What? A *year*? Why not?"

Since this was the first I'd heard of it, it seemed weird he'd had this hanging over him so long without saying anything. I wondered if the threat of eviction was the reason behind a few recent outbursts of temper on the squash court, flinging himself and his racquet around wildly.

"Why do it now, after all this time?" I asked. "What's the point? You're just making trouble for yourself." His stand on principle seemed compromised by his having already paid rent for twenty-five years.

Hugh didn't argue.

"Why don't you just talk to the landlord again," I said. "Make some kind of deal with him."

He shook his head. He'd made up his mind and whatever happened happened. I thought his reasons sounded plausible but not real, another fiction. If you went beneath the fiction he seemed like a little boy in a pout, angry at the world for being its way instead of his. Nevertheless, as frustrating as it was to see him hurting himself, I shared enough of his perversity to admire his refusal to go along to get along. If life had disappointed you in ways you were helpless to correct, why should you go along with the program? It was the Hell's Angels' attitude. If people looked at you as an outlaw, outside middle class society, then okay, *fuck it!* That's how you'd act. If they made a joke out of you and your ideas, were you supposed to laugh along with everyone else? Pretend you agreed with them? The problem was that Hugh couldn't hurt anyone but himself. To demonstrate against the values here in the Land of the Pursuit of Happiness was like hitting the Tar Baby. It sucked up your blows and held you tight, grinning at you. *What's the big deal, babes? C'mon over and grab a burger and beer. Talk some sports. Bird and Russell and Johnny U. and the Colts. So you've got a few gripes, don't we all. It's a free country! The rich get richer and the poor suck eggs. Who gives a shit, babes?* Hugh really had no choice but to martyr himself, even if it was only in such a small, stupid way. He didn't believe in violence, the real American Way. The Land of the Pursuit of Happiness had a genius for making your protest trivial. *Just tell 'em to shove it, babes. Sit down and chill, pop a cold one.* The hell of it was—as I could never forget about Hugh—that part of him, the playground kid calling out, "Hey, babes!" to his pal showing up for a pick-up game, loved ordinary, corny, egalitarian, leveling American culture as much as anyone. He could happily pop a cold one and talk sports and flirt with the girls—but what could he do with the rest of himself? The part that was uniquely him, his vzeoogby, the Kantian, the anti-Feynman human particle, the son of his genome and circumstances, the virtual parricide who read physics and poetry, did chin-ups, push-ups, sit-ups, rope-jumps, ran the stadium steps in his own daily decathlon—what the hell was that guy good for?

I quit trying to talk Hugh out of making some deal with his landlord. It sounded as if I didn't respect the immensity of all that was pressed up behind his decision. Perhaps he secretly wished to be saved, saved from himself, but he wasn't quite there, he couldn't put out his hand for help. Besides that, nothing had actually happened yet, and I kept thinking, or wishing, that maybe the landlord would make some kind of tacit deal with him, let him stay as the super or something, make it semi-official and just let the rent slide. Since Hugh was such a good tenant and such a decent guy to deal with, the landlord was behaving in a way very different from the usual script for his role too. He had even offered to forgive half of what Hugh owed in back rent to keep him as a tenant. Again, Hugh declined the offer.

As I realized the more I thought about it, the political and ethical part of his action, his non-action, was reasoned. Hugh saw the relationship between tenant and landlord as emblematic of the whole system of exploitive free enterprise and the market economy. The warped way human beings allocated value meant it caused friction at every point of contact between them. If the landlord evicted him he was obeying those forces, behaving like an automaton. Yet he had a choice as a free individual in a democratic republic not to evict Hugh; he could ignore, or defy (according to taste), the force that demanded one person pay another to live in the first one's property. It wasn't a law that compelled you to charge rent, it was a force, or a custom, one so ubiquitous it was never examined or studied or questioned, just assumed to exist, as if it was gravity. Similarly, it was Hugh's choice to ignore or defy the force and refuse to pay to live in someone else's property. If he did so and there were consequences, then he would be the human token whose movements revealed these forces at work. So, instead of participating in the system that had grown up around the rights of private property, he was rejecting it, come what may. He was witnessing his faith.

I began to see it in this more purposeful light, as Hugh's form of civil disobedience, like Thoreau refusing to pay his poll tax because by supporting the government he ultimately supported the institution of slavery. Thoreau didn't expect his gesture would abolish slavery, it was meant to make his neighbors see their own hypocrisy—they condemned slavery yet supported the government which permitted it to exist, even made it legal. Similarly Hugh didn't think if he opted out of the economic system which honored property rights as its foundation, anything would really change. Instead he was performing a symbolic act to show his peers how hypocritical they were. If you really believed the most important rights were human, and civil, not property, and that our first obligation as nature's sentient beings armed with thumbs was to the health of the earth and all its creatures, then how could you live day to day in a society based on exploitation and consumption? Instead of owning things in common to conserve resources and creating an alternative to the skinning of one human being by another, we each grabbed as much as we could, glorifying the individual as a kind of royalty, privileged to enjoy our kingdom of property while others lacked enough to live on. Biographer Robert Sullivan says of Thoreau, "Slavery is what he was protesting, though not slavery per se but the apathy of the people—the well-meaning, the righteous, the speech givers, and the ministers—who purported to be against slavery but in fact fueled a corrupt system." So instead of a contrarian, nose-thumbing, self-destructive gesture, perhaps what Hugh was doing was an act of positive self-assertion. He had finally found a way to make his indictment of American values visible and if his model was Thoreau, whether consciously or not, he was making "a personal declaration of independence," as Sullivan describes Thoreau's going to jail.

In making this declaration, Hugh was speaking to me, among others. He was saying, "My ideas really mean something—see how seriously I take them!" The fact that if he quit paying rent it might also force—a force of a different kind—a change in his life was an entirely private matter, possibly even a secret to him. In his desperation and stubbornness, he might well be disguising his deeper motive from himself, and only be vaguely, "subconsciously," aware of it. The conscious, self-aware part of the decision was his willingness to martyr his comfort for what he believed in. That it was also a desperate act, that it had to contain an element of self-damage if not self-destruction, was why his friends, like me, kept telling him how foolish he was to do it. Which he heard as our not understanding his message, anymore than his landlord had. How could his meaning be more clear? If he was hurting himself, he was doing it to repudiate the exaltation of property above life.

Did Hugh ever fantasize about really changing the world from such a small gesture? A tiny ripple sent forth into the sea of self-centered preoccupation we're all immersed in, becoming a tidal wave when, one after another, people renounce the prerogatives of property until a new spirit of community settles over the whole population and, suffused with this spirit, we all see there's another way to live. Did his fantasy end when the tidal wave broke against the puffed up chest of some grinning predator like Trump or Steinbrenner or the hedge fund operators? Or to preserve his fantasy from harm, did Hugh not let it go that far? Maybe not even whisper it to himself, just let it abide in a corner of his mind, unspoken even there.

40.

From Hugh's notebooks:
Necessity overwhelms evil.
All bad actions are compelled.
We always go to war because we have to.

41.

As things turned out, I was the one to move, not Hugh. Just before Thanksgiving the market around the corner parked a truck full of frozen turkeys across the street from our apartment and left the engine running for two days and nights to keep them refrigerated. We took the endless drone and foul exhaust as a signal that it was time to move. By chance a friend had a house he was trying to rent in a small town out in the country. The pieces were in place for a change. Hugh took the news I was moving sixty-five miles west very hard. I knew he would. It was the first thing I thought of when Kate and I talked about moving—what would happen to my friendship with Hugh? It wasn't going to be as easy to meet him for racquet sports. There'd be no more leisurely walks back through Cambridge from the tennis or squash courts, and was I really going to drive that far just to hit a ball back and forth? It was going to be a big loss for both of us.

It was typical of Hugh that he volunteered to help us with the miserable job of moving. I picked him up early one cold December morning and we drove over to the U-Haul office, then waited an hour for someone to show up. It had begun raining. It was going to be a nasty day. Obedient to his personal code, or simply being himself in his default personality, Hugh was cheerful and wisecracking. He moved furniture and boxes energetically, and made me feel, as I so often did with him, that we were kids again, enjoying the freedom of playing in the midst of the seriously stupid adult world. Yet whenever I caught his face in repose Hugh looked sad, almost bereft, and I couldn't help feeling as if I'd asked Hugh to be my accomplice in rupturing our friendship. He might even be wondering if I was secretly making the move to get away from him, and his misery. To make it all worse, the house and setting in the country were idyllic. Hugh looked at the stylish post-and-beam cottage on a plot of land that ran off into the woods as something else unattainable, just as he would never have the love of a woman like Kate. We all had dinner together, then spent the night in our new home (it even had a small guest room with its own bath!), and in the morning Hugh drove the rented truck back to the city for me, dropped it off, and walked home.

42.

Hugh was well into the second year since receiving his eviction notice, yet he continued to live in the same apartment without anything changing. It felt as if he was suspended, dangling over some abyss—the future—and that time now moved differently for him, in a teasing slow motion. He had one way of negotiating the tyranny of the clock and that was by reminding himself that when he chose he could step out of it, exit the temporal stream, and translate himself into oblivion. (Call it eternity, if you like.) This thought gave him a kind of mordant cheerfulness and from some of the entries in his notebook it was clear he hadn't lost his sense of humor:

Phrases that recur as I contemplate the end:

—Not that much can be said in his favor, although in fairness, he never watched daytime television.

—I won't miss a thing.

(I wonder if that's why I miss everything, I'm completely alive.)

Entwined with these endgame thoughts was the occasional note about women; love and death coiling around each other lethally or perhaps only fancifully, maddeningly. A note recalling Megan surprised me:

In 8 days it will be five years since I saw her. Five years and every day all serious thought is about her. I can no longer do those things which gave me such enormous pleasure. I can no longer love anyone. The teasing tenderness which once seemed so easy is now impossible. I am old. Everything is touched by the sadness of farewell.

Five years since he'd last seen her! I'd have guessed two at most. Nothing happened, the hours dragged yet the days flew by, the last female ghost his only intimate companion. Had he really thought about her every day during that time? I thought it was the circumstances which had made her so important to him—the depth of his need, not something intrinsic in her nature or character or person. Yet what did I know? "A man who is warm can't understand one who's cold," Solzhenitsyn says in *One Day in the Life of Ivan Denisovich*, describing an encounter between a Gulag prisoner and an officer in the labor camp. Hugh was always physically comfortable but his solo life may have been almost as distorting as constant, bone-chilling cold, and reading the note about Megan in Hugh's cryptic scrawl was another reminder of how easy it was to misunderstand him.

43.

Among Hugh's other friends the closest was Rachel, a fellow Celtics and Larry Bird fan to whose sons Hugh had become a virtual uncle. (I hear Hugh's voice echoing: "virtual uncle, virtual parricide, living a virtual life....") There was also Elaine who mothered him and invited him to dinner. Both women were always trying to think of a mate for Hugh among their eligible friends, but as everyone got older and acquired more history there always seemed to be reasons potential pairings got struck off the list. It was the same problem Hugh had had with Megan, in one form or another: prior bad experiences built up so much negative karma that the people desperately seeking a pair of arms to embrace them had turned so wary and sour they sent out rays of repellent. The older you were the more history you had and it was hard enough to find individuals who might be comfortably intimate with each other before considering the problem of how their separate histories might mesh. Hugh read the personals in the back pages of the New York Review of Books and moaned, "If all these women are so attractive and loving and gifted and wonderful, how come they're ALONE!" Any one of those lonely seeking hearts could have asked him the same question, and he knew it.

All of us worried about Hugh because of the hints about suicide. One night before we moved, Kate and I even drove over to his apartment to see if he was all right. He laughed at us—rather grimly, but it was laughter. I still didn't think Hugh would be able to destroy himself but we were all aware of the saying that if someone mentions suicide, no matter how lightly, you should take it seriously. His comments were too frequent to ignore.

Hugh sometimes played tennis with Donald, they watched sports on TV and had a few beers, and Hugh continued doing odd jobs on Donald's house in the South End and his other one on the Cape. Donald was droll and witty and smart, with a mind finely tuned to the absurd which he expressed in various voices (Mr. Magoo, Groucho Marx, a generic German or Russian) and was the rarest kind of friend: the worse things got for Hugh the more he tried to help, instead of disappearing. Which is probably how my flight to the country looked at times to Hugh. However unintended it was, the distance between us began shrinking our friendship, or the time we spent together anyway, so Hugh had been right to fear my leaving Cambridge. It was hard to find time to drive in for racquet sports, and several weeks might go by without a phone conversation. The lopsidedness of our relationship became more apparent and awkward; I tried to maintain the tone of sympathy but it was hard to talk to him. Any subjects we could muster seemed only a prologue to his tirades against a mis-made world and his own unfitness to live in it. The effort required to make conversation kept pushing up through the words.

Then, suddenly, I lost track of him. When I called Hugh's number I got a recorded message—from the phone company, not from Hugh—saying his phone was no longer in service. Kate called Elaine; she hadn't heard from him either. I called Donald and got the news—Hugh had finally been evicted. It had been more than two years since the first notice. Donald was irritated with Hugh's obstinance too. "I asked him if Marx paid rent," he said, adding a spritz of mock-German that sounded like one of Sid Caesar's bits. Hugh's stuff, books and bicycles mostly, were in Donald's basement and Hugh himself was at their house on the Cape. "He's replacing the windows. Greta has been wanting to get 'em fixed, and he needs something to do, so it seemed like..." He finished the thought with another spritz of vaudeville German. Donald's mentioning his wife was a good sign since she had become less and less fond of Hugh as his life dwindled, probably afraid that if he lost his apartment he might end up living in her house, which is just what had happened. It wasn't the one she was living in, their house in the city, so for the moment things were okay, but as Donald said everything was temporary. Hugh was now homeless and dependent on charity for his lodging, with even less control than before, and until it had actually happened he might not have been able to imagine what it would mean to live under the regime of this hard fact. Whatever his not paying rent had been intended to accomplish, the only thing changed was his own situation.

There was an extra aggravation too. In Hugh's friendship with Donald, Donald was the one who talked and Hugh listened. It had been that way from the start; Donald was the boss interviewing someone looking for a job and Hugh was the applicant. Nothing had altered that relationship. While with me, from the first night we talked on that charmed summer night in Cambridge when he described his father dying of a heart attack as he slid into second base, Hugh was the one telling his experience and I was the one listening.

44.

From Hugh's notebooks:
[This notebook is blank. It has no entries at all.]

45.

In the following weeks, I didn't try to call him at Donald's house on the Cape. Hugh wasn't going to talk about what it was like to be evicted from his home of so many years, and what else was there to talk about? The old familiar subjects seemed so irrelevant now. They were exposed for either their triviality or the tone of hope underlying them, and hope had become its own parody. Any ideals Hugh still lived by weren't adhered to so much by conviction as habit. Now he was doing no more than serving out the sentence handed down by some indifferent, non-existent non-Authority to live in this temporary solitary confinement, a dumb fate that proved nothing. So why embarrass him by making him respond to my voice? It was enough to know he was okay.

Then, a couple months later, after a mild, sunny fall Saturday of leaf raking and dog walking, tranquilized by the serene splendor of such prosy activities, I called Donald's number on the Cape. I just wanted to say hello, to hear Hugh say, "Hey, babes, how you doin'?" It was the weekend so Donald and Greta might be there too and I hoped I wouldn't get Greta. I did. But instead of having to make lame conversation, perhaps to hear her say he'd been evicted again—this time by her—she said brightly, "He's right here," and passed over the phone so quickly I seemed to hear Hugh's greeting in my ear as I was anticipating it.

"Hey, babes!"

"Hugh! How you doin'?"

With a strange jokey cheerfulness Hugh assured me he was all right, minimizing whatever had happened before I knew what he was talking about.

What the hell *was* he talking about?

Hugh's oblique account was punctuated by his diffident laugh, and in the background I could hear Donald's mock EMT report in a Boston Irish accent—"Man down! Man down! Traumer unit repawting a accident!" All this preceded by Greta's almost giddy greeting, so it sounded as if I'd interrupted a party to celebrate something. I began to understand that the euphoric chorus really was celebrating and the occasion was Hugh's survival, that he was alive. I finally doped out that he'd had some kind of accident on his bike. He rode everywhere, in any traffic, and never wore a helmet. Helmets are for football, not for riding a bike. He didn't wear a seatbelt in the car either, part of his fatalism combined with a stubborn allegiance to the culture of his youth when seatbelts and helmets for bike riders were unknown. If it was good enough then, it's good enough now. But the first reason was the real one: he was not going to wear a silly piece of headgear that advertised a sentimental attachment to life. Sentiment was for the middle class, it was a subsidized, phony emotion he didn't share or respect. When he rode he rode bareheaded with hair flying like a Hell's Angel on a Harley.

The accident happened when he was riding back to Donald's house from a store, a few groceries tucked in his usual small back pack, coming down a long hill on a curve ("I didn't think there were any hills on the Cape," I interjected. "Just one. I found it," Hugh laughed). He was still accelerating when the wheel hit something or the tire blew—in the background I could hear Donald's contrapuntal commentary, now switched from Boston Irish to German, real or made up, something multisyllabic that sounded like "thunderstrike"). The bike, now out of control and at speed ("die grosse Geschwindigkeit!"), shot off the road and hit something big and immovable like a tree or a pole. There were no witnesses and Hugh didn't remember. Donald's comic commentary also made it hard to hear Hugh, but the message was clear—his collision with the tree or pole or whatever it was had been serious. Somebody found him and got him to a hospital, and he was there for several days, long enough for his stay to become an incarceration. The picture I got was of Hugh lying under a tree for as long as an hour, unable to get up because of his injuries, something ruptured and bleeding internally, before someone found him and called for help. Later Donald said to me, in his own sober voice, out of Hugh's hearing and no fooling around, "He almost killed himself. Maybe he meant to. He sure came close."

PART THREE

Swim to Infinity

The Swim to Infinity was conceived on the model of a Walk or Ride or Run to Cure Cancer or Hunger or Poverty or Crime or Incivility or Tooth Decay, and as he entered the water in the bay, Hugh Prime—he could only begin the event by thinking of himself as not exactly himself, as one aspect allowed to dominate the rest of him so completely he became a kind of clone of himself—he was aware of the city but only as an abstraction, a half step to one side of ordinary reality, just as Hugh Prime was to him. This sense of abstraction included the temperature of the water, the bay in front of him, the impossible goal of the event. He was sure it must be colder than it felt, because it was almost comfortable, as if he'd already been swimming for an hour or two. He was wearing his running clothes, shorts and a shirt, and had forgotten or neglected to take the shirt off. It didn't matter, he stroked as smoothly as if he were naked.

He had entered the river at the estuary and was swimming out into the bay. The surface was striped with orange from the rising sun lighting the ripples; the sun barely a semi-circle on the horizon, flashing into his eyes whenever he glanced ahead. There was a boat way off to his right, a small one, bobbing on the shallow waves. He didn't see anyone in it. He looked back over his shoulder, feeling there was someone behind him. Another swimmer. A shark. His fellow man. That was the kind of thought that out of water would have made him laugh. There were a few people back there, way back, a few friends. As far as his family knew he was already infinite. "I'm not Boudu!" Hugh shouted inside his own head. The words of the essayist had been scratched into his heart and he knew what he was doing.

He stroked to a regular beat, not quite hard, although in this blank, stone, pitiless mood it was difficult for him to judge his level of exertion. His mind was empty of its usual competing thoughts and impressions, focused on the motion of his arms and coordinating them with his kick. He wasn't a superior swimmer, just a strong one, and had only measured his buoyancy once, not very accurately. It had been less than average; he assumed his bones were heavy for his total bodyweight, one sixty-six at last weighing. Yet this was salt and he felt rather high in the water so maybe this was going to be easier than...than what? When you got the rhythm right the swimming was more efficient. Not that he cared. What did it matter how efficient he was? The pride he felt in his strength, or the comfort he took from it, was irrelevant too, something else he was leaving behind. Something extraneous. Something to spend, get rid of. He had anticipated the obstinance of his body, its dumb vitality, which of course was a joke when you chose to pit yourself against such a goal. Even if it was just a theory, to see what would happen, to see if his opponent could be renormalized. Brought back to the norm. The norm. A man's name. It was casuistry, wasn't it, to subtract one infinity from another, the sequence of numbers $(1,3,5,7...)$ subtracted from another infinite series $(1,2,3,4,5...)$ to show there was a hierarchy of infinities, like gods, which he felt intuitively there couldn't be, that any infinity had to encompass any other, all others. There could only be one, of any kind, although he could see the specific case of a value in an equation, a kind of sidebar infinity confined to its own situation—like the rogue freezing caused by ice-nine that turned everything wet into a form of ice, froze it solid, once it began it couldn't be limited, everything froze, but everything else that contained no water was unaffected, so it was limited, a limited case, which meant although it killed everything living it wasn't boundless, unbounded, without end.

"Shamrocks' Point Guard Redefines Role On and Off Court. For someone who has changed so much of our world in such a short time, Hugh Lewis looks at first glance surprisingly normal, though there is nothing normal about him, more like a graduate student than arguably the best point guard in NBA history. That he would excel in other sports too and actually have a degree in theoretical physics from the Institute for Advanced Studies in Princeton, New Jersey, where he contributed several new ideas to loop quantum theory, while also publishing a book of seminal essays on philosophy and politics, all seems so far beyond unbelievable that even a sports writer couldn't have made it up. Nevertheless...in it he portrays the quandary, the situation of what he calls the impossible human, the 'New Babe,' a statistical anomaly who becomes its insatiable victim all while running the pick and roll to perfection. His ability to not only score from virtually any place on the court but also to make the players around him better puts Lewis in a category of his own invention and definition before one even begins to examine his other achievements..."

The small boat was behind him now and there was nothing on the horizon. The sun was clear of it too, a hot ball, and its brightness was irritating, the way it sparkled and shimmered on the water when he swiveled his head to gulp some air. Even when he kept his eyes closed, he could see it, the beam of light he was swimming into, but then he couldn't see if he was still swimming in a straight line, dead reckoning the sun which he was afraid he wasn't doing anyway, like walking in circles in the woods. That was another one, swimming in a circle, a different one than swimming in a straight line that went on forever, out beyond the cosmic horizon, 13.7 billion years back in time plus, plus another length or two stuck on the end, so it was easy to see how these competing infinities infuriated the physicists, the mathematicians, and Feynman's inspired decision to just lop them off, even though he called what he'd done hocus-pocus, he called it dippy, so exactly what was there that was what it said it was without any hocus-pocus. Do you know how hard it is to know one thing for certain? One thing that isn't dippy?

You could subtract the unknowable distance of swimming in a circle from the unknowable distance of swimming in a larger one. Infinity minus infinity prime equals what? The answer is dippy. Hugh minus Hugh Prime equals? Not everything after the equals sign has to exist. Equations can be fictions too, like stories that are plausible but never happened to anyone so they're dippy.

He wished he had his stopwatch although he couldn't really read it without stopping and he didn't want to stop once he got into a rhythm, arms and legs so synchronized they could do this forever. Like running the stadium steps. This, right now, was not dippy, the hole in time he occupied now. It could not be subtracted from any other hole in time. Not with him in it. Running, you could always glance at it, reset it, a slight interruption in pace, but not much, not on a long run. He usually didn't swim here because of the filth but today it didn't seem bad, the way it wasn't really cold either. What they were talking about was what Hazlitt meant when he said hypocrisy is the tribute we pay to our ideals. But you aren't so dippy you actually live by them. Not unless you want to end up at fifty-plus the strongest carpenter in Boston. A phee-nom. A freak. Who do you think I'm fucking well fucking? The only player in NBA history let alone All-World to have written a paper published in the Physical Review on renormalization. The Norm. Find that in the Guinness Book of Records. Heaviest bathtub carried down the most flights of stairs. In history. To be a citizen of the modern west, Pfaff said, is to belong to a culture of incomparable originality and power and implicated in incomparable crimes. The atomic bomb, napalm, phosphorus fire-bombing bringing liberty to the world. Hallelujah! You could see how it irritated people when you dropped one into conversation, like you weren't supposed to remember things. It wasn't cool to know. It was cool to approximate. Whatever. To make things up. I was reading this book—I can't remember the title or author but what it said was—and you were supposed to take something seriously someone couldn't remember. Because it had the authority of having been written in a book they'd read but couldn't remember. Whatever. I was reading this book about something called renormalization and it was really interesting, something about things being dippy. Isn't that cool? If you just lop it off it will all make sense and it will be dippy. Whatever, babes. Early one morning in 1872 I murdered my father, an act which made a deep impression on me at the time.

The reflection of sunlight on water was irritating, infuriating, a joke, a very bad joke. Using your body to its limit was a way to thank nature. The sanctified life force, a normal, mortal enemy. Do you know how deeply I abhor our custom of steadfast carrying on. The motto was scratched on the rock wall of his cave, on the inside of his eyelids. Beside a drawing of an aurochs. Crude but surprisingly good. In charcoal and blood. Do you know how hard it is to know one thing for certain? Anything not surrounded by uncertainty can't be the truth. Our Mister Sun is going to go on till midday, babes. Think you'll reach the Finnish Line by then?

Kicking the water, Hugh decided—Hugh Prime decided—next time he'd choose a cloudy day for his swim to dipfinity. It was nice there were almost no waves. Wishing for one thing led to another, and another, another repeating series. He swam harder to blank his mind again, to empty his head, and it worked. He sought blankness, the blank not the norm. He was swimming away from specificity, losing sense of time. If he swam far enough he could swim out of it entirely. Another monstrous cliche, the space time continuum. Although you had to concede it wasn't sentimental.

The feeling he had been waiting for, swimming toward, came over him suddenly, like a capsized barrel: he was drained. He rolled on his back and felt something pulling him down into the deep. Shark jaws? No, the tail of his t-shirt. It was a serene sensation, immense, overcoming, as much bigger than him than gravity. It was gravity. He felt heavy floating but the water sustained him. Neither could he sink, nor could he rise. Could he grow fins? It's strength was as much bigger than him than, say, dipfinity. So he was already here, had already swum over the edge. It could only be seen in reverse. No edge, no surface, the force and edge and surface were conventions, conveniences, like rest rooms, metaphors, Nabokov's analogies used to understand what was otherwise incomprehensible. Pretty much everything else.

Hugh Prime lay waiting for a force, an irresistible force, to take him up while he floated, swam, failed to sink.

How had he swum this far, he wondered, really not far at all, only a few laps around Walden. A mighty small, you might say an infinitesimally small percentage of dipfinity. Quintessentially zero. Let's lop it off. See what's left. The difference between a percent of some indefinably endless quantity expressed mathematically and swimming a distance that was, by definition any distance, was a lesser percent of dipfinity. Percents of dipfinity could be calculated even if they couldn't exist. Swimming and math were not the same thing. Babes.

Now his body felt unusually buoyant, as if he was being supported by the water. Which he was, of course. He was letting himself float, as if he had any choice. Somehow it felt as if he did, as if he could let himself sink. Neat metaphor for free will, the illusion of. He'd bring his Philosophy 101 class out here for a lesson in how a sensation creates an illusion we call real, how intuitive knowledge deceives, how all science and logic is based on doubting the signals we receive from our senses. Seeing is not believing, disbelieving, learning to disbelieve, until you've trained your mind to be just as useless as I am.

Hey, kids, let's go for a swim! Last one in's a rotten egg!

The mere accusation, by one of the group, by the in-crowd, was enough to exclude, to make something normal something rotten just by saying the word. By sentencing one of the group to be not of the group you could make them run. I prefer not to. The motions of the sea beneath him felt as if he were lying on the back of an immense beast who might smother him with her love. One of the saurians. The tortoise. He was just waiting. Soon he would join the enemy, slipping behind it, renouncing it as it wrapped him up in her arms. He could say anything, she didn't care. The long swells rose and fell, rocking him gently, immensely, and he closed his teary eyes against the bright blue white sky. For my next swim around zero I'll bring sunglasses. Goggles. You only make this swim once, biologically, I told Dick, so your calculations are as useless as I am. He was smiling that smile, the winning smile, punctuating his comments with bongo riffs. The drumming sounded silly at first but if you listened you could tell he was serious about it. Like certain solo athletic events. Think about it, Dick. Once you begin your swim there's no way to come back, not biologically, even if mathematically you could work it out. So you've got to keep swimming, steadfastly carrying on, even if no one could swim far enough. In this event everyone loses. When you turn back you're still going the same way toward the end so the course has a kind of ultimate symmetry to it, a universal quality. The goal is always the same no matter which way you're going and wherever it is home is zero. Time is a quantity of motion through space, right? I mean once it's explained. Or a quality. We call it distance. The faster you go the slower your clock runs. If you got to the end of infinity in an instant instead of dead you'd be the same age you are now. Virtually, I mean, as in—that's the charm of the event. So simple, so obvious. Yet it eludes the mathematicians if they try to define her. I think she's a her, she's so slippy, so to manage her they make her hippy.

Hugh Prime was stroking again, not quite hard, a regular pace. He could keep this up forever, like running the stadium steps. He enjoyed the blanked moments, the periods when it was just him in the water's arms, her classic physical embrace, cool on the skin, which he could make warm by moving his limbs, just moving his arms and legs, swimming and swimming, one of the bands of current between him and there. It would be different on a stormy day but this was the right day, he'd certainly made the right choice. The sea rose and fell, the undulations were pleasant, moving with him, they were together, stroking endlessly. It took almost no effort at all, same as the sea.

He had swum quite far, changing his vision, way out of that pitiless gaze in the bay, still not much closer to the Finnish Line (that's a joke, babes), but he was way out of the harbor and when he rolled over again and looked back with his unspectacled, nearsighted eyes, the land—the city, the shore—was a silvery blur. Staring at the sight from his back, head craned slightly up, he interrogated its reality. It was definitely a place he had come from, a place he wouldn't return to, a place he knew well—had known well, his little portion—but it was a mystery because he didn't belong there. If he didn't belong there where did he belong? Not a logical question. A legitimate one, illegitimate one. Just because you didn't belong anywhere didn't mean you belonged somewhere. There was no necessity. Perhaps he belonged here, right about here. Where there was no Here. Any number of points one might be, yet none existed. A quantum location. An event. Ah...so I get it, Dick. I made it. And if you try to say what it is, if you subtract here from there, what do you get? The distance between them? What time is it now? Depends on who's looking, right? You just can't avoid the problem. Always right there, right here, right around the corner, even when there's no corner. No wonder you have to do something dippy. There's no choice. There's always a choice. It isn't a choice. Is there any event?

Sustained by his physical buoyancy, as before, and by the immensity bobbing him, over which he enjoyed no control, enjoying the immensity, the vastness, the endless lack of control, Hugh—first and last of the Hughs, sole, unLewised, the Prime— slept, or perhaps he only dozed or imagined he slept, but instead of sinking into the liquid dimension below, he rode the waves while his mind lolled far away. Once beyond his constrained world, he felt nothing for the mortal; that was the secret of angels, their blessed indifference. We imagined they cared about us because we imagined them. They were so serene because they didn't care about anything. He felt as if it was a discovery, what a closed world it was, a very small place full of pain. Why would anyone stay there? Here? On the skin of the earth. Cheering each other on, sentimentally cheering, steadfastly carrying on, so irritating to what one can hear from here. Or let's say it's a movie where you can see how petty everyone is, and has to be to stay in it, to be visible, still onscreen. If you aren't petty, you're invisible. Poof! No one notices you for so long, you actually disappear. Somebody has written that story. Once, he felt sorry for them, helpless treaders on the mill of mitochondria.

Some unmeasured space of time later, Hugh Prime was awake again. The mood he returned or came to in was practical, immediate, sober, a banker at sea. There was nothing he could do with a mental state like this. Not out here. This was not a practical situation. Just how far was he really going to swim, for instance? When you turned the question around, when you asked it like that, it looked completely different. Instead of swim as far as you can and call it the Finnish Line—call it anything you like—the question he might ask was can you swim from here to shore? When that was the only question a mood could produce then something that hadn't mattered before mattered now. Was he really going to swim back? Second question. Restatement of the first. The Ultimate Solo Athletic Event wasn't going to end anywhere and he had to end somewhere. Right? As a human not a quantum particle. As a human address for a certain, an uncertain large number of quantum particles. That was one way to renormalize the swim to infinity. Instead of the ultimate solo athletic event it was just dippy. Just like you said, Dick. Could it be done without swimming back through all the filth? Third question. It wasn't that filthy, not really. Otherwise he wouldn't have begun in the first place. Perhaps he wasn't that close to the city. To "civilization." He didn't look back, not now, he didn't want to know. He had a sudden sensation there wasn't any city behind him. No shoreline. No silvery blur. Nothing, without end.

Hugh Prime began stroking again.

As the sun continued to rise through the sky, the surface of the sea remained quite tranquil, rising and falling in flattened swells, and after another long swim he slept for hours, or perhaps it was minutes, on the long swells, before rousing toward consciousness again. The sun was now overhead. Sort of. It was hard to tell. Without moving his head he felt the sun through his lids. His body was divided into two distinct planes, a warm zone above and a cold one, a cool one, below. There was something else too, a weight pressing down on his diaphragm. He felt no curiosity, no fear, no interest at all to find out what it was. When he did finally open his eyes, squinting against the sunlight, he saw something black, a figure, rising above him. It looked like a crow, a huge one—maybe it was just his skewed senses, he thought, trying to control his surprise. It stood on his midriff, head cocked, one dark eye studying him with a kind of irritating curiosity. The creature seemed to be mocking him.

"You're alive!" it said, sounding surprised too. "I was just about to pluck out your eyeball for lunch!"

"Lunch?" The word made him hungry. But it wasn't hunger exactly, it was more like the memory of hunger. "I'm not dead yet," he laughed harshly, still waking up to the water around him, the black bird so big in his field of vision.

"You are not dead yet," agreed the bird.

"No!" Hugh Prime tasted salt on his lips.

"Is that what you'd prefer?" said the bird helpfully. "I take my food either dead or alive. But all I've got is this..."

He stabbed his beak twice into Hugh's ribs to show what a poor weapon it was.

"Hey, hey—watch it, babes!"

"Sorry. Just wanted to show I'd be glad to help. But I'm no good at homicide."

Hugh Prime stared at the dark eye cocked at him.

"Me neither," he said.

"Too soft for this world, uh?"

"I guess so." Just like that Hugh saw everything. Too soft yet he was guilty. "Maybe it's a philosophical problem. No, a physical one. I need to get renormalized."

"Is that how you do it? By taking a swim?"

"Is it possible to lose a race to infinity?" Hugh Prime said. He laughed harshly again.

"Well, how can you win?" the black bird cackled back at him. It sounded like an imitation of Hugh Prime's laugh.

"Nobody wins," he said. "You just swim. As far as you can. Then it's over."

"Is it a race? Is that what you're doing?" said the black bird.

"Did you see any other contestants? Anyone else bobbing around in the ocean with a crow on his belly?"

"You don't have a crow on your belly."

"I don't?" Hugh said. "I'm hallucinating?"

"I don't know. You might be. But I'm not a crow, I'm a raven."

"A raven." Hugh squinted, trying to recall the difference, other than size.

"Something wrong with that? You don't like my company?" said the bird, the raven. "You wish someone else was perched on your belly—a seagull perhaps?"

"How about a mermaid," Hugh Prime said.

"Mermaid! Mermaid!" the raven cackled and sprang in the air, still cackling. The breadth of its wingspan was astonishing, eclipsing the sun before lifting the creature up and away.

The sky, the sea, were suddenly empty. The mermaid, which for an instant he felt he might conjure up from no more than the thought of her, had vanished too.

Hugh Prime turned in the water and stroked. It felt like he was in the same place. You could only go from stroke to stroke, each one the same, so it was easy to think you were staying in the same place while the earth, the sea, was moving beneath you. He stroked a little harder, speeding up the rotation of the earth under him. He was a mote, a jot, an iota. A certain degree of solipsism was essential for any original human enterprise, wasn't it? Like, to take one example not quite at random, one's own existence. It was wired into the infant, screaming for food, the most important thing. The only thing. That feeling had to be strong enough to last our whole lives. Otherwise...otherwise. Everyone seemed to think the most significant thing about the dinosaurs, besides their size (although most of them were much smaller, more "normal" sized than brontosauri, closer in size to us, Hugh Prime reminded himself pedantically, reflexively, absurdly), was their extinction. Brontosaurus and Tyrannosaurus rex were symbols of extinction. People gasped at creatures so big and so totally gone from the face of the earth. What should have struck people, Hugh lectured—his pedantry enjoying its freedom at sea—was not their extinction but their endurance. For a hundred and sixty million years—that's *million*, babes—the dinosaurs were the most visible residents of the planet. The primates have only been here about a third as long and Homo sapiens for a scant 200,000 years. And if you start our clock with civilization, then barely ten grand. So let's give the Big Guys a little credit, babes. Give me a call when you're a hundred and sixty million birthdays down the road. We'll throw a party for you. Invite all your ancestors. See how many show up.

Sooner or later, in relative terms, swiftly approaching the absolute, Hugh Prime, if that's who he was, whoever he was, was going to have to get something to eat and drink. He certainly was if the ultimate athletic event was to keep going, although the Finnish Line was only infinitesimally closer. Or was it further away? If you spent your whole life swimming were you closer to it than someone who'd never gotten wet once? Hard to tell. Anyone seen a McDonald's? Hugh asked the sky, glancing around as if even a mirage would do. I'll have a Mirageburger. With everything. Make it two, babes. And a six-pack.

He spun slowly in the water, dipping his warmed upper half into the cold sea, and looked around again for land. It had to be there. He was disoriented. Sense-deprived. The sun had passed its apex and begun its descent. He was sure he couldn't have swum that far, not beyond sight of his starting point, though as he scanned his surroundings from his low vantage point he couldn't see anything but the low rolling waves in every direction. They weren't high, the swells weren't deep, but when you were in the water you were down low. That was a fact, not a factoid. Besides his hunger, he felt a little tired too, not too bad, just enough to remind him of his ever receding goal which, to be honest, no matter how far he swam could only be a personal best.

The raven had ruined his mood. Altered it, anyway. Craning his head up as high as possible while he treaded and paddled the water furiously, Hugh Prime still could see nothing but water. The horizon seemed to be only a few yards away and he felt as if he was at the bottom of a watery hole in the sea. He rolled on his back again, feeling less buoyant now than several hours ago. A briny, metallic taste dripped into his mouth. Nothing had happened, no one was there. He felt a seizure of panic. Something else he couldn't control. His swim just might succeed after all. This was an event he could win. A shadow crossed his chest, then a seagull appeared, hovering overhead. It looked supernatural, like some kind of god.

"Hey—where are we?" he shouted at it. "Which way is McDonald's?"

The seagull tipped its head down toward the human floating below.

"Okay, Burger King! Which way?" he shouted.

The seagull flew away.

He didn't like to think he was already so addled by swimming, by exposure, he might be hallucinating, going crazy. It was imagination. He had more physical endurance than mental. He knew that. His mind was blurring the boundary between reality and everything else in his head. Even Feynman had done it, lopping off, rounding off infinities to make the math work! Torquing the numbers. Adjusting them, teasing them. Flirting with them. At least Feynman was embarrassed by it. It was false, a trick, and no one cared! So what if it's dippy! Evolution didn't care. Caring was dippy. A deficiency, a flaw in the organism. If you insisted it mattered, you were useless because you were wrong. Even if you were right. He was swimming all the way to the Finnish Line, which couldn't be done, not without renormalizing his goal and then it was no longer the original one. He was unable to deny, sooner or later, he was hungry, thirsty, weary, frustrated, bored, scared. The conviction he'd felt wading into the water was gone, leaked out of him. So perfect, so perverse. He lifted his arm to swim. His arm was heavy, both of them heavy. What a ferocious strength he'd had when he waded into the water! The size of his passion! How much he cared! No wonder he'd swum so far. Not far at all. Once you couldn't see land you were always in the same place. No matter how far you swam. Welcome to the Finnish Line, babes. You won!

The sun was warm, almost hot on his face but he was shivering, too long in the cold water. He lay staring up at the sky, on the edge of the panic, waiting to tip over into it. Mental artifact. A shadow passed over and a moment later a crow, a raven, something big and black swooped down and landed on his midriff again. He winced at the hard claws digging into his skin. He didn't believe the cocked black eye; it didn't look like it believed him. There was something sustaining about their equality. Assuring. Buoyant. There was in existence another creature who agreed with him. So to speak. His flaw, one of them, was not believing in what he believed. What he believed in was not believing. The raven believed what he believed without thinking about it. That was just an assumption. His flaw was believing too much. Which was not believing. His unbelieving made him unfit, he was maladapted. People adapted to life didn't think of such things, didn't perform unnatural athletic events. The truth was unnatural. What was true didn't coincide with what fit. What was fit. Wasn't knowing the truth enough for him? Why did he care? Was he some kind of evangelist? Was it his sense of humor? Flirting with girls? Did he have a secret need to be popular? He wanted girls to like him, yes, definitely. Or was his belief in himself so fragile he needed someone to agree with him? One being to assent to his being. A loved one. One who could read him like a book and say Hey this is okay, I understand it, keep going, keep playing, keep swimming.

The large black bird was looking off at—at whatever it was looking at; there was nothing to see but water. Suddenly it looked huge, as if it had changed size or maybe he could now see it as it really was, a force of nature so immense it rivaled or was part of the sea. The sight was thrilling. Hugh felt like part of the sky himself, part of the sea, as if he was growing fins. This is what he was swimming for! This is why he was out here! He could lie here forever, his limbs had been taken over by this force and instead of swimming against the inertia or resistance of the water he was moved by it. Even speeding up, soaring. Over the water.

"You're still here," the raven croaked.

"That's right, babes." His voice quavered as he tried not to let his teeth chatter. "How far is land?"

"You mean the place you came from?"

"Anyplace."

"Anyplace? There isn't anyplace out here."

"Anyplace around here I could get a hot dog and a beer," Hugh Prime said. He still felt part of the sea; the voice he heard wasn't his own.

The raven looked at him.

"There must be a hot dog someplace," Hugh Prime chattered.

"Perhaps you were hoping to swim to an island with no one to keep you company but corvids. Is that what you imagined?"

"Mermaids."

"Where would you like to go now?" asked the raven.

"Now?" His teeth chattered. "Someplace warm and dry with food and drink."

"Isn't that where you came from?" The raven's brisk manner had no affect, no emotion at all. It extended no empathy to his fellow creature. "You don't want some brave new world anymore? All you want is a sandwich?"

Hugh Prime's teeth chattered. Aiming at oblivion, or infinity, whichever came first, he had only made himself supremely uncomfortable. Such a cheap trick, and there was no one to call on it.

His thoughts were spinning out a swift autobiography; he might escape into an image from the past—

"Put your foot down."

"What?"

Hugh felt the water lapping around him.

"Put your foot down," the raven cawed again.

"What? You mean I can touch bottom?"

"I haven't the faintest," it cackled. "I know I can't."

The cackle was so irritating, he felt an urge to grab the raven and throttle it. Perhaps it sensed his animosity because it was lifting its wings and flying over his head. They were both moving. Hugh Prime's body had rolled in the water, spinning the gray dome above, and with an angry, fatalistic spasm—the way one might shrug—he thrust his foot down, automatically sealing his breath as the water lapped over his nose.

After so long as a human-sized cork or island—a perch for stray birds—the touch of terra firma was so novel Hugh Prime felt a rush of lost emotions. There was so much he had loved! How could he give it up? He had yanked his foot up at first contact, but now he put it down again. It felt like rough shale. Fully extended, his toe just touched the bottom if he tilted his head back to keep his nose above water, so he made a kind of balletic motion and it seemed as if the earth was sliding very slowly under each of his big toes. The purchase was slight and the globe he was trying to move beneath him was massive and heavy—an entire planet!—so his progress was maddeningly slow. If it was progress; he couldn't tell if anything was moving. The buoyancy of his body made him bob up, so every few steps one of his legs merely stroked through the water instead of pulling the globe under him. So far the water hadn't risen over his nose so perhaps he was actually advancing toward a shore. All he could see was the sky and when he took a breath and tipped his head down to look around, the wavelets stirred by the breeze or by his own motion slopped into his eyes. He was trying to do something immense—to move the whole earth itself, and these stupid irritations were thwarting him! He shouted inside his head where it made no sound at all. He felt stupid and puny himself. He wanted to wail and bawl like a baby.

His mind had become ungovernable, as much at sea as his body, although he was lucid enough to know for certain that the raven or crow or whatever it was must be a hallucination caused by swimming and exposure and having nothing to eat or drink for so long. He couldn't stop the visions of things he missed, aching with thoughts of them, the smell of baking, the poplar trees he rode his bike under, the touch of warm skin and how much he had loved those he'd abused, himself most of all. He hallucinated a kind of Eden, another trick of his brain he assumed, but one so blissful he tried to hold on to it, make it last longer, a shifting blend of impressions he loved even more for their triteness. It came unpredictably, a surprise, a sense of well being—not ecstasy, but serenity—so relaxed and natural how could it not last forever. The visual sensations that accompanied it didn't seem to fit with the feeling. They were irrelevant, and Hugh wondered if this was the brain's prologue to shutting down. You felt fine, sublimely fine, and whoever "you" were was about to exit any physical form, and at this final moment a few postcards from "home" were flashed by your eyes by some equally uncontrolled mode of memory. There was no "Rosebud." No icon from childhood or any other images of poignant significance. Instead the visual sensations were random, as if they might have been slides from anyone's life. His mind was unmaking itself. When the feeling vanished unpredictably, he was conscious again, still here in the body called Hugh, or Hugh Prime, still floating, a human hulk. At a certain point, his core body temperature would drop below what was necessary to keep his body alive. He wondered why it hadn't happened already. Was it happening now?

He became aware of a gentle tattoo on his head, something hitting him—apples, it was apples. He was bobbing in a sea of apples. He grabbed one and bit. Eating, the juice, it was like another hallucination, and putting something in his stomach awoke a wild beast. He had been beyond hunger but now he was in its cage, attacked by it. He grabbed for more apples. He knew they were going to make him sick but the apples owned him. Everything was rushing back with the wild hunger: not the desire to live but disgust and fury and the insane energy that had made him swim out from shore without any second thought, without any thought at all. He could already taste nausea. Puke and die, puke and die. He didn't puke, he dozed and slept. When a wave broke over his face he inhaled water and woke, choking, and shivering. Instead of thirst and hunger he felt loneliness, an edifice rising out of the sea, mocking him. He rolled in the water automatically and began a methodical breast stroke. If there were apples someone must have dropped them off a boat or they drifted away from shore. Could he see it? Was he close? The sky was dim, the sun behind the gray dome. No land anywhere, nothing but gray water. What was he swimming toward?

Just keep stroking.

When he rolled over again it was to look for the sun. Whichever way he was swimming it was away from the apples. But maybe not. Something was bumping his head. The nudge startled him, almost made him lift himself out of the water, expecting to see apples, a pair of jaws. Instead he saw what looked like a log or—no, it was a leg, a human! He flailed at the water, turning himself, spinning, to see—to greet—this savior. Even before he saw the head, and the face, the rising arc of the belly had loomed overhead, bobbing deadly, warning him. Whoever this had once been, it was now the wreck of a human. The face looked like wax or black plastic, as if it had been burned or melted, and perched on its brow was the raven! Or some other enormous black bird—it blinked; then swallowed the eyeball clenched in his beak.

It was an apparition. It must be, he realized a few minutes later, after his panic was spent. Now he couldn't find it in the water around him. The sea had risen, the swells were higher, not much, just enough so he was aware of a continual rising and falling, as if the water was lulling him after his seizure. That's what it felt like, as if something had grabbed him—the corpse, a floating zombie, pushing him down in the water—which now, just a few moments later, seemed so strange because when he had wanted to sink he was as buoyant as cork, styrofoam. Buoyancy couldn't be helped, it was a natural state, he reminded himself, the natural state of a body in a body of water, bodies in bodies, sustaining a body no matter what it might want for itself.

How long before he went completely nuts? Was he already? If only he had the guts to put his head under and inhale. He wasn't afraid of death but discomfort! It wasn't just guts, it was this force he couldn't control, floating helplessly, talking to birds...out of six billion plus, not one other human knew where he was. Bodies floated out here with no one to claim them. Lost, solo, unclaimed human junk. Were they on the same earth?

He felt drops of seawater on his cheeks.

Hugh Prime floated, a hulk, a repetitive beat. Thump, thump. The disgust of desire, of wanting to be saved. He could feel himself already bloating.

Something bumped him again, and as if he was Pavlov's dog, Pavlov's fish, he was unable not to react the same as before. It felt like he was being seized—he flailed and whacked at the water, and this time after the attack when he lay beside it hyperventilating, with seawater stinging his eyes, and the "log" hove into view, instead of a leg it was a hand, an arm. It was pressed against him, making a comradely gesture, making friends after his panic attack. The hand was livid, so swollen it looked like a purple balloon, and when the water swept it up to nudge his chin the cold touch and whiff of its putrid stink set off a second seizure which ended with Hugh at right angles to the corpse, kicking it with his feet to drive it away.

Exhausted with kicking and thrashing, he lay in the water panting. When his breathing slowed down he experienced a moment of clarity, like a man with his head on the block staring up at the blade who suddenly feels the clock stop and thinks, What're you waiting for? Go ahead! Drop! Drop! He was laughing. He couldn't stop. His body shook in the water. Now he was calm, emptied even more empty, staring up at the blade.

So it was not an apparition. A figment of his imagination would not assume the same form twice. Would it. No. It wouldn't touch him and smell of—he'd never smelled it before, the retching stench, and the look in its eye, the dead innocent blink as the bird swallowed what it had in its beak.

Despite his companion, Hugh Prime dozed and whenever a wave or a change in the wind roused him to near consciousness, his companion, his buddy, the stench, was there.

He woke in the dark to a child's nightmare. The grotesque images played and replayed, jagged abstract expressionist images seized and twisted by physical pain, but like the bird's eye, the tortured kaleidoscope had no passion, it writhed mechanically. The times he woke were the same except for the pain in his guts, a handle, a grip to hold on to. The physical pain was less intolerable. When he became aware of light in the sky, he was limp from the looping hallucinations and cramped guts. He lay on the sea as mindless as his companion of yesterday, not sure which sensations were conscious ones. He didn't notice whether the corpse was gone but assumed it was still there, in the trough beside him perhaps, and now felt he understood what it meant. There had been an event, an accident, something huge, inevitable, people were inured to the idea, as if it was something to be gotten over with, a taboo that had to be breached so everything could go on, just the way he had had to live through last night and walk into the water in the first place. Had he done it because he sensed a cataclysm approaching? His mind wasn't his own. Yet he had, he'd done it, although now he felt nothing, not even hunger, or pain, but only a sensation—vast, sea-sized, like gravity itself, a weight pulling him down. It also buoyed him up. He was pressed between these two forces. All that wisecracking chatter with the raven, the vulture, the black-winged thing, that could never happen again, he understood, because those were the kind of things he would no longer say, no matter what anyone said to him, or to himself. He was not the same one who had walked into the estuary for the athletic event to end 'em all, the joke on himself. The event was over. He had won, or else he had lost, there was no difference, no finish line. He could have stayed on shore and saved himself the trouble, since everyone else had gone too—

2.

The sight of the ship was sudden: close and huge. Terrifying. It yanked him back to its world so violently, he tried to shout. His dried throat choked but any sound he made couldn't be heard over the ship, anyway, the thundering engines he could feel through his body, coming up from his groin, and the shrill churn of the bow slicing the water. As hard as he swam he didn't seem to move at all; the ship was too large, it took up so much of the sea, it was so wide, no matter how far he swam it would crush him. Panic made him superhumanly strong, thrashing on top of the water. Then suddenly limp, exhausted. Something was propelling him away from the ship, the sea it displaced was shoving him out of its way and he realized he was further away from it than he'd thought. Not only was it missing him, he was so far away no one on board could even see him. How could that be? It was right there! All they had to do was look! I'm right here! He didn't realize he was shouting till he felt the pain in his throat, rasping, the thirst. He was weeping, weeping, a wet rag twisted, wrung out. I can't waste the liquid, he thought, unable to stop. The black, rusted hull was already so far away he couldn't see any human figures on deck. It might be a ghost ship. He squinted, trying to sharpen his myopic eyes, but the only movement he could see was the low-rolling sea between him and the ship. A stupid feeling of fatalism overcame him, permeating, dissolving him into the sea.

He bobbed helplessly. He couldn't swim, couldn't sink.

He was floating in garbage. Garbage! He had a grapefruit rind in his mouth! A water bottle, floating, flagrantly empty, such arrogance! A soup of garbage and trash surrounded him, oceanwide. He inhaled waste, shit, oil, smoke. Had they seen him and this was a gift? We won't save you but we'll feed you—here, eat our trash! Seen from the air—which was now the view he had of himself, from overhead—he bobbed in the gray mottled sea like another, larger piece of garbage. He could see his own hands picking up whatever they bumped in the putrid flotsam, examine it briefly, uncuriously, then put it in his mouth. He imagined being picked up himself and stuffed in some creature's maw. His appetite and his thirst were beyond taste. The bits he picked out of the sea were unrecognizable lumps in the rotten goulash. The ones that tasted too foul he spit out, the others he chewed fast and swallowed. He knew he was going to be sick from the briny taste in his mouth but the thought barely registered. He lived in a time frame of instants, each one punctuated by a mixture of extreme discomfort and contempt. From the vantage in the air over his own bobbing body he had a sense it was possible to withdraw his sight back into the eyes he was watching himself with, and in this way he might evacuate his being. Withdraw and leave this husk, whoever he is, was, just leave him behind. But before it could happen, he felt his guts rise up in his throat and he was regurgitating himself into the sea, trying to puke himself inside-out.

3.

A desperate moment for poor Hugh...yet why am I torturing him like this? Isn't there something a little perverse about this scene, and unnecessary, besides the question of whether it says anything authentic about Hugh.

True, it's only his fictional self out there bobbing helplessly, it's not Hugh but Hugh Prime who is suffering the kind of abuse he wished to inflict on himself at his worst moments of self-loathing, so no one is really suffering. But of course someone is, all the time, everywhere, Hugh himself would correct me, without adding that he could be the emblem for at least a few of them. Or maybe just one. Am I doing this to make a point, using Hugh's life as an argument, an example...an example of what? Or is this only the logical end of his non-story? Here's where you end up, if.... Or am I doing it because of some unconscious purpose, some resentment of Hugh—do I really want to see him suffer? That doesn't feel right. Hugh's suffering made me feel sympathetic, and my resentment was only that I had no power to give him what he so passionately needed. When I got exasperated with him, he was always there ahead of me, far more exasperated with himself than I could be. "I'd be really sorry to lose you as a friend," he told me once, and I thought, "You're not going to lose me as a friend, Hugh, but what bothers me is the way you've lost yourself." That wasn't something I could say. It wasn't something he could answer. In the end I'm still trying to solve the mystery of Hugh. But the real mystery is what was it that appealed to me so much about such a difficult person. Because Hugh's life isn't a mystery, it's too obvious. He's just another guy who couldn't put it together. Yet he wasn't just another guy, and despite his own pinched existence the parts of his life visible to me radiated out into all the maddening insoluble enigmas of sentient life on planet earth.

At this point, before returning to Hugh's story, to his rescue and surprise and transition back into real life, there is another voice expressing the case, fantastic though it is, against Hugh. It may justify in some way what has been done to him so it isn't so gratuitous, and may even make some kind of sense. His situation might turn out to be not so arbitrary or contingent as he thinks, but instead inevitable.

4.

"It wasn't his fault," Hugh Prime heard someone saying, apparently on his behalf. But what did innocence count for? he answered. When the tribe was inflamed, it's appetite for vengeance grew fierce; never mind the Biblical admonition, "Vengeance is mine, saith the Lord,"the Lord is just another name for the voice I speak in: I, we, the tribe. The ritual human sacrifice itself is more important than the particular human who is sacrificed. Better if he's guilty—to make the story true—but not essential. Let it be dippy, if necessary; it will still do. If you are cold enough, it doesn't matter what sacred tree or antique you burn to get warm. Hugh, or Hugh Prime as he tacitly styled himself, walked into the sea by himself, exercising "free will," so it was hardly the tribe's fault—our fault—that one of us renounced his membership and decided to swim out of the race into oblivion. If he wanted to play the role of Joseph K. that was his problem. It didn't matter if he was innocent. He wasn't innocent in the way that the rest of us are innocent. There are levels of innocence just as there are levels of guilt. For instance, was it Hugh Prime's fault Disney World burned? Was it his fault that more than a thousand tourists (they don't even know how many) including hundreds of children died in the flames, suffering horribly? No. At the same time, was Hugh Prime as innocent as those who burned? Perhaps he was trying to refresh his innocence in the sea. (Choosing Disney World as a target was genius, one had to acknowledge that fact—Fantasy Land, Snow White and Bambi melting along with the shrieking children in the playground where having fun was a virtue and people were good and evil was defeated and justice was done.) You don't have to be the one who strikes the match or sets off the bomb to be complicit. You don't have to be part of the plot or one of the conspirators. You don't have to know them personally or even be a member of their tribe. It's enough to agree that they might be justified in having a grievance against us. That's what taints Hugh Prime's innocence and separates him from the rest of us. It's only a question of sympathy, or not even that, just an opinion, one he didn't act on—but how could anyone feel any sympathy for people who murdered our children! In their most vulnerable and most innocent location—at play, doing nothing more harmful to anyone than enjoying themselves! Their little minds alight with the antics of Mickey and Goofy and Donald. Burned beyond recognition! The melting faces and strips of flesh peeling off their little bodies, and Hugh Prime actually expressed, made a case for the perpetrators—even if it was only in his own mind (where only God can see!), even so, he thought it, he said it to himself. He said what they had done was understandable if you looked at it from the point of view of those who had experienced economic exploitation by another tribe, an exploitation that subsidized a culture they felt was threatening to destroy their own. These are the sentiments of a man who is willing to betray his own tribe. A man who has already betrayed his own tribe in his heart. If he is willing to betray his own tribe in his heart, hasn't he already committed treason against them, almost as if he set off a bomb in their midst, scorching their children and their innocent moms and dads on vacation at Disney World. Of course Hugh Prime would say—he can't say anything now, his throat is parched with brine, his intestines are heaving with garbage—he would say, if he were able to answer for himself, he would say the incinerated children may be innocent but their parents are not. They are voting age adults, living the good life in the Land of the Pursuit of Happiness, and their lifestyle is only possible because of the economic exploitation of people in countries far away from their home, people they've never met who are members of tribes they know only by rumor and caricature, and even though they are barely aware of the way their rich, innocent lives are built on a foundation of poor people on the other side of the planet, they are still responsible. It doesn't mean they should burn to death or watch their children die in Disney World, it only means by participating in their own culture, by being members of a tribe which battens on the lives of other less advanced tribes, they are part of a web of human beings of various tribes comprised by Western Civilization, and that if some of those other aggrieved tribesmen, exasperated beyond reason or mercy by the situation they see themselves in—if they should decide to burn Mickey Mouse because he embodies Fun and Fantasy in a godless, decadent form, and do this in order to make a political point, then mom and dad are ever so slightly to blame. Only ever so slightly to blame, infinitesimally to blame, for enjoying the lifestyle which happens, nothing more, to be available to them after someone's forefathers carved a new nation out of the Stone Age wilderness. Only the slightest infinitesimal blame rises exponentially like a flame burning the fuel of the tribe's fondest artifacts. What happened to Mickey, to the children, is horrific, unspeakable, and the perpetrators are beyond any kind of human forgiveness, yet the moms and dads are not without the tiniest sliver of responsibility for it all. Is that a fair way to describe your position, Hugh? Hugh Prime? Yes, I know, your literal position at the moment is somewhat compromised, floating at sea in a patch of garbage and trash and excrement, inhaling diesel exhaust, but I was referring to your political or moral position *vis à vis* the atrocity committed on Disney World. Do you agree with my characterization of what you believe? Or did believe at the time you walked into the estuary to swim away from the tribe into infinity, or oblivion, whichever came first. Right now you may have a somewhat different view of the whole thing. Lying there retching in the sea after filling yourself with garbage can change one's point of view. I wonder what your opinions are now or even if you have any. My curiosity is not merciless though it does have a certain indifference, a lack of sympathy for anyone who has exiled himself, who prefers to be floating out here alone in garbage and shit instead of suffering the tainted company of the tribe. You left us, in case you don't recall. And before you left us physically, you had already withdrawn your sympathy for us. Why, in his heart, does someone abandon his own kind? You aren't a sociopath. You always seemed like a decent kind of person. Decent enough. Not a saint, not a sinner either, somewhere in between, but certainly not someone who would bomb and incinerate thousands of innocent people along with their children! I didn't say you actually did it, I just said—you know what I said.

It's impossible to think of this, of your situation, bobbing in the garbage-strewn sea far from anyone (is that laughter I hear on the soundtrack?), and at the same time, with the same mind, encompass the scorched earth of Disney World, the charred hulk of Fantasyland sitting in its own ashes with the cries of the dying filling the empty air around it, without one's mind withdrawing, recoiling, pulling even further back to take the point of view of history. Let's take a much longer view, Hugh—the history of civilizations. Who except someone living in the present, in the speciously urgent Now, is going to care about civilizations which are in eclipse? If you were an extraterrestrial tourist who came to Earth at the height of the T'ang Dynasty in Cochin, for example, wouldn't you find that more worthy of study than the Druids of England or the Stone Age natives of North America? An anthropologist might say they were all equally interesting, the way a zoologist might say a chimpanzee, a nematode, and a protozoan were all equally worthy of study, but from the point of view of the history of civilization, there's no question which is more interesting. The very phrase "history of civilization" implies a hierarchy. There have been rises and falls, there have been highly developed human cultures at the same time other tribes were living in caves. Are you prepared to say that on the great scroll of human history all tribes are the same, that the Forbidden City is no richer a product of the human imagination than Stonehenge? Or than some mud village that dissolved in the rain, its name, its people, their language, habits, customs, culture, genes, memes, all gone. If you assert that, then there is no story to tell. All facts are equal and four-fifths of a champion is just as good as the champ. You agree with that? Eh?

Hugh Prime is so quiet. I don't think he's dead yet (although he might wish he were!), but his situation has made him unsociable. Maybe he can't hear me with his ears full of sea water. Can he hear the laughter in the background? Hugh? Hugh *Prime*? Perhaps you're laughing yourself. I doubt it. Eating garbage is not funny. Swimming to infinity is not funny. Not unless you're on land.

Assuming this role of historical camp-follower, bandwagon-joiner, frontrunner, triumphalist, scorekeeper, my interest in the human experience is the flux of civilization. Which is to say the story of winners because the lives of the people in the less dominant cultures, the losers, may be richer in human drama, in meaning, in soulfulness, but so what. Soul is for losers. Ask a winner if he'd trade places with a loser if they threw in a little soul. You bet, babes. If whoever is winning right now should be toppled, if they should decay and decline and fall from their pinnacle, well then I—scorekeeper, historian, judge—would shift my attention, my allegiance, to the new winners. Because that's the trajectory of the story. The human story can be scored like a game. Pick up a history book, Hugh (as I know you have many times). What is it? It's the sprawling, messy account of a game. (Nothing like your non-story, Hugh.) Anything else would disappoint the audience's expectations. They, we, want to find out who wins. If another creature should come along more advanced than us humans, someone smarter, more powerful, more ingenious, then our interest, our allegiance—our attention as an audience—would shift to them. Human beings would become fodder for someone else's story. If that new creature's tribe could create a more complex and accomplished civilization than the ones so far built by humans then our curiosity would be more excited by them. Doesn't that violate the principle of loyalty to the tribe, the Tribe of Human Beings, which everyone was assuming was so almighty worthy and virtuous a few moments ago—the sacred vessel of sentience and consciousness we revered when we were describing the quality of your betrayal of your own tribe, Hugh? Wouldn't a shift of our attention and sympathy as an audience rooting for a new winner be a kind of treason against our own evolved species? Yes, of course it is. But as I was also saying a moment ago, the final rule of this game, the one that trumps all the others, is that we always go with the greatest power. Always. (That really bothers you, doesn't it, Hugh.) That's something not always noticed by those comfortably enjoying a peak in the history of civilization. Why should they? They take it for granted they're on top, that they have the best story. How could it be their responsibility to let their civilization be distracted by a few ethical quibbles instead of attending to the business of building a taller skyscraper or flying to Mars or curing cancer or keeping their enemies—the lesser, envious tribes—under control, and preventing their impassioned rogues from turning civilization's playground into a pyre for its citizens and their children and their harmless cartoons.

Enough of my intrusions. It's time to go back to our fish (has he grown fins yet?), to our exception to the rule, the traitor of the tribe, the refusenik of the historical imperative, the pathetic Hugh or Hugh Prime, who I see is no longer floating in the garbage and shit dumped by the monstrously big brainless prop Maru Maru, and has recovered from his convulsions of retching and is now nearly comatose from exposure and lack of food, to say nothing of the killing thirst he endures which, to remind you, is still nothing compared to the thousandfold suffering of those burned at Disney World for which, had it ever actually happened, he would be at least distantly ever so slightly guilty because of his secret sympathy, despite his abhorrence of violence and dogmatism, for the terrorist enemies' critique of our culture. The wretched, thirsty, mortally solitary Hugh Prime, having achieved his personal best long ago, yet no closer to infinity than ever, is, however, at this particular moment...

But let's see this from a vantage closer to his point of view, from some place which is more immediate, more sympathetic (speaking of sympathy) than the tribe's. Because instead of killing him, we're about to save the solo swimmer—unexpectedly, miraculously—and he would say, agreeing with us, no matter how much he loves life despite himself, undeservedly.

5.

When the arms came down toward him, Hugh Prime didn't wonder whether they were real or not. The yacht with its colorful sail flapping up into the sky so far above him, the excited voices shouting so urgently, with such alarm, then his body buoyed powerfully into the air by a force so much stronger than him, might all be another hallucination, but how could that matter? He was beyond thinking. All his mental functions had sunk below the thin layer of consciousness and whatever signals came into his brain were only perceived as phenomena. The arms were smooth, strong, warm, and there seemed to be many of them, as if a flock or cloud of beings hovered above him. How sweet if he were to be rescued by a woman, her long hair caressing his face as she wound him up in her arms. If this was someone's very bad joke—if that long hair was a horse's tail brushing his face and instead of being saved by an angel he was about to get a faceful of warm manure— that was a perversion he hadn't the energy to imagine. He had been so tortured by the elements that he didn't experience the dramatic rescue, and when he recovered enough to begin to sense his surroundings, he seemed to be in something like a clinic, a hospital or sanitarium. It must be on solid ground too because he no longer felt the sway of the sea under him. The lack of motion was palpable, as if he was stuck in the earth like a peg.

"You are very lucky to have survived," he heard her say, whoever she was. Her voice was almost affectionate, although she was scolding him, as if she knew it was at least partly his own fault.

Everyone else who came in to see him said he was lucky too and because he couldn't remember what had happened he took their word for it, politely, gratefully, in a spirit of sociability, not expressing out loud what felt like a reservation closer to his own mind. He was lucky compared to what, he wanted to ask. He could remember feeling quite wretched; the skin on his face was blistered and painful and he was so weak he couldn't even push himself up to a sitting position in the bed. But he got better rapidly and over the next few days the same people who told him he was lucky began saying he was amazingly strong, otherwise he would never have survived what he'd been through. The woman, a nurse, the first person he recalled seeing when he came back into the conscious world, wasn't the one who had saved him, she said several times, but that was how he thought of her. The association was automatic and if he was lucky to be alive, as everyone said, his luck must be owed to her too, something he felt whether it was true or not. The first impression of her face with its kindness and concerned frown and her soothing voice—the first things he'd seen or heard returning to life—were indelible and he couldn't imagine existing without them. Soon, after he recovered enough to talk and respond, he began telling her how beautiful she was and how he couldn't live without her, and she took it as teasing, the half-serious flirting the nurses often heard from the male patients. Some of them liked to pretend they were great Casanovas, a shared joke, a way of saying they were going to get well, regain their vitality, they weren't going to give up. One morning the nurse, Astrid, told Hugh he might be checked out soon, even that afternoon, and he said, "So, I'm coming home with you? The rest of the guys'll be jealous."

"Oh, no," she joshed back. "You can't come home with me, Hugh."

"Why not? You married? He can move out." He knew he was teasing; she didn't wear a wedding band.

"Because I have a cat," she said without thinking, and then laughed.

"I like cats," Hugh said. "I like the big tabbies with the golden hair and yellow eyes."

Astrid stared at him.

"That's just what mine is," she said.

"That's great!" Hugh said, smiling, as if that settled it.

She had to go answer another call, and for the rest of the morning was busy. When she went in again in the afternoon Hugh was sitting up, and grinned when he saw her as if he'd been sitting there like that the whole day, waiting for her to come back. He said something she didn't catch, only that it was about the cat again.

"All you guys tease us," she said lightly.

"I like teasing," he said agreeably. "But I'm serious."

He caught her eyes in motion and she pulled them away.

"Have they found a place for you to go yet?" Astrid knew the social worker had been to see him. Everyone knew Hugh's story. The mysterious man found at sea, where had he come from, where did he belong? When he was rescued there was a reporter from television, an interview with the EMTs and the people who found him, although Hugh either doesn't remember it or pretends not to because if anyone mentions it he brushes them off and makes a joke or says nothing at all.

"They're working on it," Hugh said. "I think they want me to go home with you."

He said it so brightly she couldn't help smiling and turned away so he wouldn't see. Everything he said to her was almost unnaturally bright, and it seemed to her this must be a reaction to finding himself here in safe hands after the trauma of whatever it was that had happened to him. Astrid was as familiar as anyone to him now, and having lost so much of his recent memory it seemed likely he was clinging to her because she was all he had, except for a couple other nurses and staff people at the hospital. But he hadn't spoken like this to any of her colleagues, not that she'd heard, and perhaps because she was alone herself she felt herself drawn to him. But also wary. He'd been through some kind of awful event and besides that he was odd in some way she couldn't quite place, a misfit or eccentric of some kind. But he had humor and also seemed very kind, even gentle. Although that could merely be gratitude.

"I think they've got an apartment somewhere. I don't know where." He smiled, perhaps so he wouldn't seem totally helpless, as if he was throwing himself on her hands for lack of any alternative.

"I know they can help people," she said. "If they need a place."

"But why should both of us sleep alone?" he said, in his bright, jokey voice.

She felt a faint blush in her cheeks. Usually this kind of flirting didn't make her blush at all, she just parried it coolly, or ignored it and kept to business.

"Ah, so that's it," she said, finally finding her own jokey voice while she pretended to check his chart. "You are just like everyone else!"

"Oh no," Hugh said seriously. "I'm different from everyone else. That's my problem. One of them, anyway." He laughed a little too loud, almost harshly.

"I think you're lucky to be alive," she said. Now it sounded lame and stale, but she didn't know what else to say. His remark about being different had ambushed her sympathy. It was just the impression she had of him, but hadn't put into words.

"You mean if I weren't so lucky I might exist in some other form?" Hugh laughed.

She wasn't looking at him so she heard with unusual clarity what he said, both the jocular philosophical nonsense and that he had used the subjunctive mood. His gentility was making her trust him a little.

Astrid looked at Hugh, at his nearly healed face. "Have you thought about what you're really going to do, now that...?" She finished the query with a hand gesture.

"Do?" he asked. His eyes showed a tiny hint of carnal desire, but so civil it seemed to be in the subjunctive mood.

"When you leave here, I mean," she said.

Returning her sober look, no flirting around, he said:

"I'm going to find someone to love."

When she heard this, Astrid felt—to her surprise—that what he wanted to give someone already belonged to her.

6.

Hugh was still sensing everything through a haze that seemed to make reality only provisionally trustworthy. For the moment that was enough. He didn't want to remember the particulars of his own history, or the extreme athletic event he'd been rescued from, or how he'd gotten into it, or anything else biographical. It was too humiliating. Something had been wrong or gone wrong in his life and it felt like a pit he might fall into again if he stepped back too close to the edge. His mind seemed to drift on its own toward a vague sense of vastness; the sensation made him feel anxious, vertiginous. From the way Astrid talked, he might have washed up anywhere, an infinity of possibilities including nowhere, although occasionally he seemed to remember an island, undeveloped and idyllic, on no one's map, where he had taught everyone to ride bikes. The bicycles had also washed up onshore, in a huge metal container after a violent storm and shipwreck, and the natives thought Hugh was another gift from the same benevolent god who sent them the bicycles. Now the absentminded god had sent someone to teach them what they were for. Until then the shiny metal contraptions had been a mystery to the wheel-less inhabitants. Soon enough, after the brief honeymoon of cycling, Hugh was in conflict with the island priests who controlled the residents' access to the gods and their blessings. Hugh had debunked the silly priests and since he had his own powers—like teaching them to ride bikes and play games (basketball, soccer, chess)—he had followers too, especially among the younger islanders. So the days when Hugh led a clutch of happy, squealing kids biking around the island in races and games dissolved into chaos and discord, he was shunned by the natives and one day they ambushed him and threw him back into the sea.

In another recurring memory he washed up on a tennis court. The brand new courts were endless in every direction, the baize green surface, the perfect white lines, the blue sky, a warm breeze, and when he hit the ball each swing was right on the sweet spot, and the pleasantly satisfying THWOCK! seemed to reverberate through him like a heartbeat. He ran back and forth without effort, each swing ending with the same percussion he could feel in his spine, in the air, under his feet. The vision ended each time in the same analytical stupor: why should striking an object produce a sensation of such complete satisfaction and equipoise?

These impressions infiltrated him unpredictably as the place he thought of as Astridistan took a stronger and stronger hold on his mind. It's a place he hasn't examined too closely, afraid that scrutiny might make it change or disappear. What he enjoyed in his first weeks with Astrid was living in the present, moment to moment, engrossed in simple chores and activities. He cooked for her and cleaned the apartment and fixed a few things, like the oven door that didn't shut properly, and her bicycle, and her car which he went over like a mechanic. When she told her friends about Hugh they were, at first, a little wary just as she'd been. Shouldn't she be careful? He'd moved right into her apartment and she knew nothing about him. That wasn't smart. Who was he really? Then when she described all the things he was doing for her they began teasing her. "Where do you find a man like him?" "You don't find them," she laughed. "They come out of the sea!"

It was funny but she wondered who he really was too, and where he had come from. At times she worried about it, and a certain wariness still underlay her emotions, although he never did anything that made her feel personally on guard or afraid of him. Instead he seemed to want to protect her, and treated her as if she was something fragile and precious. That was how he made love to her too, gently and considerately, as if he was restraining his strength or marshaling his passion, although she was aware of it, especially when he regained his full health. He was never uncouth or aggressive but his appetite for intimacy, both physical and emotional, seemed unlimited. When she stepped back out of its glow she felt overwhelmed, as if she wasn't the right woman to inspire this kind of attention, and sometimes she had to check herself from sounding as if she was mocking his behavior when she only meant to praise him, even thank him. She was old enough to have had her romantic disappointments and if now she was lucky why be a fool and question it too deeply or tear it down. But the oddness of their relationship, the missing tooth of his past, was always there—always not there.

"How old do you think I am?" he asked her. It was evening, they were enjoying a post-coital moment of shared solitude.

"I don't know...early middle age, I guess."

"What's that—what's 'early middle age'?"

"I don't know..." she said in the same cadence. "Early forties. Mid maybe." She looked at him. "How old *are* you?"

"I don't know," Hugh said. "That's why I asked."

"You don't know?" she said. She didn't know anyone who didn't know how old they were. "Well, however old you are, you're in awfully good shape."

She realized what that sounded like—out of character too—and blushed and giggled.

His body had recovered fast and he'd begun exercising. After he fixed Astrid's bicycle he rode every day. He was already jogging around the neighborhood, running really, and soon he had a routine. Astrid could see right away that exercise for Hugh was an obsession. His mental energy was abnormally vigorous and intense too. He was always up early, before the sun, making coffee, making her breakfast, going out for a ride. He overflowed with all kinds of energy and had to find something to do with it.

For Hugh the physical exercise was easy. His problem was what to do with his mental appetite. In this new situation he felt reborn and, like an infant, his mind was mostly blank. Yet he also felt wary. Just as he treated Astrid as if she was fragile, he was cautious about what he exposed his scoured brain to. It felt as if he was on one side of a dam holding back a flood of knowledge and memory and history. He was tempted to immerse himself in it, but this fresh start was precious. He earned it by his ordeal, and for once he felt at least somewhat entitled to a certain peace of mind, an equilibrium. He was also aware that his mind was in some ways ungovernable, but the appetite to ingest knowledge almost indiscriminately, just for its own sake, wasn't the same now. What he knows isn't enough but he no longer cares. Not the same way. Because he knows it will never be.

The memory of the wretchedness of thirst and hunger, the pain and fear, the seizures of panic, the burned skin and cracked lips, all that faded fast. What he retained was a kind of physical memory of the motion of the sea. If he lay down on the couch in Astrid's living room and closed his eyes he could feel it again. He had a sense of being pulled down and buoyed up at the same time, as if he was at the nexus of two immense forces, both so immense neither could defeat the other but only contend in an irresistibly powerful, endlessly dynamic tension. This was the force that underlay everything in the universe, the part he could experience—however slightly or in disguised ways—and it was also the much greater part his senses couldn't apprehend and which he could only imagine, by analogy, or mathematically. Nevertheless, during these interludes when it felt as if he was held again in the liquid skin of the earth, crushed between gravity and the levitation of the sea, the sense of his own puniness had a paradoxical and almost pleasurable immensity conferred by the forces pressing up and down on him. He was so minute, such a thin layer, that whatever he was was nearly a nullity, a vanishing point, yet in the interface between these two forces he could feel the power of the physical universe. When he came back to his own limited consciousness, lying on the couch with Astrid's cat on the window sill watching him, Hugh realized that he had won his ultimate solo event—or if he hadn't won, he also hadn't lost. He had finished it in some definite way, a way he could never exceed.

Emerging from this mental swim with its oddly comforting dual sensation of immensity and insignificance, Hugh tried to savor the equilibrium, the undippiness, the unaccustomed sense of completeness. As his self-consciousness seeped back, he felt a little embarrassed, as if he was having an experience he might scorn if another person tried to describe it to him. The wonder he felt when these forces contended within him, the liberating powerlessness in their grip, his attraction to them instead of resistance, and the escape from any need to reason them out, to explain them—all these were present in the collage of sensations that combined to make him feel he had won something. He was strangely, unexpectedly, justified as himself—as less than himself, as no one at all—and the sensation was too definite to be a transient mental artifact, a mere mood. It had the quality of an experience.

However indelible, the feeling earned by his ordeal by water was soon diluted by daily life, and the man in the mirror slowly returned. He was still able to conjure up the experience, but less vividly, more routinely, and it was during one of these repeat mental journeys that he was interrupted by the bleating of an electrical chime. It took him a moment to realize he hadn't imagined it; since the doorbell was so infrequently used, he didn't even know Astrid's duplex apartment had one. After it rang again he got up, as if arms were lifting him up from the couch. Instead of a delivery person or Jehovah's Witnesses, it was a woman, probably in her late 30s, stylish and not unattractive, her long brown hair streaked with magenta.

"Hugh Prime!" she said, as if she knew him.

"Let me guess," he shot right back, falling instantly into his flirting mode. "You're Carol and we were separated at birth."

"Close," she laughed. "Hey, I've been trying to reach you."

"Rich aunt died and left me a million?" Hugh felt a tingle of insincerity; this kind of joshing was so natural for him, especially with women.

"Hey, you know, wouldn't that be something? No, I'm a reporter—" She flipped her hand back over her shoulder and did a quarter turn. Hugh had already noticed the white van with big call letters, the microwave dish on top. "—and, you know, like, Hey, could I come in for a minute. I just want to talk."

She had one of those narrow notebooks and a pen clutched in one hand and held them up like a badge.

"Okay," Hugh said. He didn't want to let her in and didn't want to talk to her but there was something in his nature—still there, still there!—that made it very hard for him to say no to anyone who needed something from him. Besides that there was also something perverse in him that wanted to tell the press why he didn't want to talk to the press instead of simply not talking to the press.

They sat at the table in the kitchen and he offered her coffee or tea. She said, "Yes, thanks." Hugh said, "Both?" echoing Feynman, but she didn't catch it.

"No, just—whatever you've got is fine."

There was coffee left from breakfast, so he poured them both a small cup and sat down across from her.

Deirdre wasn't as pushy or manipulative as Hugh imagined press people to be, although this too was a nearly blank slate because she was the first of her species he'd really encountered. He'd met a couple journalists when he worked on the TV show but they were pundits, not ambulance chasers. It turned out there had been some footage of Hugh—Hugh Prime!—on the news just after his rescue but he didn't remember. What Deirdre wanted from him now was his "story." Who was this man from the sea? Where had he come from? How had he gotten so far out there? "You can't imagine how tiny a person looks out there in the water—we almost sailed right over him!" she quoted a crew member saying on the yacht that rescued him. All news to Hugh. The container she proposed to put his story in, her story about him, was, "After such an incredible rescue, what's it like living, you know—"

"In Astridistan," he finished it for her.

That made her laugh. "Astridistan?"

Hugh made a gesture with his hand meaning right here.

"Good for my vzeoogby," Hugh said, laughing too.

"Your what?" she frowned.

"It's my whatever-it-is," he explained. "If I have one. It doesn't have to exist to have a name. Just like me."

"Oh, right," she laughed. "No, really...what I—I mean why, how were you swimming out there in the first place? Is that what you did, you swam all the way...?"

When Hugh didn't answer, she said, "One of the rescuers said you told them you were swimming to infinity—" She made a face like she must have gotten it wrong. "Is that what you, you know...?"

She smiled again, helpfully. Her question made him feel like a child; he was being encouraged to speak.

"You mean how long is a swim to infinity?" Hugh heard himself say with a laugh. "As an athletic event?"

"Well, yeah, I guess..." she laughed too. "Like longer than a cricket match, right?"

"You want to know the rules?" Now Hugh started rolling. "Anyone can enter. Fins are allowed. Take as long as you like to get to the finish line. Start anytime. Hire a substitute."

She was laughing.

"Contestants don't all swim in the same direction. Swimming in circles is permitted. Once you're in the water anything is permitted—"

"But seriously," she tried to interrupt.

"Oh, yes, seriously. Entrants have to be serious," Hugh rolled on. "But laughing's allowed."

"You were serious," she tried to follow him. "Swimming out—"

"Everything else is serious," Hugh said. "You have to pretend to be serious to enter. The swim itself is to defeat seriousness. It's leading the fight against carrying on. It's like the March Against Gravity. Another ultimate athletic event. Walk till you're weightless. We're doing it for charity. We're going to win on land and sea..."

They were both laughing now.

"...How long it lasts depends on whether you believe you can subtract one infinity from another."

He waited for her to answer.

"So I mean—you mean it was personal?" Deirdre asked, looking at her notebook. "Or was it more—was it political like the guys to pick an extreme example who set themselves on fire, blow themselves up, you know, to draw attention to an issue..."

Hugh didn't hear what she was saying. The limits, the triteness of the available replies which could be written down in her hasty scrawl in the slender notebook, had struck him dumb. It didn't seem real that he'd done what they were talking about. He must have been someone else. He was someone else. Yet it was him. These were things he couldn't explain. They would come out wrong, they'd be translated into something else in that little notebook.

"How about music," Hugh said. "Ever heard of the Mills Brothers?"

"The who?"

"Lazy River, Paper Doll...'You're nobody 'til somebody loves you'," Hugh crooned.

"You're kind of a difficult interview, you know that?" Deirdre said, tilting her head to one side with a smile.

"What do most people say?" Hugh asked, eager to follow a digression away from the subject of himself.

"Well, most people actually want to tell their story. I mean they want people to hear what they have to say. Especially if they've done something as...you know, unusual and as committed as you did. They want people to know their reasons. Like, you know, were you trying—were you swimming away from something...?"

"Sharks."

"There were sharks out there?"

"Where else would they be?"

She gave him a schoolteacher's look.

"Most of us don't know why we do things," Hugh said. "We have reasons but they aren't why we do things, they're just something we tell ourselves to fit the story we think we're living."

"Yeah...yeah," she agreed. "So, what do you tell yourself? What story do you think you're living?"

"I don't have a story," Hugh laughed. "If I told you one it wouldn't be true."

"That's okay. Try me."

"You mean it doesn't matter if what I tell you is true or not? It just has to be plausible. What if it's stranger than fact?"

"True stories always sound the best," she said automatically, professionally.

Only Hugh didn't bat it back at her. He just sat there, not so shy now, his expression reminding her of a picture of Thelonious Monk, who her jazz fan boyfriend was trying to get her interested in listening to.

Deirdre glanced at her notebook and said:

"I mean, if you were asking me to analyze it I'd say the true stories, the ones that really happened—" She seemed surprised the thought didn't finish itself.

"They sound the best, even if they aren't really true," Hugh laughed, helping her.

"—you might even say the reason people do a lot of things that look...committed," she went on, "I think it's because they really are committed to some idea or something they want other people to know about. Something they think is true. Because they think if other people knew about it, they might have the same experience. They just need—they need to be exposed to it, to get their attention. You know what I mean? You do know what I mean, don't you?"

This is so bizarre, Hugh was thinking. Sitting in Astrid's kitchen—Astrid, someone he didn't even know a few weeks ago, and loved more than anyone now—he would even swim to infinity for her....

"Knock, knock—anybody home?"

"It's pretty weird that I'm here," Hugh said.

"I think it's very weird that you're here," Deirdre agreed, still trying to prime the pump.

She looked at her notebook again. It had a single scribbled word. An illegible one.

"I think there's something—maybe it's just me, but I think, I'd like to hear about this when you want to talk about it. How about if I come back in a week or two and maybe, who knows, or just give you a call, and if you feel like, because I think this could be...I don't know, I just have a feeling. Okay?"

Hugh felt all the analogies with a seduction. Nothing literal, although Deirdre was attractive enough, more conventionally attractive than Astrid, but his desire was attached to her. This attempted seduction was intended to get inside him, to know him in the ordinary, nosy, human way. It made Hugh think how much he did not want to be known.

Yet after the reporter left he felt depressed. When Astrid came home he didn't even mention it to her. It felt like something that might come between them. Not because the reporter was a woman but because—well, yes, partly because she was a woman and represented a temptation even if it wasn't a sexual one; but, no, more than that because her question, just her intrusion gave her, might give her access to his inner self, his hallowed, his precious, his goddam vzeoogby. He had nearly died for it. Whatever it was. Despite the amnesiac haze over much of the experience, it had left him with the feeling, he was reminded again, that he had earned something. Whatever it was, he didn't want to lose it.

The next day Hugh went down to the basement of the building Astrid's apartment was in to lift weights. The landlord had invited Hugh to use them, "Anytime, Hal. One of my tenants left 'em there when he moved out. Damned if I'm gonna move 'em!" The paunchy guy laughed, and Hugh laughed, obligated to go along with the guy. He was the type who had to give you a nickname, but Hugh didn't object. Usually, if someone got his name wrong, Hugh corrected them right away, not aggressively, but firmly, definitely. This time he let it go. "Hal" was a pleasantly superficial new identity, one more layer to hide behind. Maybe Hal could tell Deirdre how he ended up here. It was all phenomena—one more talking head, forgotten with the next click of the clicker, some guy swimming away from it all with no witnesses, no note, no message, no farewell, no cliches, no fake sympathy left behind for people who wanted to save him from what he was doing instead of saving themselves from what they did every day. If the reporter had magically appeared right here in this spic 'n' span basement counting his lifts and curls he'd have said it. Here alone, his arms so flexed with effort they hung angled, the explanation, the rationale, the passion gushed in his ears. So, why should he have to say it? Out loud. To anyone. Couldn't they see that he'd done what he'd done because of what they did, not because of himself? They were the reason, he wasn't. Yet as soon as he said it, even in the privacy of his own head, it became false. It became one of those lame accusations by the pathetic who couldn't get their own life in gear so they denounced everyone else. Had he forgotten that the swim was his own imitation, his travesty of the Run for Hunger, the Crawl for Cancer, the hip and harmless contemporary version of the walk up the cathedral steps on bloodied knees to kiss the image of the Virgin? Bow down, babes, show us you really care!

The endorphins of exercise made it possible for these thoughts to flow, this far at least, by making his inexorably returning frustration manageable, by countering it with an internal drug that infused Hugh with his right to exist. For some reason, or no reason, the visit by the reporter made him feel that his recovery from the episode was over and although he was still in Astridistan, he was also back in the world where he had begun. Deirdre had brought him back to shore. The truth, if that's what you wanted to call it, had clamped its jaws on him again. He made supper for Astrid and him, lentils with carrots, onions and bacon, and a salad, but his forced cheer leaked out of him and by the time they were done eating he was sullen. He had Astrid, a huge difference. But the impossibility of life, of his life, sat on him. It was a weight he had been able to lift only so far, then it fell back on him. The price of being rescued was the return to the finite. The dippy.

7.

It flattered Astrid that Hugh had taken solace in her company, that he trusted her, even if the times he tried to confide in her or explain himself to her was also when he seemed most remote. Instead of describing his feelings he spoke in abstractions she couldn't understand. His silences became more frequent and longer but his behavior was consistently considerate and affectionate. It was simple, she felt loved, loved and valued, even treasured in a way that could be a little embarrassing. But she did not understand him, not in any normal way.

She didn't really care if Hugh lived as her guest, although it might look as if he was a kind of gigolo—the word made her laugh when one of her friends used it—but she was relieved when he got a job because as much as he enjoyed reading and exercising it seemed to her he spent too much time alone. What else did he have besides her? He needed something.

"I need a big event," Hugh announced in the self-mocking voice he used when he was in a good mood. "So I got a job."

"A job?" she said as if that was something very few people did.

"Bagging groceries."

Astrid wasn't sure how to respond.

"Oh..."

Hugh laughed. He wouldn't have been able to do this before his swim but now.... He'd been only mildly surprised to watch himself walk into the supermarket, ask for the manager and present himself as a candidate for bagger. How had he done it? Easy. He walked in and asked for the manager. The manager was short and rounded with harassed, sincere eyes. His name was Reza, a name that Hugh assumed made him self-conscious, as if he might be accused of being an insufficiently patriotic citizen of Astridistan, so immediately Hugh's empathy was aroused and he adopted the manager with affection ("Hey, babes!"). Reza showed him the job himself, as if it was so important that the manager had to instruct him, which Reza did in almost parodic detail. "Always put the eggs in their own bag," he cautioned. Hugh nodded and smiled. "Right. One bag for each egg?" He was suppressing a laugh. "No, no. Like this." Reza carefully slipped a carton of eggs into the plastic bag and set it to one side of the other groceries. "Then you put it in last. In the cart. On top of the others. Like this."

It really was a big event. Hugh had never had a job that suited him so well. He flirted with the cashiers—"How come you're all named Ashley?"—especially the fattest one, making it a challenge he had to win to make her smile, and he helped the customers, particularly the old ones, with his jocular courtesy, and he befriended a fellow bagger named Bobby whom everyone assumed was retarded. Hugh discovered it was the speech impediment that made people think he was slow. He made it his mission to communicate with Bobby. It sounded as if his palate was malformed because his words were missing syllables and the consonants were so softened the words lacked shape. But Bobby could be understood if you listened carefully and he was so grateful for Hugh's attention he became talkative and animated around him. He liked to talk about his previous job as a landscaper. He'd had to quit when he hurt his back, Bobby told Hugh. The more physical, manly work seemed to represent a high water mark for Bobby's working career, and he loved to tell Hugh about his former boss. "He wath amahing!" Bobby exulted. Amazing, Hugh got on the second try. The crew boss was one of those high-energy guys who is always performing, Hugh intuited, but he was less interested in Bobby's portrait of the man than in how Bobby felt about him. His childlike admiration for the boss seemed to answer a real need in him and there was no one like that in the grocery. It was not a stage for vivid, vigorous characters. "Thi-hh guy..." Bobby began, shaking his head in anticipation of what he was about to tell. "What was his name?" Hugh asked, thinking it would be easier to follow the exploits of a proper name instead of a pronoun in Bobby's hobbled speech. "Paw!" Paul. Paul drove the big truck, the one with the crew cab and the hydraulic platform on the back, putting it places you couldn't believe. He had nicknames for everyone, he talked back to the owner, he had eight children. "Eighhh shil-hen!" Bobby smiled, showing his missing front teeth. He and Hugh were standing in the back of the store, the day shift done, replaced by high school kids at the bagging stations. "Do you still see the guy?" Hugh asked. "Now that you're not working there, do you ever see him?" Bobby's face changed. He looked perplexed by the question, as if Hugh was the one with the speech impediment. Hugh wondered if maybe he shouldn't have reminded Bobby of the admired foreman in the job he couldn't do anymore. "Paw keeh himell," Bobby said. "What?" Bobby tried again. The third time Hugh got it. "He killed himself?" Bobby nodded. "You're kidding. The guy with all this, this..." Bobby nodded his head. "...vitality," Hugh finished. No, Bobby wasn't kidding. His face had the same perplexed expression, a child who had lost his big friend to an evil force he couldn't understand.

As Hugh rode his bike back to Astrid's apartment, he felt accused by Bobby's loss, as if by having taken his inexplicable swim—made his own attempt to escape—he'd somehow broken faith with Bobby too. What was Hugh's grievance compared to living your time on earth in Bobby's body and mind, with his limitations? But that was a false analogy. Bobby fit and Hugh didn't. His gifts were a problem, not a blessing. He thought of the superfluous men of czarist Russia, the privileged class with nothing to do. They drank and gambled and wandered around Europe complaining and chasing women, the artistic ones created a cultural boomlet, they wrote pamphlets and novels, or were dilettantes, members of the audience squirming in their seats, applauding the artists with envy and frustration. Some who were discontent became political activists, even terrorists like the ones who blew up Czar Alexander II, others were killed or sent to Siberia. But the phrase was really meant for the idle ones, the educated upper class sons without any role who whined through their lives with fashionably aching consciences. Hugh could only feel hostility to their kind. They lived on someone else's labor—a luxury that made their discontent possible—and wanted everything to change beneath them while still maintaining their privilege. To be superfluous was trivial, a social malaise, but to be useless because you were wrong even though you were right was a profound quandary, an indictment of nature, not just society. It negated any but the slenderest natural basis for justice and ethics. Its fragile legs couldn't stand against brute evolution. Adapt, fit in. To get along, go along. The struggle against this primal force wasn't natural, it was man-made. An artifact of the very life produced by evolution. And what if you were unable to believe in man? You could not be forgiven. Not by the same fellow man. To say it, even in the privacy of his own mind, still made Hugh churn with fury and frustration.

The novelty of the job bagging groceries soon faded down to routine and boredom. The sight of so many trashy, overpriced "consumer items" rolling down the conveyor belt every day was depressing to Hugh. Every time he picked up a bag or box of elaborately packaged and processed junk food he saw entire industries rising up behind it. The industries fed appetites programmed by nature and conditioned by advertising to consume junk. So what was new about that—another dreary fact, connected to a juggernaut of dreary, invincible facts. The customers looked misshapen and unhealthy, the women with rolls of stored calories bulging out of compliant stretch pants and tank tops, men so lopsided with hanging guts they shuffled with baby steps to keep their balance. Even some of the young ones were so obese they looked like freaks. The junk, the waste, the toxic excess, rolling down endlessly into his hands to be bagged and set in the cart with a smile—as if this was a cheerful, innocent activity instead of a voluntary mass poisoning—it was beginning to bring back the ache that had sent him into the sea. Even the store manager's voice made Hugh feel dizzy—the harassed and amiable puppy-eyed Reza announcing on the PA system a special on super-soft bathroom tissue or two liter bottles of soda or extra lean ground beef or any of the other thousand products offered for your shopping convenience. The infernal engine that produced all this had no mind of its own, no kind of intelligence or consciousness of its existence that one could confront and appeal to, and instead of anyone noticing this vast superpower driving them, reaching into their lives in every way possible, into their minds and bodies to alter them chemically while they fed it their money, their time, their labor—their lives! Instead of noticing this they were rediscovering an invisible power which didn't exist at all except in their heads. God himself was reappearing everywhere, even in Astridistan, and not in something like his medieval majesty but as a kind of metaphysical club to hammer into oblivion the doubt engendered by science. God was something people rooted for, like their favorite sports team.

Ritual praise for religion had re-entered the stream of memes that wafted through the air, in an even cruder form too. Once it had seemed that the illusion was fading and those who still believed in it, if they were intelligent, kept quiet about their faith to avoid being embarrassed. Now they testified to their belief in public and were proud of it, proud of their attachment to this vestigial organ of tribalism, proud of their faith in the supernatural, all because it enhanced their own importance as specially favored pets of an imagined deity. It also attached them to the power of patriotism. The pious regard for a flattering fantasy accompanied by the mindless yet very real Demiurge that drove everyone's corporeal lives made Hugh feel almost insane at times—why couldn't everyone *see* it?—and all he could do with the energy produced by the clash in his thoughts was to pedal the bicycle harder and longer, or lift more weights, or do more sit-ups and push-ups. He tried to keep these thoughts to himself, afraid of where they would take him—back to the sea!—but when he was silent too long Astrid would sometimes begin to quiz him, gently and slowly, as if she were opening the lid on a vacuum-sealed, pressurized jar. If he was frustrated enough he would soon begin to describe the turmoil inside him, his voice dropping so low she had to lean close to hear him. What he said was usually cryptic, but familiar, once she learned the language of his private tirades. She said very little, conscious that her sympathy could sound patronizing. Once, when they were sharing an especially pleasant post-coital bubble of intimacy she dared to express a thought she often had about him.

"If we lived in a Catholic country with monks in monasteries, or an Asian one, up in the mountains...maybe that's what you'd be."

"A monk?" Hugh made a soft sound of amusement. "Not unless I could have you there with me. I'm not an ascetic—not at all," he laughed.

"No, no. You're very passionate. That's part of your problem. In having to live with it, I mean. You don't seem to have any...brakes."

"Look, Ma—no brakes," he quoted from childhood, and squeezed her.

The strength of his embrace was reassuring. It made her feel that someone so strong couldn't be overwhelmed by whatever was going on inside his head, despite what she knew about how she had met him. She had many thoughts that bothered her too, but they seemed to be out on the fringe of her mental world. There was a ring of chaos out there somewhere, out beyond the small protected island she lived in. Within was a place she could be quite content, even more so now that Hugh was in it with her.

One evening when he was in a breezy, silly mood, whistling "Paper Moon" while he made dinner for Astrid and himself, she said, "Do you think you'd be happier if you didn't go to work at the market every day?" He'd had the day off and she connected his mood with his holiday. She had assumed it would be good for him to get out and spend time with other people, that the social aspect of work would distract him from his thoughts, but lately she'd wondered if it had become just the reverse. Stationed at the market in the rectum of the Demiurge, as he had called it in a rare vulgar moment, where the product of labor, money, and resources was exchanged for excrement disguised as nourishment, this activity was looking more and more like a poor choice. "No retreat!" Hugh answered jauntily, pouring pasta into the boiling water. But Astrid had signaled him he had an alternative, and he had begun phrasing ways to disappoint Reza with the news that his outstandingly talented bagman was going to retire.

Hugh had made up his mind but he procrastinated. Facing the decent humanity expressed in the manager's face—a decency so exploited by the mercantile system of which he was such a minute, sincere part—in order to tell Reza he was quitting and would no longer earnestly man his post at the ass end of the cornucopia of products for kitchen, bathroom and home, was going to be much harder than it had been to walk in and ask for a job. Reza was prince of the supermarket, he believed in the aisles upon aisles of gaudy goods, and Hugh was rejecting it. It was at this indecisive yet slyly opportune moment, that Hugh looked up from the box of Count Chocula Breakfast Cereal he'd just slipped in a bag and saw someone he knew. Or should have known, should have recognized. Was it someone he'd known long ago—back there before the swim? The thought mortified him; to have to go back and be that man again, or worse, deny him, explain him and his absence, and his presence here....But then he remembered who she was and his relief poured into his greeting.

"Deirdre?"

"Hugh!" she gushed back as if they were an act. "What're you—you're working here?"

"I volunteer. It's a charity. I donate my labor and the shareholders agree to give all their profits to the Kingdom of Ends Foundation."

"The what?"

"Are these yours?" Hugh deftly scooped up two small cans rolling down the chute into his hands and held them up.

"For my cat. Tiberius."

"The emperor." The cat Hugh saw in his mind was Astrid's sublimely self-sufficient tabby.

"Of course." She cocked her head. "No, I mean really, this isn't, or is it, you know—?"

"No, it isn't. But it is."

"But do they know who you are? The people here..." she flipped her hand toward the cashier.

"Do your viewers know who you are?" Hugh smiled. "I bet they don't know you live with an emperor."

"You know, listen. Hugh, this would be a terrific, you know, we see you here bagging and this is the guy who survived such a— we've got the footage, really good stuff—you haven't seen it, have you. We could talk a little about, you know, the 'big swim,' your current life—what do you think, could we do that?"

"The Kingdom of Ends? Dangerous territory," he said in a teasing voice.

"Whatever. Sure. I mean, the footage of the rescue really is terrific. One of the guys on board had a camera. He got it all—you haven't even seen it, have you?"

Hugh was shaking his head which she took as a response to her most recent question, not as a belated reply to the prior one. But as stubborn and forceful as Hugh's mind was, it had its semi-permeability, and one of the characteristics of the trait was how unpredictable it was. The last thing he wanted was for his colleagues—Bobby!—to think of him as the swimmer, a curiosity, an oddity, some lost soul found at sea—no. That wasn't him. But the breach that let Deirdre and her film crew enter his life was linked to the one he had walked through when he stepped out of his running shoes and walked into the water in the bay and began stroking. An extreme desire for something. A need for relief from his entrapment in a cycle of thoughts that led him every time to the same conclusion: he was right; but that made him wrong. Wrong because he was right, the more right, the more damned as wrong. All he could do was make his life small. Very small. Treat anyone who came into his orbit as well as he could. Live as an example, if to no one else then to himself. And yet, and yet! That left everything out! The cycle of thoughts spun him helplessly. Maybe the reporter with her notebook and camera were a way out. He hoped with his emotions even if his will was against it. So he was left to find a reason for saying yes, to permit himself; perhaps it was simply not to disappoint Deirdre, since he already knew he was going to disappoint Reza, and Bobby, and he couldn't disappoint everyone.

8.

"Is it possible to subtract one infinity from another?" Hugh began, standing a few feet from the camera, leaning against Astrid's bike, his bouffe of electrified hair faintly aquiver, dark eyes staring toward the lens but not focused on it, in space. Deaf to whatever it was Deirdre had asked him about the swim, the rescue, the whole thing, he took his cue from the fact that she had stopped talking and seemed to be waiting for him to speak.

"Mathematically, yes," he went on, "if you renormalize, although I think there can only be one infinity. If it exists, no matter how many exist, there's only one, since anything infinite would have to include everything else or else it wouldn't be infinite. Although that infinity still wouldn't necessarily have to include the answer to every question. For instance, is it possible to understand life as other than a progress? If there's no progression, is it intelligible? Because a life is knowable to the extent it makes sense. Which is circular, like an infinity. So you can't know your life if it doesn't make sense. And it doesn't make sense if there's no progression. It's random events and impressions—phenomena. And every time you try to make sense out of it, you tell a different story, and the stories you tell are equally valid—they're all equally true, or equally untrue—"

"Hugh! Hugh!"

"—unless they're dippy."

He stopped.

"It is true you were rescued at sea, right? You were found floating or swimming or whatever, after how many hours or days, and if that's true, if that's a fact, unless you fell out of the sky then there must be some reason why you were out there, I mean in the first place. What about that? Can you talk about that? Like, how you got there? Can you tell us?"

Hugh's eyes glanced briefly at Deirdre, then found the spot in space between him and the camera he'd been addressing before.

"If there's a first place there must be a second and third, a progression, and if there isn't it must be because anyone's life is knowable only to the extent it makes sense. Life can't really be grasped except as a progress."

"Progress—okay!" she interrupted. "So, how did you get out of the water? We can come back to how you got in. Because that was progress, wasn't it—someone saving you?"

He was looking at her but she couldn't read his expression.

"I mean...give me some help here, Hugh."

He reminded her of her boyfriend's dog who just stood there when you said fetch or come.

"I mean, was it like a beautiful woman," she suggested. "An angel of mercy or something. And she came to rescue you? Was that what it felt like?"

"An angel? Something with wings? How 'bout a vulture?" Hugh laughed.

"No, just, you know, someone finding you, pulling you out of the water...I mean, wasn't that like really—for Christ's sake, Hugh— why the fuck were you out there...?"

"It was an athletic event," Hugh said. "My private charity." He laughed.

"A charity?" Deirdre made her eyes wide, encouraging him. "Was someone else out there with you? If this was—No? Did they leave you? Were you out there all by yourself, no one else, nobody tracking you in a boat...? What did you think—were you lost, is that—? I mean, what kind of athletic event? Can you describe it?"

"I was swimming to the Kingdom of Ends."

"The Kingdom of—yeah, right. I thought you were swimming to infinity. Jesus!"

"It includes everything, even the things that don't exist."

Hugh smiled.

This is what she got for trying to make a story out of a kook.

"Okay, look, tell me about—" Deirdre sighed. "You know, Hugh...I need something a little more, you know, meat and potatoes. Our viewers don't tune in to see theater of the absurd."

"They don't? You know that for sure? Maybe that's exactly what they tune in to see. Maybe all the trouble you go to to create a progression so your story is plausible, maybe that's just what they reject as fantastic. Maybe they watch thinking of all the ways your story doesn't make sense. Maybe they think it makes too much sense to be true. That's what happens as soon as someone tells our story. All of our stories are bad novels but once someone tells them we're in them forever. After a while we even begin to confess to them because all of us feel doubt that we know ourselves at all."

Hugh was quoting, paraphrasing a few lines from a novel he'd read. Equipped with someone else's lines, he was like an actor who is suddenly animated.

"And because we don't know ourselves, we feel guilty to exist. To be is the crime we commit, and anyone will confess to it."

He stopped. There was more he could say, much more. But he realized it sounded like he was confessing. He'd said enough, more than enough.

9.

Deirdre could tell he was done. He'd finally found a groove but it was over almost as soon as it began. Unusable, anyway. He just couldn't see what was interesting about himself. At first she was pissed but now she almost felt sorry for him. The guy wasn't exactly made for the medium. The cameraman filmed Hugh riding his bike around Astrid's neighborhood, just in case. Sy even did a long tracking shot from the van because the guy looked so good on his bike and Sy liked him. He had a weakness for people who didn't get being on television and managed to turn the whole thing on its head. The ones who'd do anything for their fifteen minutes of fame were all the same.

A wasted shoot, Deirdre thought, when they were done. There was always a chance it would look different in the editing room than when they filmed him. She had the rescue footage which really was terrific with everyone shouting *What is it? What is it? It's a body! A dead body! No—he's alive, he's alive!* The pretty girl shrieking, the guys hauling him up. The whole piece would be an update at most. "He won't talk about this incredible rescue when they pulled him half-dead out of the frickin' ocean, and he won't let us film his girlfriend or workplace, so what the hell have we got?" she complained as she and Sy drove away in the van. "He said we could film her cat, his girlfriend's cat," she snorted. Then she laughed. "The cat would be a better interview!"

"A little weird for your average viewer," Sy said, "but the guy was putting it all out there. In his own way."

When they looked at it in the editing suite, Deirdre wondered about her own judgment. "It's all because of that frickin' great footage—people screaming, the camera looking all over the water, and suddenly there's this body! Sunburned so bad he looks microwaved—it's frickin' ghastly! Then he comes back to life right in front of your eyes! He's alive! Well, almost alive. You can't believe it! They're all heroes!"

Hugh's voice on the screen, almost whispery when he became intense, sounded oddly intimate recorded on camera, and his hooded eyes under his electric hair made him look madly vulnerable.

"Stone weirdo," Deirdre said. "I blew a whole day on him for nothing. I mean it's not *Perfect Storm*, but it could have been a very nice little piece."

"Guess he didn't want to be famous," Sy chuckled.

"Everyone wants to be famous," Deirdre said. "Except the ones who're already rich."

"Like you said...stone weirdo."

Sy winked from behind his goatee.

10.

A strain of fatalism had created the mood in which Hugh let himself be filmed. It was a seductive fatalism, a sense that what might happen by yielding to the flux of events was more true to other people than it was to him. So this reversal—going along with Deirdre instead of his own inclination—might connect him to other people, even to that unreal being, the public, in some otherwise inaccessible way, so he had to let fate or accident give him its little nudge in the back.

When he stood in front of the guy with the camera and Deirdre asked him a question, she listened in a way no one had ever listened to him before. He didn't have to hold her attention, she held it for him. They were all so attentive it was manipulative, and he wondered if they were patronizing him, making him into a child or a freak performing for them. This kind of attention operated on him like an anesthetic and the only thing he remembered distinctly was Deirdre's voice shouting, "Where's your helmet?" when he rode around on his bike while they took pictures after recording him talking. He hoped he hadn't said, "Kingdom of Ends." In those words, using those words. Deirdre said she'd give him a call. Let him know when it would be broadcast. Not that he'd watch. If he did he'd only regret it. Seeing himself packaged as part of a show with commercials and hyperventilated introductions and all the swooping special effects would make him an object of his own scorn. Yet when a few days passed, then a week, and she hadn't called, it forced him to think about it more than if she had called. It also forced him to think about it differently. Instead of dreading seeing himself on TV, seeing pictures of someone who was not really him, now he had to think about how this was another non-event, one that seemed to exist and not exist at the same time. He had the feeling that something he'd done excluded him. It was a joke on him, like applying the rules of membership in Groucho's club to the one person the club comprised. *You're no longer a member of your own club, babes. We didn't throw you out, it just never existed.* Or he was like Schrödinger's cat. He was on TV and not on TV at the same time. If you tuned in, he was there. Or else he wasn't. Neither outcome existed until you tuned in. As time passed and the experience changed shape in his mind, Hugh continued to feel something was owed to him, yet it was something he did not really want. It was also easy to flip this feeling so he was the one who owed someone something. Those people who pulled him out of the water—did they want something from him? Like his life. Did he now owe it to someone? What would they do with it?

The experience, the non-experience, with Deirdre had made it easier to tell Reza he was quitting his job. They both had their disappointments. "I knew you wouldn't stay with us very long," Reza said, shaking hands, his brown puppy eyes looking quite businesslike. "You are what we call overqualified," he smiled. See, Hugh thought, Reza even expected it. I wasn't born to bag, eh, babes? He waved goodbye to Bobby and all the Ashleys and walked out of the market feeling a gust of freedom, as if he'd escaped from the cornucopia of consumer products itself. It was a bogus sensation, he knew, and wouldn't last long, but if he didn't examine it too closely, it was something to savor.

Despite the ambivalence Hugh felt about whatever he'd said when the camera was pointed at him, and all the misunderstandings that might be spun out of it, if he had seen what Sy shot when he was riding his bike, he would have been surprised. It would have been something for him to savor. It was a portrait of Hugh's most authentic being. It was Hugh in action, the athlete. A view of himself he'd never seen. The shot went on for blocks as the camera, tracking along in the van, followed the extraordinarily fit and youthful middle-aged man on his bike. Spurred by Deirdre's cries of concern—"Where's your helmet?"—

rendering in the abstract a woman's love for a performing, risk-taking hero, his crown of Einsteinian/Hoffmanesque hair tossing in the wind, his Olympic-sized thighs pumping with the strength of a sprinter, Hugh pulled the tracking shot along with him for blocks, as if the camera were tied by an invisible cord to the cyclist and couldn't lose him. He flowed past trees and pedestrians and joggers and other cyclists and dogs and cars and two cute girls waving, waving at Hugh and his electronic witness which made the girls assume he was important, someone special, famous, worthy of tribute, and as he flashed past them he glanced back for an instant and the camera which had zoomed in for a close up caught a few frames of his grin.

It was that shot which ended the short piece Sy had edited for his own pleasure, and through the easy magic of digital editing he created a frozen image of Hugh's grin, his helmet of hair, his pumped up legs, his torso turned toward the camera with one palm resting carelessly on his thigh—the whole form arrested in motion, immortal. A nice contrast to the opening shot frantically scanning the water before finally finding a mostly dead, half-submerged hulk of a human. Then the excited cries and shots of the limp body hauled up by several young, tanned, male and female sailors—out of the ocean and onto the deck of a carbon fiber-hulled catamaran under an enormous flapping sail. The sound of its flapping was nature's indifferent, imperial, deafening voice, underscoring the shouts and shrieks of young, innocent, beautiful bodies pulling a fellow creature out of the mouth of death. It was an unstaged human interest moment, spontaneous and even miraculous, just as Deirdre was saying yet again as she watched the finished piece over Sy's shoulder.

"If he'd just said one frickin' thing about being in the water, we could've used it!"

"Yeah," Sy nodded. "But I don't care what you say, Dee..."

Both of them were staring at Hugh's frozen image on the video screen, the cocky, flirting, ageless athlete grinning back at them.

"...any guy who can look like that, I mean, shee-it..."

He turned and looked up at Deirdre, her arms crossed, staring at Hugh on the screen.

"...no way he was out there trying to drown."

"Then what the fuck *was* he doing?" she answered.

11.

It's an ending, the end of Hugh Prime's story, but it's not the end of Hugh's story, his non-story. I haven't yet solved the mystery of his death—which isn't a mystery anyway, only a kind of McGuffin—but there's more to tell, a coda, before Hugh's fictional clone is sloughed off entirely. Sy's freeze frame of Hugh echoes the shot Truffaut ended *400 Blows* on, the boy Antoine running on the beach, suspended in an eternal instant, intensely romantic when compared to daily experience yet true to the stop-motion of memory. It's a technique imitated a thousand times since, and paradoxically it's a reversion, turning a motion picture back into a still photo, as if to say we don't really understand things while they're moving and need to stop everything and hold them in place to grasp them.

Even if life can only be grasped as a progression, as Hugh said.

The frozen frame of Hugh riding away on his bike is so fetching, capturing the playful, flirtatious man inside the unhappy anti-carpenter/philosopher, and it really does evoke its own truth (while ignoring a number of others), so I have to look into it for just a moment, even if the van is now stuck in traffic and the helmetless bike rider, having finally outridden his video escort, is on his way home to make dinner for the woman of his dreams—his mature dreams, the angel of his desperation who is coming home hungry and happy to see Hugh after a day at work. This is conventional happiness, which we know Hugh can't have, not conventionally, but if we stay with the hair-flying, helmetless, pedaling man flashing a grin, we can ask: Where would he go if he could carry the rest of Hugh's existence anywhere? If there really were some other place for Hugh besides Astridistan, some place he could fulfill himself, what place would it be? In other words—words I've been avoiding having to say—what would a Kingdom of Ends actually be?

We have to leave aside some endlessly complicating factors and renormalize, just as the physicists must do to avoid the dreaded dead end of infinity. So, cheating a little, hoping not to sound too dippy, we hit the Play button to unfreeze Hugh again and follow him pedaling into the Kingdom of Ends. I'm not going to try to describe the physical features because it doesn't have any—it's a philosopher's concept, not a theme park—and invoking no magic at all, which is not allowed here, we follow Hugh on this detour before he goes home to make dinner for Astrid. Kant's own description of this ideal world is abstract, as it must be, and rather dry, as you also might expect. In the philosopher's imagined Kingdom of Ends, no one takes advantage of anyone else or uses another person as a means to get something. Everyone respects each individual as an end in him- or herself and also respects that person's right to fulfill themselves too. Kant's Kingdom sounds like a Misteroger's Neighborhood for adults. It conjures up a sea of reasonable people all considerately measuring their own actions so each thing they do can pass the test of universality. No one does anything unless everyone else could do it too. In theory, there is plenty of room for personal freedom and even originality, but a moment's reflection suggests that an awful lot of human behavior would disappear, starting with anything we can do using our economic privilege for comfort or convenience. Compared to someone lacking that privilege, anyone who has it is enjoying a luxury, and therefore—in some way that might not be directly connected—that person is taking advantage of someone (even if he doesn't know who they are). To avoid this difficulty (a little renormalizing, again), the inhabitants of Kant's Kingdom seem to have been assumed to be of his own class—the educated, the genteel, the carriage trade—much the way his contemporary Thomas Jefferson's democracy didn't include what we now call people of color. A universal theory that leaves out so many people is obviously a paradox, a rather devastating one that negates the theory. Those were different times, granted, but Hugh felt he had to try to figure out what Kant's social blinders allowed him to finesse. Could Hugh do it? Could he recalculate—imagine—an actual Kingdom of Ends? Right here on earth? Without Kant's negating paradox? No. He could not do it. Instead of a creator he could only be a critic. All he could do was notice, yet again, and point out, how much of what we do exploits someone else, something we would have to acknowledge if we really thought about it instead of assuming—slipping behind the assumption—that it's just the way things are. Evolution confirms that someone's got to be on top and if it's you, babes, go for it. (If it's not, join the revolution.) Evolution can teach many other things too, subtler ones, but the blunt force of fitness for adaptation to things as they are is always trump.

Money provides a compensation for using other people for your ends instead of theirs, or being used yourself for a paycheck. That's why Hugh had such an ambivalent attitude toward money. No, not ambivalent—hostile, contemptuous. Money made you aware of the interlocked deals one had to make constantly, all based on getting someone else's attention or time or skill or service, one they might not want to give you at all unless you gave them these markers representing the available resources to achieve your, or someone else's, ends. Worse than the transactions conducted in money, there were the ways all human relationships including intimate ones involved subtly manipulating the other person to get what you wanted. Even if you kept the books in your head carefully balanced so neither person took advantage and turned the other one into his or her means to happiness, it required a constant accounting and made you aware that the Kingdom was a marketplace of another kind too. The most spontaneous act of generosity could set the cash register ringing. Added to these nagging difficulties, was another overwhelming one. To respect another's dignity and never use them as a means to your advantage might be possible, but to give everyone the space in which to fulfill themselves—there weren't enough resources for that. Some people to fulfill themselves just wanted to go fishing, and a few altruistic ones wanted the spiritual joy of helping others, but too many needed to use other people to reach personal satisfaction. They needed an audience, other people to pay attention to them (instead of themselves), or, in a complete collision of goals, they needed to give other people directions, boss them around, manipulate them or even cause them pain—the accounts turned into chaos when one began doing the arithmetic of pathological desires. Had Kant noticed that he himself could only be fulfilled as a philosopher if people read what he wrote? And took it seriously. That required an effort, someone had to give him their precious time. It meant his Kingdom could only function if there were a considerable number of people in it whose personal fulfillment would come from being consumers of what others created. What if there weren't enough willing consumers? Look at art—all the works created by the educated, leisured class who wanted to cultivate their talent for self-expression and whose only audience was people like themselves doing the same thing. There was no shortage of people displaying an esthetic response to life and many of them had at least a dollop of talent; there was however a lack of fresh, hungry consumers of esthetic products.

This is only the beginning. What about the ecological cost of everyone achieving their ends? Obviously, it can't be done, so what kind of system could distribute rewards equitably to everyone? And who would create it—since any such system would mean the creators would have to accept less than a mandarin's pay to achieve a universal average?

Where did these deal-breaking problems leave the Kingdom of Ends? Was Kant taking his own swim to infinity when he conceived it, trying to do something he knew couldn't be done, unable to prevent himself from attempting it anyway? It was at this point that Hugh needed his bike. Or his weights, or he had to lie down on the floor to do a few hundred push-ups, or sit-ups. Under the stress of physical exercise his mind was clarified—or hazed—by endorphins, and he could feel that the swim to infinity was stroking toward the Kingdom in some ineffable way. Or, to view his experience through reality instead of fiction, his wild ride down the hill on Cape Cod had been a less willful and more ecstatic means to the same end. It wasn't oblivion he'd been seeking on his swim, nothing as trite, nothing as absolute and final as that. To find a place that didn't exist he had tried to push his body through an ultimate exercise in a dumb hope it might somehow take him there. It couldn't be other than a desperate act. He had to face that fact. He had done it because there was no other way. There was no reason in it. Nothing of reason at all, even if reason led to the same conclusion. Instead of coming out in the Kingdom he'd suffered pain and shock and nearly died before been rescued, by chance, by people whose only end at the moment, as role players in his life, was to save him. To them he was not a means to anything. They obeyed a human instinct to help someone in need. They performed their strict duty. So for that moment at least he had passed into the Kingdom and felt what it was like to have arms reaching out for no other purpose than to save him—to save him for his own ends, and no one else's.

What were those ends? He didn't know. It could not be known because it didn't exist, except as fiction, as something made up. And he was still unable to invent any story for himself which he could believe. Was his obsessive pursuit of knowledge an attempt to answer this question, to fill in this blank? Was it the mental counterpart of furious physical exercise, the perfection of a body which could never be other than flawed no matter how strong? To fill his brain with knowledge which could never assume a narrative shape, so the constituent parts might be true but in sum didn't signify anything? A sense of urgency came over him when this thought filled his mind. If Kant could believe his own story, why couldn't he? Hugh thought. Was Kant more credulous? Kant, the hypochondriac? Was it a function of ego, a solipsism? The power of Kant's mind, his vzeoogby? But that could also be the power to deceive oneself. To convince oneself that something was whole when it was not—to believe a fiction as convincing as fact. More convincing. Much more.

Hugh's mind spiraled around and around on this point until, as usual, he escaped through a bout of physical exercise. Yet it was all waiting for him when he wound down from tripling his heart rate or using a set of muscles till they were melting with the heat of exertion. Most disturbing of all when he got caught in this spiral was Kant himself endorsing a bad idea, God, the mother of all bad ideas (the only worse one was Money), because a world without God would "upset his servant," as one facetious wag put it. Obviously his reasons were deeper and subtler than that but for the young acolyte in Ann Arbor immersed in Kant's world for the first time the insubordinate quip stuck. Ever after it stood in Hugh's mind for the human preference for comfort over truth. Earlier in his career Kant had dissected the hopeful traditional arguments in favor of a deity but later he refined his philosophy, and a critic said, "denied knowledge to make room for faith." Hugh interpreted this as admitting the implications of reason were not for everyone. The most austere truth was only for connoisseurs, and the concept of God was the original renormalization. It was dippy. What bothered Hugh personally about all this was the *Hey, babes* question it raised—if Kant was willing to put God back into his universe to make his servant happy, would Kant have cared that it made Hugh so unhappy? Was Kant's servant more entitled to happiness than Hugh? Obviously, in some way, he was. He represented a part of society or an aspect of mind Kant did not want to upset with the truth. (Or was his servant's peace of mind only an excuse Kant used for doing something he wanted to do anyway, like Pascal's wager?) But what good was the truth if only some of us knew it, if it couldn't be consumed by everyone? Especially in a democracy where comforting fictions could became fatal flaws, flattering the mob with its own misconceptions.

Lying on the floor doing sit-ups beside the desk in Astrid's spare room, Hugh finally left Kant behind. Through the purging process of physical exertion he reached the end of the Kingdom of Ends, as he always did, his mind sublimely perplexed, his body endorphined. Objective truth was never the point; belief in your story was. In other words, babes, renormalize and be dippy.

When he sat back down in his chair, abdominals warm and comfortably taut from the flexing, he felt almost happy, a little— yes—dippy. It was bizarre, or at least curious, that he needed to imagine an ideal with features that pleased his own sensibility. Why should that be? Why assume his own sensibility's needs exactly fit the requirements of an ideal human society. There might be several qualities of his own that didn't fit. But who'd ever heard of an ideal that didn't match the desires of its designer? No one would go to the trouble of re-imagining the world unless the new version put themselves on top as the epitome of the new order. If he followed that thought out to its conclusion and back to its source, perhaps he could imagine a new, ideal world which had no place for its creator. It was the Groucho Marx Club again, the one you'd refuse to join if they wanted someone like you as a member. Imagine that universalized!

The sit-ups hadn't done enough to elevate Hugh's heart rate so he bounced up again. Already over his quota of push-ups for the day, he did an exercise he'd designed, a modification of stepping up and then down from a chair or ledge, a kind of stationary Stairmaster. Hugh did it with a small pack on his back loaded with weights. He put in a hundred pounds. Actually a bit more since the two weights were in kilos, twenty-five each. Just hefting the individual weights, the two of them, gave him a satisfaction as he placed them in the padding he used to keep them from shifting against his back in the pack. To be aware of gravity, the way it pulled you against the hugely superior weight of the earth, made Hugh feel he was in touch with a force that was definite and had nothing in it of fantasy or fiction. His feeble efforts to pull away from it, repeated again and again in Sisyphean cycles which never took him more than a few inches further from the heavenly body that held him in its gravitational embrace, were a ritual which inspired a droning thought in Hugh's mind, perhaps akin to the meditator's mantra, the push/pull of all puny human effort against the immeasurably greater force one strained to overcome yet always had to give in to. Gravity was vastly weaker than the other cosmic forces yet paradoxically the strongest power we lived with every moment. By performing his ritual efforts to escape it each day, Hugh paid it homage, he gave it its due, and acknowledged that even though the ritual could increase the strength of his own muscles and possibly even extend the length of his life, his many repetitions of lifting the totems of gravity in their measured kilograms had no effect, nothing, zero, on the force itself. The effect on him might approach the ecstatic or the sublime if he excited enough endorphins but, except for this boon, the activity was useless. It was the epitome of uselessness. Perfect.

When he was lifting weights Hugh felt most like himself. There was a brief period of effort at the start before his body slipped into a groove and then, as strenuous as it was, he felt he could do it almost forever. This probably coincided with the onset of the endorphins, releasing a sense of self-worth and confidence. Elevated by his private drug, his thoughts flowed: Utopia was a gated community. The Kingdom of Ends could never be larger than one individual. Instead of mentally pressing against things-as-they-were every moment, Hugh could unshackle himself from harness and carry only his own body. Perform spontaneous acts of kindness. Open doors for old ladies. The laugh track was running. He saw Groucho Marx waggle his cigar, raise an eyebrow. "Say the secret word and collect a hundred dollars." Down came the parrot with the word in its mouth. Groucho croaked, "Congratulations!"

He measured push-ups by number, chair-steps by time. The timer made a faint DING at thirty minutes. Hugh slipped off the pack and sat down on the armless wood chair, feet flat on the floor. With the stop watch in his left palm, he pressed two fingers of his right hand on the vein in his left wrist. The number would be above triple his resting heart rate, forty-two times three equals—

If Hugh Prime has been reabsorbed into Hugh, and the Kingdom of Ends can be no more than a detour only one rider can pass through, what happened to Hugh riding on a different bicycle, his own, after he ran into the tall, vertical pole or tree that nearly killed him?

PART FOUR

Hugh sauvez d'eau

Donald had fallen into the role of the bookseller in Renoir's movie, the well meaning, bourgeois liberal who dragged Boudu out of the river after he jumped off the bridge. Donald hadn't actually saved Hugh himself; the EMT crew had done that, and unlike Boudu, Hugh had been too badly hurt to protest—barely conscious, if aware at all, with only a hazy recollection afterward of what had happened. The mangled bicycle gave the most eloquent testimony about the violence of the accident. After Hugh came back from the hospital he stayed in the spare bedroom at Donald and Greta's house on the Cape. It was the same place he'd been living while he worked on the house. Now, of course, things were different. Greta may have wanted to chuck the invalid out, but Donald was enjoying Hugh's company and even the role as a nurse, to which he soon added the job of financial advisor and coach. The body itself Hugh would take care of. Despite the smashed ribcage and lost blood from internal injuries, he had begun exercising as soon as he could. Donald's department was work and money, and the goal was to save "a hundred in thirty," a hundred dollars a month. This Hugh could do easily if he just accepted some of the odd jobs offered to him, ones which Donald was happily lining up. Hugh was soon well enough to work a couple hours a day and began finishing up what he'd begun before the accident. It seemed surprising that Hugh was letting Donald manage his life, but besides the appeal of doing something that helped someone, there was real affection for Hugh in Donald's motives. He was also shrewd enough to cast the effort in athletic terms which they could both joke about while Donald cajoled Hugh's Darwinian person back into functional shape.

A few weeks later, after Hugh moved back to Donald's house in Boston, I drove in to see him. The first sight was jarring. His unusually wide, level shoulders were angled several degrees down on the right side, making him look asymmetrical, and he didn't move with the same easy, feral grace. Nevertheless, for someone who'd hit a tree or telephone pole at speed with no protection at all and nearly been killed ("Der grosser Guy habt winken at him," Donald said), he was surprisingly whole. Hugh slid off my questions about the whole drama, including his recovery, only admitting to a few lingering symptoms. He signaled I'd asked enough questions by saying, "I'm okay, babes. How you doin'?" The part of the experience he wanted to talk about was the wackiness of modern medical practice. That was how he could vent his emotion. The medical system was utterly screwed up—agreed—but, once again, people got everything wrong! Medical costs were so high because hospitals were run as if no one was paying for anything! It was insanely impractical, a game played with funny money. In many cases Hugh's opinions were developed from afar; he read an article or a government report or saw something on television, but this time he'd been smack in the maw of medicine himself. He appreciated the emergency care they had given him, although he didn't want to admit they'd "saved his life" (that thing of such dubious value) because it sounded so melodramatically trite—how could you be important just because you'd had an accident, which by definition had nothing personal in it and could have happened to anyone; you could only laugh at the bogus significance of the whole thing. Yet once they got him into the hospital and did the actual job of saving his life, after that, instead of releasing him, they insisted on doing all these additional tests. Hugh had nothing to say about it. He was trapped. The doctor didn't ask what he himself wished to do but assumed his body was theirs, perhaps because they had "saved" it—a different twist on owning someone you'd saved from the situation in *Boudu sauvez d'eau*. Some of the tests they performed were invasive or painful, and all were expensive. Hugh couldn't afford a roll of gauze, a box of Kleenex, even a toothbrush at marked-up hospital prices, so the experience became surreal. He felt like the subject of medical experiments, not done to advance science or heal the patient, but simply because that's what they did, that was their function, doing tests. The staff and equipment were right there, ready to go, and he was a handy candidate. So who was going to pay for all this? The taxpayer, that permanently aggrieved abstraction. The Commonwealth had a fund for "indigent patients" which compensated hospitals which had these pathetic uninsured victims dumped in their emergency rooms. This, vented Hugh, was how the medical care system ran itself, another product of the exploitations of "free" enterprise, fed by the ready supply of people who got sick or hurt and had no insurance. Somehow Hugh's "debt," much of it incurred without his approval, and which he could never repay (and how much it pained him to be in anyone's debt!—such an offense to strict duty) was absorbed by the same chronically pissed off taxpayers, many who were against "socialized medicine" because it was supposedly so inefficient. What could be more inefficient than what Hugh had been through? Nobody cared. Nobody even saw it happening. Yet it took place in plain sight, in front of everyone! There was no point in the process when he, the alleged beneficiary, could have said, "Wait, stop, I don't want this." The current improvised system was tolerated so that hospitals could continue to exist and doctors could enjoy big incomes, even though everyone knew something was wrong and the "delivery" of health care to the citizenry was incoherent. The illogical mess was based on a reverence for the profit motive—in this case a profit donated by the state—instead of the task of making sick people well. What made the mess worse were the multiple levels of self-delusion about what was going on, which was inevitable as long as people believed that making a profit and healing the sick could be accomplished by the same rules! Hugh raged in his whispery voice. His tirade was a sign of his own returning vigor so in that backhanded way the medical industry was continuing to heal him. It was all as absurd as Boudu having his life saved when he was trying to throw it away, although it wasn't as funny.

Hugh wasn't back at his own level of fitness yet but by the time I saw him he was running again and could do a day's work of carpentry. What he couldn't do was chin-ups. His shoulder still hadn't entirely healed, perhaps never would, and describing it was the only time during our several hours together when his voice dropped into a minor key. He had wanted something to change, and it had. He hadn't erased the whole blackboard of his life, just a small corner; he hadn't met any Astrid in the hospital, only Donald had been there to comfort him with jock talk as Groucho and Mr. Magoo.

By Labor Day, dutifully following Donald's "coaching," Hugh had five times the first hundred in savings, and had moved into a spare room in his friend Rachel's house. They were glad to have him. Her husband Steve and Hugh argued companionably about most any subject. It was their form of tennis. Steve was amused instead of irritated by Hugh's contrariness and to their sons he was like an uncle or older brother. When I stopped by one Saturday to see Hugh they were all playing a game he and the boys had invented using the driveway and yard in back of the house. They played with a soccer ball and could score in an improvised goal or by throwing it through the basket above the garage. I didn't see it played long enough to figure out the baroque rules. I was more interested in watching how Hugh related to the boys. Instead of the pedant, a role he fell into at times, he was playful and boyish himself. If they wanted to alter a rule, he didn't object but embraced the change, gave it a new name, made it part of the fun. With Rachel's boys, Hugh could be a boy too, and all the great weight of whomever he was, or was supposed to be, all that blew away. I felt a whiff of his peculiar happiness, brief as a crow flying over our heads.

2.

The mortal innocence Hugh had lost by being saved after his traumatic yet hazed glimpse of infinity had advanced him to an even more rarefied level of contingency: if all this might have been over when he careened down the hill on his bike at a speed just over the edge of control, how could he take this remnant of life as seriously as what he'd so recklessly risked throwing away? His outrage at the way everyone silently conspired to accept things as they were had dwindled, or morphed, into this redistilled cognac of irony, and where before he'd have made a long, whispery, exasperated critique of some abomination, now a look of resigned anguish was his typical response. The tirade on medical practice had been a way of exorcising the twisted emotions left after the event, but I didn't hear anything like it again. If what he felt now was beyond words, it also meant we had little to talk about. Running through all conversation like an electric current is a belief that it matters, at least enough to fill the moment. Without it, what's there to say? Our racquet sports had become history too. Hugh's damaged shoulder, the right one, meant that besides having lost chin-ups as part of his routine, he couldn't hit an overhead serve. Equally disabling was our mutual lack of interest. We tried once to go out and hit a few balls—no game—but the pale imitation of what had once been a nearly perfect recreation was distasteful. Instead of the grace of the smacked ball and the athletic dance steps on court, we felt like impostors. As tennis players, we'd become impotent.

Hugh continued working as a carpenter and handyman, accumulating his small but adequate bankroll whether he liked it or not, and most of the time I didn't worry about him. He was living at Rachel's and to the extent he had a family it was her, Steve, and the boys. Hugh never called—I always had to call or write him to make contact—and at one point I realized I hadn't spoken to him for several months. I was busy working and glad to leave him in Rachel's hands. So when she called trying to find him herself it was a surprise. "I thought he was living with you." "He was," she said. Then he moved out abruptly, just left a note on the kitchen table saying thanks with no explanation for his exit. "He could've stayed as long as he liked. We had the room on the third floor and the boys loved having him here. They did think it was kind of odd sometimes because Hugh was so different from anyone else they knew. One day Brian said, 'Doesn't he have any family?'" Rachel laughed. "But he knew he could stay here as long as he liked. So I don't know. I was kind of hoping he might have been in touch with you."

He hadn't.

A couple weeks later Rachel called again. She'd found him. Hugh was living in Methuen, in an apartment building that let rooms by the week. She had a number for him. I called and got the rental office. I left a message and to my surprise Hugh called back later that night. "How you doin', babes?" I heard in the receiver. Almost a year after being self-evicted and then almost self-destroyed, a survivor in spite of himself, Hugh's temperament sounded as if it was pitched lower but also steadier. He wasn't waiting to see what happened next, leaning his back on the inclination of fate, he was just getting through each day on the treadmill. Not diminished expectations, no expectations. He was living in a small furnished room—much more expensive than the one he'd been tossed out of (Did Marx pay his rent?), but he had enough money, still doing carpentry and odd jobs, riding around on his bike when there wasn't too much snow and ice on the ground. "I'll come out and see you some time," he volunteered when I said I wanted to see him. "You're gonna ride all the way out here?" I said. He could do it physically, no question, but not in this weather. "I'm getting a car," Hugh said. "This guy was going to junk his Honda Civic and I told him I'd take it. It needs brakes.

I'll fix it in the spring." We laughed, simpatico, but I pictured fifty-something Hugh lying in the winter slush under a junkyard car. If you took your strict duty too seriously, that's where you could end up. "Rachel said she was disappointed you left," I said, making a tentative thrust at that subject. "Ah, you know, babes. I'd been there six months. It wasn't right."

A few weeks later, in the spring, I found my way to Methuen, an inner suburb of Boston. The building was big, almost modern, and out of place in a neighborhood of working class houses. Hugh and I sat in his room having a couple beers. It wasn't as depressing as I'd imagined it would be. The room was small, almost cloistral with two people sitting in it, but the paint was fresh, the furnishings were functional but not dingy, and sunlight poured in the one window. It made me think again of the comparison with the recently collapsed Soviet Union. If you were a refusnik there, someone who rejected the authority of the state, you were arrested and sent to the gulag. In the U.S., an enemy of the unofficially established state culture, the G.N.P., ended up in a corner by himself, ignored and anonymous. You didn't suffer horribly, you merely withered. At least Hugh had stopped his descent. It wasn't the bottom but he was no longer falling. He'd landed on some kind of ledge, or even pulled himself up to one. I also noticed that Hugh no longer kept up a running commentary on himself, a constant self-criticism which had always invited another comparison to the totalitarian regimes, to China and its Cultural Revolution where "backsliders" with "bourgeois tendencies" denounced themselves publicly. Now Hugh was less talkative. Instead of an open book—*Here, read my non-story, see my justified doubts!*—he referred cryptically to the strange person he had become. Had I just met him for the first time, I'd probably have thought that the reason a middle-aged man of his intelligence and presentable attractiveness and obvious abilities was living alone, down near the bottom of the socioeconomic heap, was opaque, a private mystery, that he was a kind of Lord Jim, crippled by some youthful act or event he felt complicit in. Not a bad guess, although now the last thing he'd have volunteered to describe was how he had "killed" his father when he was sixteen. When this occurred to me—when I remembered that night on the patio in the dark so long ago—I thought it was odd that that personal revelation, his confession of parricide, could so easily slip out of my present picture of Hugh, and settle down to the bottom, out of sight. You'd think it would always be the first thing I thought of when trying, yet again, to make sense of Hugh's life. But there seemed to be a point when the experiences of the past lost their peculiar power and mystery, a kind of statute of limitations on their potency. To figure them out now would no longer make any real difference. It was like hoarding a treasure too long. There were so many things you might have done with it but you forsook them all in favor of its potential, and to choose one now would be to lose such a large piece of your imagination no reality could compensate. By this time his father would have died of old age, even if he'd had a healthy heart, even if he hadn't argued fatally with his son—as his son thought. So the great drama of Hugh's life was history. He had kept the possibility of redemption alive so long that it no longer mattered whether he was guilty, or whether his father had died sliding into second base or on the eve of Christmas.

When I left the neat small room in the bland concrete building in the drab suburban neighborhood, I couldn't see around the corner of this kind of existence; I couldn't imagine where Hugh might end up next. This felt like a perpetual, even a terminal waiting room. Nothing came, nothing went, while you sat contemplating the sum of your days until some outside force—not forgiving and merciful but mechanical, disinterested, dumb— moved you on to your next stop. Or just left you here, quietly dangling and dwindling. Hugh no longer talked about meeting a woman who wasn't so crazed by feminism or so scarred by experience that she hated men; he no longer urged me to write out a story situation which had occurred to him, and his peculiar state—alive, yet outside of life—was no longer a source of wonder and outrage but a fact which didn't need repeating. As I'd thought before but never with such finality, Hugh was now a remnant of Hugh; not the best part of him, not the worst either, still a recognizable form of himself but faded and shrunk. Before, when he denounced himself, I could at least play the role of advocate for the accused. Now all that was unspoken, or referred to so briefly in passing it was like a message in code. Any encouragement I offered had no context, so it sounded gratuitous, as if I thought his situation was so sad I had to do some cheerleading. All it did was mock the little dignity left to him. There was a moment sitting in his small rented room having a beer when it felt as if we were two friends of someone who'd died, meeting to remember him. Since we had both known him so well there was little to say, just the silent companionship of a shared loss.

Then, when I left, there was Hugh's super-strong handshake, not to show off his strength but to convey his feeling, and his helpless vitality. After everything, it was still there. A few weeks later when I called him just after the Boston Marathon, he said he'd watched it in his room and celebrated the event by doing push-ups from start to finish. "You did push-ups during the whole race," I said. "Two hours and ten minutes or something?"

Hugh laughed.

"My cheek got so sore from touching down on the floor I had to start turning my head to the other side."

Now, his hand in mine, I squeezed back hard, trying to reciprocate the emotion if not the strength. But the grip—so familiar, so feral—was too strong for me, and my fingers crumpled in his as I heard his ritual sayonara:

"See ya, babes."

3.

If this could turn out the way I wanted it to, the last seven years of Hugh's life would be a fantastic reversal. The agent of the reversal, coming when everyone including Hugh himself had given up on any dramatic change ever happening, would be a woman, a beautiful woman. ("Keep tellin' it, babes," I hear him laugh. "I love it.") With her vision clarified by love ("Hazed, blinded!" Hugh is still laughing), she would see his best qualities and inspire him to blossom so the world could see them too. Hugh would also find a function, perhaps as a teacher of some kind. Not in any ordinary school, but some kind of private one that wasn't run by the deadly "doctors" of education, a place where inspired teachers taught gifted kids. Or maybe a place for "challenged" children with some physical or mental disability where Hugh's gift for games and his inventiveness and instinctive empathy for those outside the mainstream might be appreciated, even cherished. The years when everyone else is declining toward retirement would be Hugh's prime time. He'd be appreciated for what he was and it would no longer matter to anyone, including himself, that he had once been useless or even a parricide. His atonement would be a private matter, the moral debt no one but Hugh himself felt he owed repaid every day by his gift of knowledge to young people. A private Kingdom of Ends. Now I've gone too far, this is really a fantasy, and Hugh is laughing. "Maybe I can run a five minute mile, too, babes. At age fifty-five! Play HORSE with Bird. And win!"

What in fact happened was nearly as unexpected, as unbelievable, yet it was not a fantasy at all.

"I'd often thought about introducing them to each other," Rachel said about Hugh and her good friend, "but Naomi had been through a bad divorce and she was really wounded, and the last thing I wanted to do was have her get hurt again. And you know Hugh—he's so hard on himself and the next thing you know he's belittling anyone who's foolish enough to care about him, that kind of thing. So I never did. Then Naomi called to see if I knew anyone because she needed some work done on her house and I thought, well, I'll just give her Hugh's name and if she calls he probably won't call her back anyway. But he did. It isn't a fairy tale but doesn't it feel like it's almost a miracle?" she laughed.

It was some time before I met Naomi myself. It seemed as if Hugh preferred to keep us apart, to separate his old from his new life. I could understand that, especially when I saw him in the house he was now living in with her. An exile in Soviet Methuen, the survivor of a violent collision with an adamant object that too obviously, too stupidly, stood for everything he had futilely fought against—all that was gone. Almost as soon as it vanished behind him, it became clear to Hugh how humiliating his life had been before, and just how sorry his friends had felt for him. Even he felt sorry for the person he'd been. And for all his self-criticism, Hugh never wanted anyone to feel sorry for him. He was a jock, an athlete, and there was no crying in baseball. Sitting across from me at Naomi's house ("How 'bout a beer, babes"), on the patio which he had rebuilt for her while they were falling in love, both of us enjoying the sunshine, I saw a transformed man. It made perfect sense that the door would be shut on the past. Why go there? We both knew it too well. When I exclaimed over the house, how nice it all was, I saw the smile on Hugh's face, an involuntary smile which he tried to control, just as I shut myself up when I realized this might embarrass him. He had been rescued from his solitary confinement in a rented cell by a woman who owned an actual house in the city, where real estate values had exploded into the stratosphere and only the rich or very lucky people could afford to live. This sudden good fortune could cast him in the role of gigolo, if he were seen as cynical and calculating instead of sincere, so I followed his lead away from the subject. Instead we talked about all the work he'd been doing on the house which seemed to give him the right to have moved in with the mistress of the manor. Hugh may also have been disguising from me just how romantically in love he was with Naomi because it too didn't fit with the unworthy, unlovable man he had felt himself to be for so long. The shadow cast by that molted wretch also revealed that his portrayal of himself hadn't been a clear-eyed appraisal. Instead of the final verdict on Hugh, it might have been only a "phase," a temporary situation, or affliction, an aberrant form. If it hadn't been true that he was useless and worthless, then perhaps it hadn't been necessary to denounce himself either. Much of his suffering and punishment had been self-inflicted. Why had he despaired so? Why hadn't he kept the faith? Why hadn't he nobly and bravely persevered—steadfastly carried on? It showed him as a man who gave up too easily, one who ran to extremes. This kind of happiness might have been his years ago if only he'd kept his head up and looked around. There was something to be said for optimism after all! Who cared if you sounded dippy if you found happiness?

But all that was irrelevant. The clear conclusion of hindsight is the most seductive deception of all. Anyone's life can be fixed in retrospect. Putting two people together who can make each other happy is magic, and magic—real magic—is unpredictable. If there were a formula, we'd all know it. Hugh had spent endless, empty hours trying to deconstruct the mystery of love and after so many years in his own purgatory he had his reward.

4.

"He treated me almost as if I was fragile," Naomi said later. She said it with wonder in her voice, as if she could take a lot more than he imagined, but of course what Hugh was afraid of was not that she would break but that he would hurt her somehow and ruin it for both of them, burst the bubble they were in.

That was part of the miracle and I'd seen it the first time I saw them together. I was in the city on business and met them for an early dinner alone, without Kate. When I arrived at her house for my second visit I was a little apprehensive about what I was about to see. I'd called once before and invited them to come out to see us in the country and while talking to Hugh I could hear her saying in the background, "Tell them we can't make it." I wondered if she was afraid of meeting Hugh's old friends, not out of possessiveness but from a fear of a past that had been so difficult for him. Why go back there? I never divined the reason for her reluctance, apart from a certain reserve in her nature. All the ways to misunderstand each other! So our meeting embraced several levels of self-consciousness; just as Hugh was treating Naomi as if she were fragile, I was treating Hugh as if he and his new relationship were fragile too. After what he had been through, if this should break Hugh would crumble. But during the evening I spent with them there were no signs of the man who needed to trash himself by criticizing someone else, especially any woman unwise enough to care about him. There were no verbal fights, he didn't mock Naomi; to the contrary he listened respectfully when she spoke. We ate at the table in the large kitchen and when she lightly touched his arm to interject something or finish a thought, he listened and took her seriously and made appropriate jokes which kept everything lighthearted. He was playful and funny, and instead of a political tirade or denunciation of the immoral state of the world his criticisms were expressed with irony and satirical laughter. I knew this man, I had seen him before—but not for more than twenty years. After wandering all those years in his own wilderness, it was as if the original Hugh had returned, the humorous, sociable guy who loved life and loved women and baseball and physics and puzzles and poetry and the smell of poplar trees in the spring. I wanted to laugh or weep for him. There was no emotion that fit. The situation, the drama, the non-story was too long and too layered, it included too much and it also included too deep a void to be encompassed in a single emotion.

Hugh had washed up on this shore, and now that he'd found it, now that it had found him, and we were all sitting at this specific table in this one and only kitchen eating dinner together, it looked as if it must have been in plain sight all the time. I knew what an illusion that was. *Post hoc, ergo propter hoc*, Hugh would have said, naming the fallacy: because something happened, it must have been caused by what preceded it. I knew better. Sitting there eating the pasta Hugh had cooked, noticing the looks he and Naomi exchanged that bespoke this tender emotion that hadn't a name—none more specific than love—I kept thinking this was the opposite of the inevitable; as an outcome it was precariously contingent, a blessing. Or, as Rachel had called it, a miracle.

5.

We were standing in Rachel's dining room at a gathering to honor Hugh. Although she had lived with him for the seven years since we all had dinner in her kitchen, Naomi and I were still barely acquainted. Now, after Hugh's sudden death, we needed each other and were talking confidentially in a way that wouldn't have happened if Hugh were still with us. Describing how they had gotten together, Naomi said, "I asked him what he wanted from me and he said he wanted someone to love."

The house was full of people, most of them friends of Naomi, and earlier we had all sat on the long porch surrounded by greenery where people described memories of Hugh. It felt awkward because of the performance aspect. Twenty or thirty people, many unknown to each other, sat listening to the speaker describe a memory, a few of us feeling a strong emotion behind it, a degree of intimacy, the rest only acquainted with Hugh through Naomi. It was the kind of situation which Hugh, had he been there, could only have made fun of—like recalling that his old pal knew how to use a fork, a skill he wouldn't be needing any more. Donald stood up and told us Hugh was the one person he could tell anything to, and did, including his most private and secret thoughts (possible perhaps because of the difference in their social status, the way a valet knows his master intimately). What he said was heartfelt and I knew how much he had done to help Hugh, but his reminiscence was more about him than Hugh, so it was an unintentional reminder of how empty of event Hugh's life had been.

Elaine, who had known Hugh as long as any of us, was moved by the loss to join Hugh with another of her friends, a man who had recently chosen to endure a last desperate treatment for his cancer. Describing the other man's courage facing an extreme illness, Elaine didn't seem to notice that she was no longer talking about Hugh but about a person whose relationship to mortality was the direct opposite of Hugh's. "Do you know how much I abhor the steadfast carrying on?" he had written in his notebooks. At the time he was deeply depressed, no doubt, but Hugh had always been ready to satirize mankind's most trite sentiment. It was a trick nature played on us, extorting our praise for the gift of life while she tortured us, and for Hugh it was a vestige of religion, of the ritual thanks to God, the fond obeisance also expressed in the pep talk and greeting card. Elaine's conflated tribute was so inappropriate when applied to Hugh that it could only fit perversely, as an unintended salute to the way people got things wrong and then took them to heart. That it was done unaware—a live demonstration of a fallacy Hugh had so often despaired of— might have amused more than disconcerted him: *This is for me? Glad I'm not here, babes.*

When Kate stood up to take her turn, she described how she had met Hugh while jogging in Cambridge, and during their conversation—aided by the discovery of having a mutual friend—he seemed so bright and humorous she suggested he call Donald who was hiring people for a new program, the one Kate was also working on. Which Hugh did. (For those keeping score, this is the first of two critical phone calls Hugh made which significantly altered his life; the second was, of course, to Naomi when she needed someone to work on her house.) So their chance meeting had gotten him a job in television and introduced him to nearly all the people who were gathered here at Rachel's, including many who became so important to him. Contingency and running, those were two themes that had jogged all through Hugh's life, and Kate enjoyed taking credit for having spotted his talent and urging him to call Donald.

Another woman, no doubt intending the compliment generously, regaled us with Hugh's skill at fixing things. Let's hear a cheer for Handyman Hugh! Such a useful guy to have around! A Swiss Army knife kind of guy! This was turning into a burlesque. Maybe I really should tell everyone that Hugh knew how to use a fork—and tell it in context, so people could laugh and be a little shocked by how he treated his mother. What seemed more evident in this woman's "eulogy" was her envy of Naomi for landing a man with so many useful skills. The philosopher-handyman. Would you like some Wittgenstein with your new faucet washer? I also couldn't avoid noticing the irony of hearing useless Hugh praised at his death for his omnibus utility. You'll miss me now, when you can't get that door latch fixed!

Since the subject was the semi-inscrutable Hugh, maybe it was inevitable that so many of us would get him wrong because when I spoke I heard myself adding my own layer of misunderstanding by saying Hugh had been brought back to life by Naomi. I didn't go quite so far as to say she was the princess who kissed the toad, although the silly image occurred to me and I thought how Hugh would have laughed at the idea of being a toad ("Sure it wasn't a cockroach?"). I was giving Naomi more credit than she was going to accept, especially in public, because even when I added that she couldn't lighten the darker corners in Hugh's mind, she almost shouted, "No, no, they were still there! They were always there! I couldn't change that at all!" It was modesty, and honesty, on her part. Naomi wasn't going to take any sentimental credit for something that hadn't happened. She knew his demons were there (the demons were us, we were the way things were!) and she had suffered from them too, no matter how Hugh tried to protect her from them. Maybe that made her almost as sad as losing him, because she knew that if he were still here everything that tormented him would still be here too.

While we were all testifying I could see Hugh in his running shorts and polo shirt up in the tree above one end of the porch. As he listened to the tributes and speculation about him—all of us poking at his soul, his vzeoogby, to make it pop out and reveal itself—I saw him smiling, shaking his head, laughing his shrill, strong, critical laugh. "No, no, that's not it, babes. Not even close!" Or maybe in a voice that once would have sounded exasperated but now was only amused: "See—no one understands anyone! Are these really his friends? What do the people who *don't* know him say?" If someone's comment did do him some justice, especially if it was meant humorously, he might laugh again and say, "You're gettin' warm, babes. Keep tryin'!" But he wouldn't have meant it. He didn't really want to be known, even if he did want to be loved, and there on the porch with all the people who knew him, or were connected to him through other friendships, I felt a kind of semi-permeable rush of Hugh's hostility to psychology. Fascinated, yet hostile toward the specious science that claimed knowledge of our most private self, Hugh had wanted to remain an enigma, to pose in person one of those puzzles he loved, the kind that expressed the only metaphysical truth he could believe. As much as he insisted on his own view of everything, beginning with his view of himself, he wanted to exit as a conundrum. Had he really, literally—no, figuratively—killed his father, and that was what crippled him? "Search me, babes," he laughed in the slang of our youth. "But why would that have blocked him from having anything like a normal career? Was it a kind of cancerous guilt?" "Good question," Hugh laughs again. "Were his ideas just too exalted, too unrealistic, even too childish, and he was too stubborn?" "Could be, babes," Hugh agrees in a tone that says go ahead, suggest anything. Sooner or later it might occur to us that he doesn't know the answer either. Or he does but can't express it in words. Not without bending it out of shape, distorting it into something false. But that doesn't matter. What matters is that Hugh died with the question intact, in less time than it would take to trace your finger around a question mark down to the final *punkt.*

Something else matters too, something far from insoluble puzzles and Viennese psychoanalysis and Kant's ethics. Ordinary life. Naomi and I, with some others, were standing in the dining room after the scene on the porch. I was waiting for my turn to look at the photo album when I heard Naomi describing to Kate how Hugh got along so well with her children, now in their twenties. "He didn't fight with them?" Kate asked like an instinctive reporter. "Oh, no. Not at all," Naomi said. "They got along beautifully. He could understand my daughter's research in a way I never could. And Jonathan's work really interested him too. They would sit up late talking whenever they visited."

"So that was a real change for him," I said, wanting to hear more about this side of Hugh.

"Well, I guess so," Naomi said. "I didn't know him before. But you know what I think was different for him—when he was living with me, and he saw my children on holidays—he began discovering a kind of ordinary, an ordinary side of life he'd never enjoyed before. I think he began...it made him think about what he'd missed, and maybe if he'd lived a more ordinary life he could have had children of his own, the way he talked to mine now as adults..."

"He'd have fought with them, he could be so pedantic at times, and so argumentative," Kate said. "I don't mean to insult—you know what I mean."

"Oh, yes, I know. Although he was always very gentle with me. But those were—he had to live with that. And I think he enjoyed some of what he experienced, just..."

"Like the trip," I said, looking at a page in the photo album. The shots were of the Grand Canyon and there was Hugh, not quite like any other tourist but a tourist nonetheless. "How did you ever get him to go on a vacation like that?"

"You know what I did?" Naomi laughed. "I told him, 'I'm going on this trip because I've always wanted to do it and you can come if you want but you don't have to.' Then we had this big argument about how much it was going to cost and you know how with Hugh there were all these arguments about the waste of resources and how expensive it was and he said he wasn't going to go. So he sulked around and I said, 'Fine, I'll go myself.' Then the night before he threw a few things in a bag and off we went!"

"Look at this shot of him!" I was looking at a photo of Hugh sitting in a chair in the sunshine, his sneakered feet up on a rock, gazing off at a picturesque sandstone mesa. The tourist on holiday.

"You can say what you want, Naomi," I told her, "but anyone who got Hugh to do this has done something to change him!"

He might have felt ironic inside, may have been mocking himself, but he was there. Some force—love, curiosity—had lifted him up out of his stubborn environment and dropped him down far from home. The trip had required him to do many things he disapproved of for idealistic or dogmatic reasons, like eating in restaurants, flying on airplanes, renting a car, gawking at spectacular scenery. But Naomi had arranged things with a sensitivity to Hugh's prickly frugality. They stayed at a place that looked like a campground where lodgers cooked their own meals and the snapshot of Hugh standing over an outdoor stone fireplace, holding a beer and supervising the hot dogs with a parody of a smile, gave me a slow rush of vicarious pleasure. For that one moment, at least, he had let himself succumb to what was in his terms the squandering of resources in exchange for fun. If everyone else did it, then why not you too, Hugh? Well, there were good reasons not to, like that's who you were, the person who did not do what everyone else did.

The next thought wasn't so happy.

What if it turned out—and in precisely what scenario could it be revealed in a way that would make any difference?—what if it turned out that Hugh had been guilty not of his father's death but of exaggerating his own importance. The two of them had argued the way teenagers and parents do, then his father slid into second base and had a heart attack. Then he died several months later (after more arguments), just before Christmas. Feeling he was responsible was only a youthful mistake, a vanity, the kind of thing an impassioned adolescent does because he fills his own world so completely, without any distance between himself and his own selfish motives, which is why the mistaken conclusion, the guilt, feels so right at the time. Under the sway of the opera of grieving and loss at sixteen, Hugh could come to no other emotional conclusion. In that way his guilt became an historical fact, one that grew more solid with time, and the potent mix of a powerful ego with a semi-permeable sensibility combined, like the ingredients of an epoxy, to glue him to the psychological spot where these forces had first come together.

Perhaps.

But that would mean his guilt wasn't true. It was a fiction. A story he made up and believed. I stood by the dining room table in a reverie. Naomi interrupted it, ambushing me with another surprise.

"You know, Hugh thought you were a minister..."

"What?" I didn't think I'd heard her right. "He thought I was a *minister*? You mean like a—"

She was nodding.

"You're kidding!"

"No. He really thought you'd become a minister."

"How'd he get *that* idea?"

"I think it was because you sent him a letter and the return address had 'Reverend' on it."

It took a minute but then I remembered. It had been a joke—a solicitation I got in the mail, sent on by my mother, I assumed (she was still trying to get me back in the church after all these years), and when I replied—just replying was already a joke—I mischievously checked the box for a title that said "Rev." instead of "Mr." Later another letter came in the mail with a sheet of return address stickers printed with my name and the title Rev. I must have used one on the envelope I sent Hugh. But how could he have not read it as a joke? That I couldn't have sent it *unless* it was a joke!

"He actually thought I got a degree in theology? Got myself ordained?"

"I guess so," Naomi said. It sounded as if she meant yes but didn't want to say it.

Incomprehensible! It was a joke, Hugh, it was meant ironically—you understand irony, don't you? It was playing off the impossibility of it's being true! That's what made it amusing, even if it was a little lame, a little adolescent. But how could he think I'd actually done it? In our time, weaned on science, children not of God but of technology, of antibiotics and the Bomb—it was cheating to try to escape from the real world into religion. For Hugh it was a diabolically dishonest dodge because what he wanted more than anything was to live in a just world presided over by an omnipotent being. He wanted Judgment Day, a final accounting when virtue would become visible and it would be rewarded. Heaven on earth! Since all that was a child's fantasy—the greatest fiction of all—for a serious person to believe it was a personal insult to Hugh. All of his diatribes about the raw facts of human existence colliding with the dream of an ultimate justice could be distilled into a single complaint: There is no God! There was no moral intelligence or power above us; there was only us. If there were a higher moral intelligence with the power to reward and punish, then Hugh's life would have made sense! He had lived as if such a metaphysical being did exist, as if some unseen eye saw all, and if there were a way to make this witness manifest, he might have felt his worth was valued, that his behavior was more than futile and solipsistic, that he had an audience. But he didn't, there was no audience, no Higher Audience of any kind, and to say so was a travesty of the truth that defined the human condition.

This was a statement Hugh couldn't make directly because, again, it lost all its sublimity, its authenticity, its poetry, if it was expressed in ordinary speech, worst of all if used as an excuse. To say it out loud betrayed the meaning behind the words. It sounded dippy. If the ancient Hebrews had been unable to speak the name of their Yahweh out loud, Hugh was unable to name the absent metaphysical being or abstraction which could redeem him, had it existed. He never referred to the Kingdom of Ends. If he didn't curse, he also didn't speak in capital letters. He might make a joke, but to be true to the sacred—to the dimension and significance of the vacuum its absence created—the most Hugh could say was nothing. In that sense he was the preacher himself—but one who'd been struck dumb. His silence was the tribute he paid to what was missing.

I went back to the piano in the dining room where the photos were laid out on the lid. I had a sudden need to see Hugh, to remind myself what he looked like, as if I might not be able to trust the images in my mind after all this misunderstanding. I was feeling a new sadness: If Hugh could have believed this about me, it meant he didn't know who I really was. I may have talked like a believer at times, a believer in *something*, some kind of spiritual dimension even if it was only a human one—another fiction, with no reified form—but how could he have not seen the foundation, the slab of skepticism it rested upon?

Standing by the piano with all the thoughts about Hugh gently bumping each other like boats moored together, the photo my eyes rested on was a simple portrait of Hugh with Naomi. His arm was around her, holding her beside him, just there, a companion, and she had one arm up diagonally crossing her chest, inclining her slightly toward him. With her serene smile, she looked like a woman who feels loved and secure. Hugh is looking at the camera with an expression I recognized as typical. Sometimes cameras lie, but not this time. It was him. Resigned yet alert, ready to make a wry wisecrack and laugh. Okay, babes, this is what my life is, I hear him say. Then he goes on to say—but this is only a thought, he's not going to say this out loud either—that he has done what he could and for reasons too stupid and absurdly contingent to explain, this is how things turned out. Most of all he is not going to say anything to harm the person beside him, however destined they were to end up in a photo together. We're all destined to end up in any particular photo, so what's the surprise that we're here in this one?

My eyes shift and I'm outside the photo again, looking at them as a couple. He may have screwed some things up but he is loyal to her and to the dictum to do his strict duty. He is as much at peace with the world as he can be (is the world at peace with itself? Hugh asks in reply), and this look which also expresses his intelligence, his critical discernment, his willful, involuntary clash with things as they are, says the code must be observed, it must be steadfastly carried on, even if the world is unjust, ignorant, greedy, and gluttonous. Because I know what I know, I add my knowledge to the portrait, and feel Hugh's burden, the moral weight he lived under in a world which considered him irrelevant. A world where so many others who had large busy responsibilities felt no weight at all. That was a mystery that tormented him every day, one he could never slough off or resolve.

6.

It was one drink later and enough people had left Rachel and Steve's house to make it feel as if the ones still there had really known Hugh. After getting another beer I'd come back in the dining room, hovering near the photos as if I expected Hugh to come to life in one of them if I stared at it intently enough. Lying on the piano lid beside the pictures from their trip west was another album I hadn't noticed before. It was smaller, with a dusky red cover, and it was set off to one side so I couldn't tell if it was one Naomi had brought or belonged to Rachel and Steve. No one seemed to have looked at it and I was ready to ignore it too when Naomi saw me staring at it.

"Oh, look, you've got to see this," she said in her mild, kind voice.

"These are Hugh's too? There's more?"

"Look." She opened the album and took out a small card laminated in plastic. It was darkened and brittle with age.

"What is it?"

"His driver's license."

That was strange. Suddenly Hugh had a past, like everyone else. My eyes jumped around the new evidence, trying to gulp it in.

"Must have been his first," Naomi said with amazement, as if she hadn't seen it before either.

It was a Michigan driver's license, issued to Hugh when he was 18 or 19. In the faded black and white photo sealed under the lamination he looked like a very young Abby Hoffman with wild dark curly hair; except Hoffman always looked mischievous and Hugh's eyes had a feral intensity. Yet the picture wasn't the surprise. It was the address. Above "city or town of residence," it said, "Grosse Pointe."

Grosse Pointe?

Not lunchbucket Detroit, but the city's cushy suburb?

I looked again. Grosse Pointe. Grossy Pointy, with its two dainty silent e's. The kind of mannered and useless luxuries Hugh loathed, everything he abominated. They were the name of his hometown! The working class neighborhood I'd always pictured him growing up in vanished. But it didn't vanish. It was still there, lingering with a persistence of vision I couldn't blank out. I still could not see Hugh in Grosse Pointe.

Yes, I could. Because to confirm the address, to solidify the upper middle class image of Grosse Pointe, was the most startling photo of all. From the same small album, Naomi took out a 3x5 Kodachrome print. A boy about ten with short thick dark hair growing low on his scalp, giving him a narrow strip of forehead between hairline and eyes, accentuating his frown so it looked like a precocious glower, wearing a white shirt, jacket and tie, stood in front of a spacious brick Tudor house with a curved flagstone walk and neatly trimmed shrubbery. There is no doubt where we are. We are in an upscale suburban American neighborhood. And standing beside the boy is the proud paterfamilias. Gauged by the height of the front door, if not the small size of the boy, the man is tall. He is broad shouldered and straight. He looks so well built he might be Clark Kent, Superman disguised as a reporter. He is a brick Tudor house in human form. Comfortable, solid, respectable, perhaps even hearty, heartily normal in values and style, and supernormal in physique is what the snapshot conveys to me. It contradicts utterly the picture in my mind created by Hugh's story told in the dark that long ago night in Cambridge. But, I remind myself, the hard, intense, working class man in industrial grays sliding into second base came from my history, not Hugh's. This man might be many things that don't show up in the photograph—and, of course, my new assumptions might be just as skewed as my former ones—but the one thing "Clark Kent" does not seem to be is Hugh's father. Not the Hugh I thought I knew. Yet, here he is, the epitome of a type so fulfilled he might be the original, the reigning prince of the Land of Pursuit of Happiness. To feel you were responsible for bringing down a pillar like this might well make you see yourself as a retrograde being, someone demonic, unfit for human society, no matter how justified your critique of his realm.

I put the photo back in the album, feeling I had looked too deeply into Hugh's past, that the impressions I had of him now should stay unchanged, even if they too were factually wrong, in some opaque way. Yet there was also his misconstrual of me, thinking I was a minister (had he wanted a reason to reject me and the part of his past I represented?), and if I could go back and correct that I certainly would. The desire to know more, to get things right, was unquenchable. I opened the album and looked again, trying to absorb it enough to get over my disbelief that I was looking at Hugh as a boy. I stared and stared, as if maybe it would reveal something else about him, or his father, or his background, something that would make the image in my mind and the one under my eyes coalesce.

The parent Hugh resembled must have been the gay and frivolous one, the flirt, the one who partied and played bingo, the one who taught him how to use a fork and snatched books from his hands. The snapshots Naomi is showing me now are from Hugh's bus trip to Florida. These aren't going to be shocking; we've moved from tragedy to comedy. The family is sitting around a kitchen table. Hugh's two sisters seem recognizably related to him when Naomi identifies them, there's a brother-in-law sitting on a couch behind and holding up an empty vodka bottle, upside-down, as a joke. The table is crowded with beer bottles, and sitting beside Hugh, then in his early 40s, is Mom. She's got the dark hair, dyed now, and distinctive low forehead of her son, but her eyes, instead of intense, look—yes—flirtatious! Mom is ready for fun. She's almost a pixie. Her grin seems to end under her ears. In the midst of this merry company sits Hugh looking as if he knows he's the answer to the question: What's wrong with this picture? The man in the middle with the dark frizzy receding Abby Hoffman hair, surrounded by all the fond women and a jokey brother-in-law, is receiving their attention and tolerating this situation with a little humor and a lifetime of ambivalence. He's been joking with them, they've been teasing each other, no one is poking around in the past, they're just having a good time. What the hell, life's a party! Everything that Hugh is and has tried to create in himself is submerged, absent from the photo; it doesn't belong and cannot exist here. Riding down in the bus he probably knew this, must have anticipated suffering some new form of this old estrangement, a fresh reminder that despite his genome he must be some kind of changeling. But he isn't, he's theirs, blood and bone, and besides the biological form inherited from flirty Mom and Clark Kent in front of the suburban Tudor mansion, he has their history too. Even if I couldn't see it, Hugh always knew it was there.

He'd given us a hint the time he and Kate were jogging through upscale Cambridge past houses like the one in the photo and he told her he'd always assumed that when he grew up he'd own a house like one of these. Remembering that incident again, I thought even if he didn't really want it himself, the vestige of the assumption had still been there, the house behind the boy in the photo with Clark Kent was a part of him, a fact he couldn't change.

The sudden jump in Hugh's socioeconomic background would take some time to seep into all the impressions and memories I had of him. Seeing the driver's license had felt like an unfair disclosure this late in the game, an unsportsmanlike withholding of facts, like the fresh clue the author reveals near the end of the story when the mystery is unraveled in a way you could never have guessed. You feel somehow cheated, betrayed. Yet there had been two other passing clues, if I'd chosen to pursue them. Tennis was usually an upper class sport when Hugh and I were kids, and Hugh had said his father was an amateur champ on

Long Island. By the time he mentioned this the image had already been fixed in my mind by his father's slide into second base, and baseball was a working man's sport. It was what the men played summer nights behind the school a block up the street from my house. The second clue I might have picked up was Hugh saying his father was an engineer. Instead of asking What kind? I'd taken the other road and asked about location, not his profession. "I thought you lived in Detroit, not Long Island," I said. "This was before," Hugh said. His father was champ before they moved to Detroit. Or rather, Grosse Pointe. As usual after one follow up question he didn't want to say more. So perhaps due to the caprices of conversation, my wrong impression stayed intact. This random or unpredestined "choice" of what question to ask was not unlike the way Hugh saw the contingencies of evolution—the momentous as well as the trivial could shift on a whim. The picture in my mind persisted and Hugh's father remained an engineer who ran machines or drove trains, not the kind with a college degree and a country club membership.

7.

The game of disclosure could be played in many ways, as Hugh knew well, and most mischievous or diabolical were the revelations and coincidences which hadn't been arranged by anyone but merely happened. In his case the discovery that he had been granted some kind of reprieve in finding Naomi, a last lucky chance, and could now enjoy some of the features of ordinary life was inexpressibly welcome but it also confused him. It was a privilege he was supposed to have earned and Hugh had not yet fulfilled the potential of his abilities. On the March day when he stepped off the bike riding machine and sat down with his stopwatch to measure his pulse and felt it stop a second or so before he felt nothing, he was still training his body and mind for a test designed only for him. If he passed the test—a test with rules and a goal never disclosed to him (speaking of disclosures)—then he could rest and enjoy things like anyone else. Yet he also knew that this was just another illusion, to imagine the test and that it had rules. Because if there were any test its sole ironclad rule was that there were no rules, so there was no way he could ever pass it. Nor could he stop taking, and failing, the test, the swim to infinity.

Nor could he resign from belonging—*not* belonging!—to Groucho's club.

You spent your life here, on this planet, always feeling like an outsider in the most crucial ways, and then you died. That was when you realized that being an outsider was such a joke on you. Because you died like anyone else, without any special dispensation. And the role, the fact of being an outsider, had been understood—in the story Hugh could not help hearing somewhere in his head—as a necessary condition for knowing the truth, along with the inherent hope that something would change because of the light your witnessing shed on that truth. That was the emotion underlying your allegiance to it—everyone would recognize you were right. Only it didn't happen. You died like everyone else, except they were the ones who had understood the game the whole time. So you blew it. Missed your chance. Now it was too late to do anything. You were going to be dead. Your life had been the useless absurdity you always said it was. You spent it pedaling furiously, lifting and swimming and running, waiting for the unseen reality hidden behind the absurdity—the invisible order hinted by the golden mean or the Fibonacci series, maybe—to precipitate out of the chaos or rise up out of the dung heap. Instead, nothing happened. The smart people, the wise ones who were on to the game, took life as it was, did what they could do, savored what could be savored, loved the one they were with, and didn't trouble themselves with ideals or strict duties or infinities. They left their DNA behind in their children and grandchildren, not bothering themselves over how fast their unique biological legacy dispersed itself in the population and became statistically nil because we were all part of the Family of Man anyway, and what was the Family of Man but another greeting card ditty, a sentimental mask we could wear while obeying the dictates of selection. The cunning ones, the ones who knew how to game the game, how to send and receive their greeting cards with a titrated drop of sincerity, accepted the need to climb over a few others to survive; it didn't mean gouging someone's eye or standing on their neck, it just meant doing your work—some portion of the world's work—and steadfastly carrying on, hoping for the best and trusting to luck. What it did not mean was going around telling everyone—even if you couldn't help thinking it, even if it was true—that the way we all lived was wrong. And the image that expressed this renormalized truth was the picture of you, Hugh, lounging with a beer while you gazed at the spectacular western landscape and made jokey ironic comments about being a tourist to Naomi who stood just behind you with the camera, smiling at how silly and stubborn and funny you could be at the same time.

PART FIVE

Alterity

It was about a year after Hugh died when Naomi asked me if I wanted his clippings and notebooks. "There are a whole lot of them, and articles from magazines—but most of the notebooks are blank!" she had warned me, and I heard the exasperation in her voice whenever I got near the box. Prepare to be disappointed, it said. It was natural she would resent whatever it was that prevented Hugh from being content with her and their life together; it had become her inadequacy to complete him despite his wanting "someone to love," even if she knew it wouldn't be possible.

If Hugh's demons left such a slight trace on paper, did they even exist? Of course they did. One of those demons erased his words as he wrote them, or would have if another demon hadn't paralyzed his hand before it could pick up a pen. What was odd was his buying so many notebooks, starting to fill them, then stopping and leaving all the rest unused. Hugh was frugal and leaving all those blank pages was a waste. It seemed out of character. Did each notebook represent a new attempt to record himself, then after a few pages of actually doing it, something squelched him? Maybe each time he felt a need to start over, hoping the cast of his mind had somehow changed, so he bought a new notebook. Doing this again and again made him seem like a Beckett character obsessively moving the stones in his pocket from one to another and back.

Most of what Hugh wrote in his notebooks were quotations from books he was reading. The few original passages were often disappointing because they were short and sometimes written in a slightly self-conscious literary voice. Another few were in his "philosopher's" voice, using the language of that discipline, so if you were looking for something that expressed the essence of Hugh, the quality of his mind, his talents, his uniqueness, the notes were mostly a tease. Apart from his gloomy scribbles about ending it all, only a few of the entries penetrated into real feelings.

There was a second large box half filled with clippings Hugh had saved, articles from the Atlantic Monthly, New Yorker, New York Times magazine, mostly on politics and public affairs, a number of others on science—physics, math, and biology—and a few on psychology and sociology. There were also government publications he'd sent for, reports and policy statements on subjects like nuclear preparedness. Two articles I noticed particularly were by the same author, Sally Tisdale; the subject was obsessions, with fire and pornography. Had Hugh had a fascination with forces and passions that could overwhelm you, consume you, take you out of your head, beyond reason, beyond self? Make your hallowed, imprisoning vzeoogby melt into a liberating mass? For a moment the notion of Hugh subsumed into a boundless force flickered in my mind. His whole story, his non-story, had been a futile pursuit to fulfill a great need, but there was nothing in all these papers—nothing besides the two articles—that showed a particular attraction to the flame or impersonal carnal desire. Perhaps he was curious about people who were obsessed by some force of nature and could find consummation by giving themselves up to it. He might even have envied them for the simplicity of the means of relief, but there was no evidence it was for him.

Basketball was a very different kind of obsession and he had saved an issue of Sports Illustrated with Larry Bird on the cover. The article extolled Bird as the complete player whose combination of physical and mental skills made everyone on his team better, just as I'd heard from Hugh many times. Looking for some extra clue about Hugh, I noticed that his ideal player had the name of a class of animals. Calling him *Bird* seemed to confer some special power on him, some superhuman ability comparable to flight. But this whimsical overtone of Bird's name only reminded me that as whimsical as Hugh himself could be in his lighter moments, he had no interest in the fantastic or supernatural. His measure of man was always what was human. I tossed the Sports Illustrated issue back in the box. Except for Tisdale's articles on obsessions, which in our free, uncensored culture seemed rather tame, the subjects of all the papers he'd saved were familiar from our conversations over the years.

Then, in the middle of this heap of articles, I found something else. It was a dog-eared manila folder. On the outside it said cryptically, "The Case," in Hugh's tight scrawl. The title told me nothing, and I set it aside till I got to the bottom of the articles. Then I picked up the folder again. When I opened it there were typed pages in lines arranged into what could only be poems.

I closed the folder. I was afraid to read them. What if they weren't very good and made me embarrassed for Hugh? Except for the notebooks, I'd never read anything he had written and I was afraid what was inside the folder might be awkward or mannered, not the real thing. When Hugh talked he didn't impress you with his gift for language. He was articulate but what was original in him was his way of thinking and seeing the world, more than how he expressed it. I didn't want to learn that my friend with all his complexities had been, as a poet, mediocre. There was something else too. He had left some poems elsewhere and told Naomi to destroy them without reading them if anything happened to him. She did. Was I under the same request? His privacy had been important to him and I didn't want to betray it. I already had, in a way, to the extent "Hugh" was a real and not a fictional person. I could insist he was a fiction and open the folder. But the very fact that I hesitated shows the question was being asked in the real world, not in the realm of post-modern literary casuistries. "Hugh" wasn't exactly the real person I'd known, but he was as close to the man as I could portray him, and he wasn't merely a "text" either. I hoped I had caught the vzeoogby of a flesh and blood man, something I could only do, it turned out, by making him fiction. So the question of how real "Hugh" was had no simple answer, even if the sheets of paper I was holding had been written by my late friend, an actual human being.

I stood there with the unopened folder, waiting until my feelings settled and a decision became clear. I already knew what it was. Eventually I was going to look inside the folder; I was going to look because it was the human thing to do. It was the natural response to curiosity, to the desire to know what could be known. More than that, it was opting for life over death, for something instead of nothing. It was choosing existence instead of oblivion. Naomi had done the human thing too; she had respected their intimacy. The choice in front of me was different. Hugh didn't know I was going to write his story, the non-story he'd been unable to record for himself: "to step out of the universe in order to rearrange it," as he described the process of writing in one of his notebooks. He had often suggested stories for me to write, and I was finally doing it. To finish the portrait of Hugh I had to read what he'd written himself. Not looking in the folder would be like adding more blank pages to his notebooks.

2.

For the reader—if anyone is still with me—the surprise will be the identity of the author of Hugh's poems, and it jolted me too. Along with it came another surprise, the more welcome answer to the anxiety I felt about their worth. They were youthful productions, certainly, and as a whole incomplete—in other words, a beginning. But many of these were the real thing, sprung from his own feelings and experience, using language in his own way, physical and playful. There could be no question about the honesty of what they expressed.

The Swim

I lie on my back
in bright threads of moon and water.
When blood pumps out of my heart,
I am as thick as a layer of oil.
When blood is sucked in,
I am as thin as sour pee yellowing.

I look along the islands of my flesh.
My breasts swell like two jellyfish.
My toes are ten soft withered oysters.
My fingers slide
through cool air
toward the green moon.

I roll over and look down
toward the warm roots of the lake.
I swim under water,
nodding my round head
over a round rock.
I am near sleep.

I swim underground
in the tunnels of my body,
find my way into my heart
and out into blue veins.
I give birth in the water;
my forehead grows from my womb.

Take Part

I love
spring skunk cabbage
because it's the first up after the snow.

A green buzzing sound
comes from the core of the plant.

My eyes are very close
to the leaves unfolding
fast enough for me to believe I could stop them
if I wanted to.

Projected View of 2000

I will be an old woman in a red cotton dress riding a bicycle.
Behind me I will tie two wicker baskets filled with tulips,
ducks and quick dogs, a small garden quacking and panting
behind me.

I will wear rouge made of cherries on my cheeks and a yellow
sunflower on a garter snake chain around my neck.
I will eat seeds and peach pits and celery hearts and drink
elderberry wine in stables full of straw and cobwebs.

I will scratch the cow's back and the horse's ear and sing
off-key to them, "Bringing in the Sheaves," and "Mint Julep."

I will carry a pearlhandled revolver in my cardigan sweater
pocket, loaded with sunflower seeds.

I will tell more huge purple lies than thin white truths, so people who have small eyes will open them wider.

I will campaign for the man who has the darkest and softest beard for president, or else I will marry him.

I will grow as many wrinkles on my body as I possibly can, and I will throw my two floppy wrinkled breasts over one shoulder when I play basketball.

I will live in a house made of stained-glass church windows.

I will put oysters and amber spiked bonbons in small goblets on the cemetery gravestones.
I will pick my nose in company, and I will play the fiddle.

When I die, the gnome and the elf from Norway will make me into small leather shoes and little leather aprons for the children of a nearby mushroom dealer.

There is no way to know when these were written except for one dated 1975, when Hugh was 33 or 34. They are all typed on Hugh's ancient manual typewriter (or one like it), on the same kind of paper, and numbered in sequence. Some pages are missing and a second smaller batch is unnumbered. With only this much evidence I'm assuming they were written in his twenties and early thirties and prepared in final versions, maybe to submit to a journal or magazine.

This next piece won't be included in Hugh's volume of Selected Poems, but I'm reading these for content first, then as artistic productions. It has echoes of the "Hey, babes" Hugh, along with this other surprising authorial identity, and also sets up the piece that follows:

The Dog in the Bar-Room Mirror

Unexpectedly a mirror reveals me
as I am, a country hick, pure ham
and potato spuds and beer. Unabashed
the toothy grin stands forth, and
the large-breasted body and the childish chin.
Compose yourself, I say, this is not
the best day on record as the Almanac (Farmer's)
and the faces at the bar have said. Joy is dead.
But beside me in the mirror a friendly dog
steps forth, rollicking the tiled floor,
nearly unhinging the door with glee. Flapping
ears hang free. This is me?
Restrict that giggle, you. There's no
room for a wiggler in your booth. It's uncouth.
Go back to where you sit with teachers
drear and fat debating in their drink.
I turn to go, but first I bend
to give myself a quick, consoling pat.

The Man Who's No Good

He reminds me of brown,
brown like the skin of the sun
unraveled over a dirt road,
and the color of blue sky over the flatlands,
as if someone in the distance sang a high note
and held it for a long time.

At the falls
his body,

braced against the curt waters,
to the certain drop.
Then into the open, into light,
dark traveler.

Something plummets from my throat to my chest,
a choked call, carried on my blood.
I never told him I liked him.

The unexpected—to say the least—voice these pieces are
written in has several modulations, and lacking a chronology I've
arranged them according to what they reveal about the author.

The Man I Never Met

Rabbit brains bitten
from the delicately smashed skull
keep him fat all winter.
Abrupt love making,
fern-covered cross of two bodies,
takes the fat from him summer.

He comes from under the earth
and enters my yard through the oak tree stump.
When he lies beside me,
his fingers grow between my breasts.
I am aghast at his freedom
to trust the wildness to me.

Male Poets

My mother
knows
about poets.
"Oh these poets,"
she says,
"Keep away from them."
Gawking through doors and windows,
they call the turkey a phoenix,
call the mashed potatoes Mountains of Myrrh,
call me Sappho.
They become murderers, rapists
or shoe salesmen
at will,
or, god help us,
horses,
or the ghosts of horses.
They travel long distance
to write odes to each other
at the ocean
without touching water or foam,
until the following Saturday
when they bring a cup of cool beer
to their lips.
And what would one
make of me
in bed? padding
my good lines,
editing my best lines,
fiercely counting
my feet?

Using images from the un- or subconscious (by the cerebral Hugh), the female narrator imagines being made love to by a wild, subterranean creature. In the piece called "Male Poets," the author is identified as Sappho. The ancient Greek female poet's name is given to her by the dangerous, unreliable poets who inflate and romanticize everything. The Hugh who is his mother's son is mashed potatoes and turkey (not Sappho), and his mother may be the same mom who grabbed books from her son's hands (so he wouldn't become Sappho?), sending him outside to play. The dangerous, shape-changing poets will pad and cut his lines (and so ruin them?) and count his feet fiercely to see what kind of being this is. To consort with them is a deep risk (what do they want to do in bed?), and in the next pieces the author is angry and helpless. And desirous.

I Hate You, You Man

What in the world
did you mean
when the smoke in your mouth
filled the tunnel of my throat?
What did you think
when you lifted me, kiss,
and turned me, kiss,
and mashed me playfully,
and followed one of my blue veins
through my body
to my heart
with your finger?

I tell you, man,
I was there.
Like the ham bone in the paper bag,

like the rock near your eye,
like the sand flea on your wrist
were there.

Lake Nubanusit, New Hampshire

I swim from shore alone.
I look back toward three men on the sand.

Water laps at my lower lip.
A water drop on one eyelash
is as large as the head of one of the men.

They are lounging
and sucking beer
and roaring with laughter
about a breast joke.
One watches me,
another kicks up his heels,
a third tilts his throat to the sun.
I hang
in green.
I look down.
My dim hands
tend my body.
I finger the scratch on my outer thigh
and the stretch marks on my inner thigh.
I press my swollen breasts bobbing.
I lace my fingers in my toes.

I am a water animal
on watch in the weeds of my hair.

I am a fish and they have poles.
I am a web foot.
They are tooth and nail.
I am the frog's throat bulge.
They are the prongs of stars.

I love them.
They would save me from drowning and
they think I am beautiful.
I heard them say so
across the water
with the huge cones
of my coral ears.

The salmon-colored flowers of my body open
and tremble
in the lake water.

What an image this ends on! Is it more ideally drunken writing? I'm thinking of the lines in Hugh's notebook: "I am never sufficiently sustainably drunk enough to write. I have had, arguably, readable thoughts, but they never pass review of my fully awake mind...." The rest of his note had some illegible words, and I'm not sure if any of it was relevant to these pieces because he was describing how writing prose was blocked by the critic who lived inside him. In the notebooks he never says anything about writing poems, and never comes back to the idea of using an altered state of consciousness—drunkenness—to open a remote part of his mind.

The images of being dominated, taken over by a stronger force, are in obvious contrast to the prosaic Hugh's independence and willfulness. As in "Male Poets," this sensual attraction to predators is mixed with wariness, although it certainly ends unambiguously. It's hard to know just how to read these when the author I know is so different from this sensibility. Then it occurs to me that that may have been just how Hugh felt too. Who the hell was "Sappho," he must have wondered. Where did she come from? Had she first appeared in a bout of drunken writing and Hugh didn't want to say so in his notebooks, which are only guardedly confessional. He never says anything about how he discovered his female voice or how she made herself known to him.

Billy and Bones

Bones. Bones is dead.
He had black hair.
Sang a song called, "Long black veil."
Ribs in his chest
thrummed
like a harp
in an undercurrent.
"Oh la la la, Oh la la, la la."

Bones made love to me last night
under a hollow tree
with wet lips and teeth
and plump thumbs.
He rose above me
like a hungry tornado.
I lay back in the rain,
my hair falling
like shagbark
behind me.

Once, Bones, when you lived,
I heard you
make love to your bone self

in the next bed.
I sweated.
I had a meek hope.

Bones,
Billy is alive.
He made love to me
inside an egg.
He has a pony tail
and teeth that can cut lips.
He is gone to California
in a red flash.
I want him here.

Bones,
go get Billy.
Tell him to come here.
Send him to me wrapped in a scarf.
Tell him to love me
with wonder at the wrinkles on my wrists and neck
where the sun locks me into the world
beside black water
where Bones
sleeps and rubs and spirals
away.

"He is gone to California/in a red flash." More than once in the midst of reading these hallucinated lines I felt the ground shifting under my feet—under Hugh's feet—and perhaps it was a flash of what he went through when Sappho spoke through him and some of these images and feelings appeared. There is a word for this state of mind, a word that appears in Hugh's notebook: alterity. Alterity, he wrote, is "otherness; specifically the quality or state of being radically alien to the conscious self or a particular cultural orientation."

Hugh would have acknowledged otherness as a mental climate he lived in every day, especially when he felt irritated or oppressed by the culture around him. But discovering that otherness also meant you were in some way—possibly even essentially—a different gender was a surprise of a different order and magnitude. It cut deeper into the private sense of self than social alienation. What was the balance between his familiar male person and this other? Was she a truer Hugh than he was? Bursting forth in a form who expressed herself so sensually and physically when he picked up a pen, was she a signal that his metaphysical being—his soul, his vzeoogby—was female?

How crazy this was! No one was more definitely his own physical self than Hugh. As a sexual person he never showed any signs of ambivalence. He loved women, he loved their bodies, he loved making love with them, yet this female portion of him seemed entirely separate from, other than—there's that word again—what aroused his sexual appetite for women. Sappho has her own strong desire which seems directed at men just as unambiguously as Hugh's was directed at women. This female persona has no confusion about gender and isn't portrayed as a threat to his masculinity either, which like Hugh himself doesn't exist in the poems (with two exceptions, yet to come). Nor was there any uncertainty or ambiguity about this female identity in the poems either. The voice seems naturally and wholly itself. It's the flip side of Hugh as a man. There's a bright line between them. They exclude each other, although he includes her in some way because it's Hugh who experiences alterity, not Sappho (again, with an exception).

While I read I wondered about the narcissistic element in Hugh's preoccupation with his honed and cultured body. It wasn't the same stripe as the pumped and oiled bodybuilders, grotesquely muscular, working out in front of mirrors. Hugh always seemed motivated by what he could do with his body, not what it looked like. But maybe both were goals. Performance to satisfy his athletic ideal and appearance to please his vanity, his sense of proportion and beauty—and perhaps to satisfy his other side too. Instead of compensating for a secret sense of inadequacy as a male— something I never heard him refer to, even obliquely—was he perfecting himself physically to win the admiration of the female sensibility within? If the female within him was as distinct an entity as his maleness—as definite as the differing dexterities of his left and right hands—perhaps the total, unified Hugh was trying to satisfy both audiences, his male vanity and his female desire. And failing to do so. Besides this frustration, there was a more worldly, practical one. Sappho might be the source of his inability to act on his own behalf. To express it this way requires characterizing the female as passive and receptive, as when Hugh writes that Bones "rose above me/like a hungry tornado." That was the cultural model Hugh grew up with. The one inculcated by his father the athlete and his mother grabbing books from his hands and sending him out to play. It could be that Hugh's peculiar passivity, his reluctance to impose himself on anyone, on the world, was due to this spirit. Maybe it wasn't reserve or lack of confidence or paralyzing guilt for killing his father that made him unable to grab the reins of his life and lead it somewhere. He couldn't do it because his spirit wasn't the kind that seized control, it was the kind that was itself seized by some force and carried away. And because the rest of Hugh, the male mind and body, couldn't abide being in the grip of anything or anyone else, he, the whole Hugh, the complete organism, was stuck in place, the battleground of these powerfully contending, canceling forces. This formulation might mean that Hugh needed guilt over his father's death to explain his private burden, his handicap, to make it part of the story of a man whose life is afflicted by a psychological curse. To accept a curse like that almost willingly, out of need, was taking a lot on oneself, but it fit with the normal male persona. To be a virtual parricide was something that would be understood, not ridiculed, in the locker room. Conflict with one's father was the original male myth, one of the first stories men told themselves. It was the crime you could own with pride. Compare confessing, "I killed my father," to pleading, "Sappho is the reason I could never be the hero of my own life."

After I read the poems the first time, I didn't want to have to read them a second, a third time, and feel again the disparity between their author and the man, the person I knew. It was too disorienting an experience, the poems too authentic, too original, to be denied. My discomfort reading the poems reflected what I imagined was Hugh's own reaction to being their author. The first time Sappho emerged from his pen, what did he think? Was he afraid that if he let this voice speak through him it would gain strength—to the point that he might lose his "own" identity? Like Dr. Jekyll who progressively became more and more Mr. Hyde until the original self was swallowed up? If that was the risk then trying to become a writer wouldn't be the simple fond dream of a poetic young athlete. Instead, trying to express his deepest self could become a fight for that same self, with no indulgent youthful posturing as a poet possible. It could lead to exactly the reverse—a need to hide the poetical self. While other young struggling aspirants were trying to find something to write about from their scanty experience, Hugh had too much of a subject, an overwhelming one. Yet, looked at another way, Sappho could also be seen as a gift—if he was willing to risk his middle class, Grosse Pointe mind there was a deep sea to plunge into. If he had the guts to do it. Did he really love the muse or was he just another young dabbler?

Or was he really someone else entirely—a philosopher, the acolyte of Kant, loyal to strict duty because it was the only way he could signify life as a human being? His respect for logic and reason as the highest, the most excellent use of one's brain was of a piece with Hugh's reverence for excellence in any human activity, but perhaps it became even more vital to him after Sappho appeared. It gave him something solid to hold on to so he wouldn't be pulled under by her irrational, inexplicable power.

Trying to suspend any judgment, or opinion, about either Hugh or Sappho, I went back and re-read the poems. I began to appreciate what Hugh had found—his dubious gift—and the form it had taken in both voice and character. As I re-read, and re-read again, I began wishing Hugh had showed me the poems when he was alive. Then I could have said, or written—it could only have been said in a letter—"Of course it's upsetting to discover you have this kind of double and to think of yourself as secretly someone else entirely, someone with the opposite gender, but look at what it's produced. These are wonderful!" I'd also have told him this was a private not a public matter, that he was the same person to me as a friend, whether Sappho was part of him or not. That was true, but how lame it would have sounded to him. With good reason. I'd have sounded as if I was just being nice, minimizing a situation that would have been inextricably complex and disturbing for Hugh. Sappho couldn't greet someone with "Hey, babes." She didn't belong in the locker room—and in the back seat just who was in whose arms? To feel as if you secretly want to be seduced by a powerful male or swept up and consumed by an overwhelming natural force, to lose yourself, to lose control and autonomy and reason to the irresistible—if that's what he had to contend with—was a desire completely at odds with his daily, conscious, face-in-the-mirror character, the cerebral, rational man called Hugh. The disparity between him and Sappho tied him in a psychological knot that can't be talked about in ordinary language. Hugh was expressing it the only way it could be expressed, and again, the more he went back to it the stronger Sappho might become. Is that what he wanted? Wasn't he already conflicted enough? Hugh didn't want to host a secret metaphysical female whose strongest desire was to yield herself to a Billy or Bones. It was enough to have mated with Megan, which Hugh said had briefly been sensual perfection, before he began struggling against her so she wouldn't destroy him, as if she was Sappho embodied and he was Billy or Bones, gone in a red flash.

Hugh survived his secret sharer but may have done it at the cost of silencing himself. To be exposed in such a way is a vulnerability no one wants. Yet preserving his *Hey, babes* self might also have felt like another failure to Hugh. He was quite aware one of the roles of poets and artists was to go down to the source of emotions like shame and fear, to confront one's vulnerability by plunging below the self's defenses to show us what the raw vzeoogby is made of, to discover and dissect the quintessential stuff that makes us ultimately all one being. Some of these pieces sound as if that's exactly what he is doing, as spontaneous as the inspiration may be. When it becomes possible to map the brain thoroughly perhaps we'll learn that this unprotected vzeoogby resembles the state of the brain at an age when we are physically helpless—an infant—and that's why it can be so unsettling, even terrifying, to receive a message from it. We scream for some force to sweep us up in its arms, to absorb us into its power and merge a puny raw self into its infinite embrace.

So a possible conclusion is that Sappho's emergence was an opportunity Hugh bravely, even curiously, took up for a while and then dropped. He may have sent these carefully typed and numbered drafts to a few magazines. Or just one. Or maybe with a crazy exuberance he sent them out to a hundred literary journals. Why not? "What can I say, babes—I'm just a poet! Let the world figure me out!" All this is easy for me to suggest, but it doesn't sound like Hugh. He was so reluctant to promote himself, and would have taken any rejection to heart. All the more so because of the content. Experienced writers learn how to expose themselves poetically and professionally; they learn to grow new skin over the flayed vzeoogby, so exposing oneself becomes part of the act, an act in itself, transforming the risk-taking writer in the process. Hugh never got that far. He only took the first one or two steps.

However, he did get far enough to express different things in Sappho's voice. In the next short piece she almost sounds as if she could say, "How you doin', babes." Or maybe in this silly ditty Sappho and Hugh are singing together. Then the piece following plunges back into complexities.

Sam's Balls

Alls
I know
is
Sam's balls
hang out of his new underwear
but I never notice.

The Evil Things I Think About Men and Do Not Say

He might
stay awake all night
and flick away my dreams
with his hand.

How does he know
I'm not dreaming to become
a fat snake or a blue eel?

I admit
I smashed an eel once
flat as a pancake.
Rolled it up and smoked it.

I imagine him soft
like an overbaked Cornish Hen.
I imagine him shrinking
into my stomach
whenever I need him.

I reach down,
pull him out,
cradle him,
diddle him on my knee,
feed mashed beets into his toothless mouth.

You will never know the most evil thing
I think about men:

I hope their whole body falls off.

This piece could be a feminist screed. The man who "flicks away" Sappho's dreams denies her autonomy, her self. He's the male as needy baby, whom she wishes would lose not just cock and balls but all physicality. It's the feminist in Hugh, not expressed intellectually or politically, but as an emotion. Living with this somewhere in his being, how did he feel when he heard a woman complaining of male sins against her? Even if she wasn't blaming Hugh, he might have felt unjustly accused as both genders. As a male his response would be, "That's not me," but whatever he felt he couldn't go on to say, "I understand completely, let me tell you about Sappho." He hadn't the language to say it, not out loud, not as a man.

When Sappho hopes the entire gender might be nullified, their whole bodies falling off, did that include Hugh—did he live with a desire to eliminate himself in this way too? Was that part of his flirtations with suicide? Or maybe I should ask how he lived with Sappho's desires? Were they cordoned off within him, like separate partitions in a hard drive? Did Hugh feel he was either Hugh or Sappho, but couldn't assume both sensibilities at the same time? Or was she like a liquid or gas flowing throughout his being, pervading his maleness, and suffused by it too?

In Hugh's notebook is a short entry written in his philosopher's voice simply noting the pairing of opposites. He says:

Consider the sometime stated condition that ideas must exist with their negations—

particle/antiparticles
truth/falsity
good/evil.

Typically, he doesn't say more; just states the bare thought. And curiously, the word he uses isn't "opposites" but "negations." So perhaps he felt Sappho was a negation of Hugh, a creature who cancelled his other self when she was present, instead of existing beside it.

However Sappho made Hugh feel, she isn't a blatant negation of the male—except in this one piece. Instead her opposite or counterpart seems to be necessary—vital and dominant—although sometimes unwanted in her world. If you were host to both "Hugh" and "Sappho" you'd certainly feel the tension between the two beings; they would not make a happy couple. Sappho is a sensual, physical woman who is both attracted to men and hostile to them. Just like Hugh with women (some of them, anyway). A piece he wrote called *She-Thing* includes these lines:

She worries
where the things she can't watch anymore
will go
and where the things who can't watch her anymore
will go

and what will happen to the woman
the things watching her see,
and what will happen to the man
she sometimes seems to be.

The female in Hugh is aware that at times she is male. Sappho contains her opposite too. It's another inversion; neither is negated by the other, but instead is doubled. Or negated at times and other times doubled. The balance between Hugh and Sappho is dynamic, never settled, inevitable for these twins joined at the head and groin.

The discovery of Sappho in his person must have required a kind of paradigm shift in Hugh's view of himself. I use the phrase as Thomas Kuhn—another favorite author of Hugh's—did to describe the revolutions in scientific thinking, like Newtonian physics subsumed by Einstein's theory of relativity. We resist these paradigm shifts because they mean re-thinking our view of the way things are. Not only is it unsettling to feel forced to re-learn what we think reality is, it's even more unsettling to notice the principle underlying a paradigm shift: that these mental earthquakes can happen any time, that this kind of instability is inherent in everything we think we know. Because Hugh had trained his own mind to be ready to question anything, he believed paradigm shifts were inevitable, and that instead of rejecting these cataclysms we had to embrace them if we wanted to know things more deeply. To get closer to the truth, we had to risk discovering something that exploded our settled views of ourselves and the universe. So when one of these paradigm shifts happened to Hugh personally with his discovery of Sappho, he would have had to accept her validity no matter how much she threatened to shatter his sense of himself.

Denial was not an option. He was trapped by his own open mind.

The tenth and last stanza from a long poem called *The Decathlon* shows how Hugh attempted and, I think, succeeded—in art if not in life—in resolving the intimate conflict between himself and Sappho. This rendition also locates the two genders in the same person, but they are now ideally unified in the author, whose body subsumes his mind to resolve other pairings of opposites too. The author is now Hugh, not Sappho, and the piece ends with a rare statement of conclusion. The duality reconciled is both male/female and mind/body:

> The Decathlon
> reminds me of
> the man in the woman,
> the woman in the man,
> the aura in the body,
> the bone in the tree—
> reminds me
> what I want in me:
>> The body in motion,
>> driven by the mind, to leap, twist,
>> roll, until a break-through,
>> when the body takes itself
>> on a real trip
>> to where body is wiser than head,
>> where mind would suffocate
>> what's growing, what's glowing,
>> in the body core.
>> But the mind re-introduces itself,
>> to ration energy flow in ten directions,
>> calculate the efforts of others,
>> put limits on one event, save for another.
>> Mind, so occupied by body,
>> that the shape fits the spirit,
>> the sculpture fits the dream.

The "break-through" Hugh imagines leads to a physical wisdom and unites the elements of his being in an ideal form. The genders are one and the mind is so occupied by the body that the body fully expresses the spirit within—the spirit it can now be understood which Hugh was unable to express fully except by a physical act, by "the body in motion/driven by the mind." The last three lines describing the fulfillment he was trying to achieve should be carved into the air marking his passage through life.

In the piece I've placed next to last there is a hint of a state of mind like anorexia nervosa, as if the person Hugh saw in the mirror was not the same one the rest of us saw. This might add a third pair of eyes to Sappho's and his "own" when he studied the reflection of the human form his mind lived in. Whomever he saw, he certainly could never be fit enough to fulfill his ideal, just as he could never know enough to satisfy his desire to comprehend everything.

Coordination

I am taking the fat test in the mirror.
I was doing calculus a minute ago.
I try to differentiate a few curves,
Integrate my body.
It's odd that mathematics requires pencil and paper,
While solving one's life is done in one's head.
When I analyze an equation, I begin
At the end and try to remember
That zero equals zero.
Life needs pencil and paper and maybe an eraser.
My eye tries to graph the body.
The form changes or my eye or both.
I cheat by standing straight, by breathing
to erase the form that would depress.
There is some shape, some size, some function
That I must be. Or just the opposite.

3.

Hugh's love of puzzles and respect for the random and the contingent take on new weight when seen through his poetical female spirit. The conundrum of his own identity teases him without mercy, yet puzzles are a lighthearted way to broadcast—to share occultly, symbolically—his hidden uneasiness. To scratch the itch for some relief. As for making ordinary sense of the inexplicable: Hugh knows this is futile but how can he help wondering about it the way someone on a long, forced march dreams of an easy chair, a place to sit down. Instead he has to keep running, lifting, climbing, biking, on and on, while his rational, logical mind scorns how flimsy anything he would dare be sure of must be. Flimsy, transient, windblown...so what can one trust or hold on to except mute beauties like the golden mean, the Fibonacci series, puzzles themselves in their mysterious symmetry and regularity, their abstract certainty. They defy the chaos around them, silently, self-sufficiently. They don't need us.

The few times Hugh was able to write, the strange genie that flowed out of the end of his pen was the reason—or the feeling—that he could not write, and the fact that he could not write is the reason, or the feeling, that he couldn't have a career, or a wife and children, a normal life. The eternally returning mystery was why this was so, even after he learned to see behind, or around, the unwinnable fact of the game. Why did he have to circle himself endlessly, why did he spend his days rotating in wonder, muscles swollen, endorphins pumping, dendrites tingling, while he ran, pedaled, and swam toward a transient, unwitnessed, unachievable ideal.

During the last years with Naomi, I think Hugh would have settled for renormalizing his life so it didn't run off to this endlessly maddening infinity, that he would have almost gladly embraced the dippy, if he had known how to do it without denying himself.

It's that self, the one who steadfastly refused to embrace the dippy, who was Hugh, whomever Hugh was.

Divine Sloth

> There's a story I read about a sloth
> Who did not respond to his own death.
> I see this sloth
> As the essence of identity or
> As the identity of essence.
> So immutable, so perfect, was his identity
> He could not be nor cease to be.
> In all of us there is a supreme being nonbeing,
> An unmoved unmover, a tar baby,
> And he don't say nothing.

www.ingramcontent.com/pod-product-compliance
Lightning Source LLC
Chambersburg PA
CBHW070659280626
47159CB00022B/995